I0603451

THE DECEPTION COLLECTION

STELLA BRUNO INVESTIGATES

PETER MULRANEY

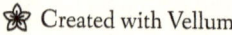 Created with Vellum

THE MELROSE CASE

STELLA BRUNO INVESTIGATES

WITH HER HIKING boots firmly laced, Stella left Brian in the car park at the start of the Mt Remarkable Summit Trail in Melrose. He was in no condition to undertake the three-hour trek ahead of her, despite the time he spent on the golf course with his mates. Thankfully, he'd known better than to protest when she'd told him to take a look around while she visited the crime scene. She had no desire to be the one calling May to inform her Brian had expired from overexertion in the course of his duties.

Stella followed the constable waiting for her up the mountain to the crime scene, keeping a wary eye out for snakes, even though he'd told her it was too cold for them to be about. She wasn't as confident as her guide about the first week of May aligning with the start of the reptilian hibernation season in the Southern Flinders Ranges.

On a curve in the path, Stella stopped and took in the vista across the Willochra Plain, a sea of dried grass stretching into the distance as far as she could see. The monotony of the view only broken by lines of green, where trees marked watercourses snaking across the plain away from the mountain. After a moment, she resumed following the trail ever upwards, as it wound its way through ancient trees and skirted steep rock-strewn gullies.

After an hour and forty minutes, they arrived at a group of trees marked with crime scene tape, where several members of the crime scene investigation team were packing equipment into backpacks.

'The bodies are down there, Sarge,' said her guide, pointing into the steep gully that fell away from where they stood on the walking trail. 'You'll need to use that rope.' He pointed to an orange nylon rope secured to a tree a couple of metres beyond the area cordoned off with crime scene tape.

'Anything up here I should know about?' said Stella, taking a moment to catch her breath before descending through the trees to the rocks at the bottom of the gully below them.

'Signs of a scuffle,' said one of the constables, pointing to several marks in the leaf litter around the edge of the rocky outcrop next to the trees they'd marked off.

'Any sign of the drone they were supposedly using?'

'Not up here, Sarge.'

Stella pictured the victims standing on the rocky outcrop at the edge of the path, intent on the drone flying out above the gully, and imagined someone pushing them over the edge. The drone could have crashed into the rocks below when they'd gone over the edge or continued flying until its battery died. She hoped they'd find it as she peered into the gully.

Stella couldn't see the party waiting for her below. 'Who's down there?'

'Sergeant Rice,' said the constable, 'with the body retrieval team. You'd better get going, Sarge. They want to get down from here before dark.'

Stella looked at her watch. It was fifteen minutes past two. She'd been warned it would be dark a little after five on the eastern side of the mountain, where they were already standing in the shadow of the peak.

'How long will it take me to get down there?' said Stella. 'Looks pretty steep.'

'Five, maybe ten minutes,' said the constable. 'You'll be okay, Sarge, as long as you don't let go of the rope.'

'Thanks for the vote of confidence,' said Stella, laughing. She walked up the path to the rope and made her way down the side of the gully, going from tree to tree, until she arrived among the rocks at the bottom, about thirty metres down from the trail.

At the bottom of the rope, she was met by a constable who directed her to where, Dr Steve Wright, the police pathologist, was standing with a group of officers amid a pile of equipment. Stella realised the rope was there to help them manhandle the stretchers carrying the bodies up to the walking trail.

As she approached the group, Stella recognised Barry Rice, who she'd worked with before. 'What do I need to see, Barry?'

'I'll show you what we have and then Dr Wright can fill you in,' said Barry.

Stella followed him around a large rock that blocked their view down the gully and watched as he lifted the sheets covering the broken bodies of a man and a woman dressed in hiking clothes.

'Search party initially thought they'd fallen from the path, until they got down here,' said Barry. 'Look at the heads.'

Stella stepped closer to the body of the man and looked down at his head. The back of the skull was a mess of crushed bone and brains. She looked up at Barry.

'The rock used to crush their skulls was tossed into the bush over there.' He pointed towards the undergrowth to their left. 'We've bagged it.'

Stella looked at the tears in the jackets and trousers on the bodies. They'd obviously collided with the side of the gully on the way down. 'Surprised the fall didn't kill them, Barry.'

'Someone wanted to make sure they were dead, Stella. There's a trail through the trees made by someone coming down and going back up,' said Barry. 'Possibly more than one, going by the amount of damage.'

Stella stepped over to the body of the woman. The side of the head was caved in, as if she'd been hit with something solid, and the rocks supporting her body were splattered with dried blood. She studied the scene, taking in the rocks embedded in the side of the gully and across its floor. 'Where's this path through the bush?'

Barry pointed up to where they could see the crime scene tape tied to the trees up on the walking trail. 'Look along this line. The undergrowth's been disturbed and twigs have been snapped on the smaller bushes?'

Stella stared up along the line he was pointing out, starting from where they were standing next to the bodies. She could just make out a line of disturbance.

'So, you're saying it looks like they were pushed off those rocks up there and then their killer came down and finished them off?'

'That's what it looks like to me,' said Barry.

'Anything in their pockets?'

'Wallets, car keys and the key to a cabin in the caravan park,' said Barry.

'No mobile phones?'

'No mobiles.'

'Any sign of a drone or its controller?'

'No luck with that, Stella, I'm afraid,' said Barry. 'Bloody thing could have ended up anywhere if they were operating it at the time they were attacked. Then again, it could be back in their cabin.'

'Guess the killer could have taken it if they'd had it on them.'

'Or it could be stuck in a tree or smashed on the rocks further down this side of the mountain.'

Stella wondered if they'd ever find it or if finding it would make any difference, since she had no way of knowing if they'd been filming when they were attacked or that they'd captured an image of their assailant.

'Has anyone checked their cabin?'

'It's secured. We're looking at that after we get down from here.'

They walked back around the rock to where the others were waiting.

'What's your opinion on cause of death, Steve?' said Stella.

'Appears to be a sharp blow to the head with that rock over there.' Steve pointed to one of the bags in the pile of equipment. 'But, I can't be sure until the autopsies. The fall itself could have killed them.'

'No chance of it being an accident?' said Stella.

Steve shook his head. 'Even if the fall killed them, Stella, you don't get those sort of head injuries falling this far down the side of a mountain. Someone's definitely had a hand in this.'

It was growing dark by the time Stella returned to the car park at the start of the summit trail. She was pleased to see Brian waiting for her in what she hoped was a warm car.

'How did you go?' said Stella, as she slid into her seat and closed the door. 'Find us somewhere to stay?'

'I've booked a couple of rooms at the North Star Hotel,' said Brian. 'That way you won't have to put up with my snoring.'

'I'll keep that in mind when I'm doing your next performance review.'

Brian laughed and started the engine to fire up the car's heater.

'The crime scene boys are staying in the caravan park,' said Stella, 'where our victims were staying.'

'I spoke to the manager,' said Brian. 'Uniform have someone on site securing the place.'

'What did you find out?'

'They booked in early Monday afternoon and were seen leaving on foot Tuesday morning, around ten. No-one was aware they hadn't returned until Mrs Washington rang the manager after her husband didn't make his normal seven o'clock call to let her know he was okay.'

'The manager hadn't noticed?'

'He thought they'd walked up to one of the pubs for dinner after their hike,' said Brian, rubbing his chin. 'He raised the alarm when he realised Washington's mobile phone was ringing inside his cabin and nobody in either of the pubs had seen them. Anything come from your hike?'

'Nothing we didn't already know from the initial report.' Stella watched as the bodies were loaded into the coroner's van. 'CSI found a blood splatted rock they think was used to bash their heads in, and there are signs someone made their way down to where the bodies were and out again.'

'Are they sure that wasn't the search party?'

'The search party didn't go into that gully until someone spotted a hat in a tree below the edge of the trail, and they marked their way down with a rope tied to the trees.'

'Did they find any cameras?'

'No,' said Stella. 'I suspect our killers might have taken them, and the drone.'

'Drone?'

'Didn't you read the notes? One of the reasons they were here was to use the camera in Washington's new drone.'

'Must have missed that bit,' said Brian. 'When I saw they were landscape photographers, I thought they'd be using those fancy DSLR cameras with gigantic zoom lenses.'

'You need to keep up with the times, Brian. It's all aerial footage these days.'

Brian moved the selector to drive and followed the coroner's van out of the car park and back into the town, where he parked in front of the North Star Hotel.

***

The front of the North Star Hotel was lit up by the media's bright lights. Stella and Brian got out of their car and joined Inspector Pence, the officer in charge of the search and rescue operation, in the glare of the lights as the reporters gathered with their microphones.

'The bodies of missing hikers Robert Washington and Judy Redding have been retrieved from the national park behind us here,' said Inspector Pence, 'where they were located after an extensive search by officers and volunteers this morning.' He stopped talking and looked at the cameras. 'The nature of the injuries sustained by Mr Washington and Ms Redding suggests their deaths were not accidental or from natural causes.'

'What do you mean?' said one of the reporters.

'We're treating their deaths as suspicious,' said Inspector Pence, 'and Detective Sergeant Bruno from Major Crimes is here to lead the investigation to determine what led to their deaths.'

Stella stepped forward and stood next to Inspector Pence. 'If you saw Mr Washington or Ms Redding or interacted with them in any way since their arrival in Melrose on Monday afternoon, or were in Mt Remarkable National Park yesterday, especially on the walking trails, please come forward and speak to us or call Crime Stoppers. We need your help to find out what happened to them after they were seen leaving the caravan park around ten o'clock yesterday morning. If you have any information that could help us identify who they may have met on the walking trail yesterday, please come forward or contact Crime Stoppers.'

Stella stepped back.

'Are you treating this as homicide?' said the reporter from the ABC.

'We're treating it as suspicious,' said Inspector Pence. 'We'll have further information for you as it comes to hand. Thank you.'

Inspector Pence turned his back to indicate the interview was over and the glare of the lights shifted to focus on the reporters, as they recorded their updates for the evening news. Stella found herself standing next to Inspector Pence in the relative darkness of the lights of the hotel's veranda.

'You don't seem to have much to go on, Sergeant,' said Inspector Pence.

Stella smiled. 'It's early days yet, sir. Let's see what turns up over the next few days.'

'Anything in the place where they were staying?' said Inspector Pence.

'We'll know more tomorrow when CSI have examined their cabin, sir.'

'Be surprised if your killer is a local, Sergeant. There's so little crime in this community we don't even have a presence here.'

Stella shrugged. 'I'll keep an open mind on that, sir. You never know who's living in small places like this until you have to look.'

'Their deaths probably have nothing to do with the people living in Melrose, Sergeant. I suggest you focus your attention on their connections down in Adelaide.'

'I'll see where that leads me, sir.' Stella knew better than to contradict a senior officer, especially one she'd only just met, but she had no intention of ignoring the possibility of the killer being from Melrose.

Inspector Pence beckoned to the uniformed sergeant waiting to join them. 'This is Paul Sleep, Sergeant. He'll take care of things here so you can concentrate on the Adelaide end.' He waited while the two sergeants shook hands. 'Now if you don't mind, I'll leave you to it. It's been a long day.' He turned and walked to his car, where his driver was waiting to take him back to the Local Area Headquarters in Port Pirie.

'I'm based in Booleroo,' said Paul, 'about twenty minutes from here. Melrose is part of my patch.'

'Guess the locals will feel more comfortable talking to you than me,' said Stella. 'Did you hear what your inspector was saying?'

'I wouldn't pay too much attention to what his nibs thinks about it not being a local,' said Paul. 'He's got no idea what goes on this side of the mountain. Today would be the first time he's been to Melrose in any official capacity.' Paul pushed his hat back and smiled.

Stella thought she'd get along just fine with Paul Sleep. He had her kind of energy.

'Besides, not everyone living around here these days is what I'd call local,' said Paul.

'He could be right, though,' said Stella. 'People tend to take their troubles with them but, let's see where the evidence takes us, shall we?'

Paul nodded. They exchanged mobile numbers and Stella introduced him to Brian.

'How long do you think you'll be here before you head back to Adelaide?' said Paul.

'We'll see what turns up tomorrow,' said Stella, 'and go from there.'

'Okay. I'll catch up with you in the morning, then.'

As Paul walked towards his vehicle, Stella turned and reached for the door of the hotel. 'I hope they serve some decent food in here, Brian. I could eat a horse.'

CHAPTER 2

AFTER A QUICK HOT shower and change of clothes, Stella called Josh to see how things were at home.

'I'm fine, Mum. Shaun said he'd come to watch me play this weekend. Are you going to be back by then?'

'I hope so, sweetheart. I'll have a better idea tomorrow. Have you done your homework?'

'It's all under control, Mum. I gotta go. Nonna's got my pasta ready.'

'Love you, sweetheart.'

'Love you, Mum.'

And then, he was gone. Stella laughed. He was just like her brother had been as a teenager, when nothing had stood between him and food.

She slipped her phone into the pocket of her jeans and went downstairs to join Brian in the dining room.

'What's on the menu, Brian?'

'Regional produce,' said Brian, passing her a menu. 'Think I'll have the steak.'

Stella scanned the list of choices. She wanted something substantial after her hike up the mountain. 'Might join you with the steak.'

Over dinner, they learnt from their waitress that the victims had eaten in the North Star on Monday night, along with a handful of other tourists, none of whom had stayed in the hotel's accommodation.

'Did any of them seem to know each other?' said Stella.

'There was one foursome, but the couple that died sat by themselves over there.' She pointed to a table across the room from them. 'But I did see them talking to some of the others before they left that night.'

'Did you hear what they were saying?' said Stella.

'I wasn't paying that much attention,' said the waitress. 'It was after they'd paid their bill.'

'Is it always this quiet?' said Brian.

'Not always,' said the waitress. 'We had a good crowd for the tennis over Easter, but it won't get busy again until the Fat Tyre Festival on the June long weekend.'

'What's that about?' said Stella.

'It's a mountain bike festival,' said the waitress, as she picked up their empty plates. 'There'll be hundreds of people here that weekend. They come from all over the place.'

'Sounds like fun,' said Stella.

'It's a lot of work,' said the waitress, 'but it keeps me employed. Now, do you want to see the dessert menu?'

Stella looked at Brian. He was supposed to be watching his weight. He shook his head.

'No, thank you,' said Stella.

The waitress turned and carried their empty plates to the kitchen.

'Think I'll get an early night, Brian. We could have a long day ahead of us tomorrow.'

'I'll get a list of places where people can stay in town,' said Brian.

'Breakfast at eight?' said Stella, standing.

'Suits me. Sarge.'

After breakfast, Stella and Brian made their way to the caravan park to meet with Sgt Barry Rice.

'What are we looking for Stella?' said Barry.

'Are there any signs the cabin or car have been broken into?' said Stella.

Barry shook his head. 'They're both locked. If anybody's been inside either they used a key.'

'That's pretty unlikely,' said Stella, 'given the keys found with the bodies.'

'The manager told me no-one's been into this cabin since he reported them missing,' said Brian, 'and we've had a guard on it since the bodies were found.'

'Let's start by confirming we have the correct keys,' said Stella.

Barry took the car keys from the evidence bag he was holding and pressed the button to unlock the Toyota Land Cruiser parked outside cabin number four. The indicators flashed. He opened the driver's door with his latex gloved right hand.

'No obvious sign of disturbance,' said Barry.

'Let's check the cabin,' said Stella.

They walked to the door of cabin four, where Barry inserted the key they'd found in Robert Washington's coat pocket into the keyhole and turned it. The door opened. They peered inside.

'No obvious sign of disturbance here either,' said Barry.

'Focus on what we can learn from what they brought with them,' said Stella, 'and see if they left their drone in here.'

'There's supposed to be a mobile phone in here somewhere

according to the park manager,' said Brian, peering over Stella's shoulder. 'There's only one bed, Sarge. I thought Washington was married to someone else.'

'That's what it says in the case notes,' said Stella.

'How old were these people?' said Barry.

'Early seventies, late sixties,' said Stella. 'See what you can work out about their sleeping arrangements.'

Sgt Rice briefed his CSI team and they started the search, while Stella and Brian waited outside in the late autumn sunshine.

'How many places can people stay in this town?' said Stella.

'There are ten places, including the caravan park, listed on the town's website,' said Brian.

'Well, we know no-one was staying at the North Star on Monday night,' said Stella. 'Shouldn't take too long to check out the others.'

'There wasn't anybody else staying here, either,' said Brian. 'The manager told me the victims were the only people staying here on Monday night.'

'Did he say how long they'd booked in for?'

'Right up to Saturday morning, but he also told me this wasn't the first time Washington had been here. Apparently, he'd stayed here with the same woman around this time last year.' Brian smiled. 'He thought Redding was Washington's partner and was a little surprised when his wife rang to ask where he was.'

'Hmm. Sounds like we could be having an interesting chat with Mrs Washington when we get back to Adelaide, but I guess he wouldn't be the first bloke to have a girlfriend on the side, would he?'

'God, one woman running your life is enough,' said Brian.

'Oh, come on, Brian. You have two of us running yours.'

'This is not quite the same, Sarge. Besides, May would have my balls for garters if she thought I was messing about with you.'

'I'll keep that in mind.'

'Careful, Sarge, you don't want me reporting you for sexual harassment.'

'I think you might have missed your opportunity there, Brian,' said Stella, laughing. 'Your balls are safe for now.'

'Thanks,' said Brian, turning as Sgt Rice appeared in the open doorway of the cabin.

'Anything?' said Stella.

'The only piece of equipment that seems to be missing is the drone,' said Barry. 'I've got two mobile phones, two laptops, and two fancy looking cameras with multiple lenses.'

'What else did they bring with them?' said Stella.

'Only what you'd expect people to bring for a week away from home, Stella. Clothes, a couple of books, toiletries,' said Barry. 'But, there's no sign of a sleeping bag, and there are two sets of pyjamas under the pillows. I'd say they both slept in the bed.'

'Interesting,' said Stella. 'I wonder if his wife knew what he was up to with Redding.'

'Guess we'll have to ask her,' said Brian.

Possible motive, thought Stella, knowing she'd need some evidence before she could bring it into the light. 'Can we access the laptops or the phones, Barry?'

'Not yet.'

'Would be helpful to know what's on them,' said Stella.

'Might have to ask family members for assistance on that,' said Barry, 'unless we get lucky.'

'I'll check in with you later in the week,' said Stella.

'Okay. I'll get this lot packed up and back to Adelaide.'

Stella and Brian spent the rest of the morning chasing up details of the visitors who had stayed in tourist accommodation in Melrose on the Monday night before the murders.

By lunch time, they'd spoken to the three retired couples who had eaten with the victims in the North Star Hotel, and heard that Robert Washington had openly discussed with them his intention to film the mountain with his drone camera on Tuesday morning.

All three couples claimed they had chosen different activities for the Tuesday and had not followed the victims up the mountain. Two of the couples, who were staying in the Melrose Holiday Units in Whitby Street, claimed they'd spent the Tuesday together visiting the nearby attraction of Alligator Gorge, while the third couple, who were staying in Yates Cottage, said they had spent the day with friends in the neighbouring town of Wilmington.

After lunch, they caught up with Paul Sleep, who had spent the morning interviewing people living in houses with a view of Joes Road, which the victims had walked along on their way from the caravan park to the start of the Mt Remarkable Summit Trail. He told them no-one remembered seeing the victims going on their hike or noticing anybody else either walking or driving along the road that morning.

'Is there any other way the killer could have come?' said Stella.

'There are stacks of walking trails in the park,' said Paul. 'He could have walked in from Mambray Creek or Alligator Gorge, but that sounds like a long shot to me.'

'Why's that?'

'How would he know where to find them?'

'Guess it could have been a prearranged meeting,' said Stella.

'You'd have to be keen to come in from Mambray Creek, though. That's a two day hike both ways.'

'Might be worth exploring just the same,' said Stella, 'along with searching for their drone.'

'Okay. I'll work on that,' said Paul.

After speaking with Sgt Sleep, Stella checked in with Crime Stoppers. No-one from Melrose had called in with any information.

'The only call we've had, Sergeant, is from a man who wouldn't leave his name. Claimed Washington had got what he deserved.'

'Trace his number?'

'Public phone in the Elizabeth Shopping Centre, Sergeant.'

'Send me the details. We'll see if they have it under CCTV.'

Stella closed her phone and slipped it into a pocket. 'Think we're done here, Brian. Let's head for home.'

CHAPTER 3

FIRST THING FRIDAY MORNING, Stella went to visit Steve Wright for a briefing on his post mortem examination of the bodies retrieved from Mt Remarkable. She wasn't a fan of the post mortem process and was glad she'd missed the actual cutting and probing of the bodies.

As she walked along the corridor to the pathologist's office, the overpowering smell of disinfectant, a permanent feature of the place, triggered the feeling of dread she felt every time she entered the morgue. She took a slow breath and made a quick sign of the cross, touching the fingers of her right hand to her forehead and three spots on her chest. She pushed the image of Rick's white face back into the depths of her mind, where she'd kept the memories of her young husband since the day he'd been knocked from his police motorcycle by a drunk driver.

'Not much to tell you I'm afraid, Stella,' said Steve, when she entered his office. 'Both victims suffered significant injuries from their tumble down the mountain. The male's got a broken leg and a shattered shoulder. The female has a broken arm and pelvis, and they've both got bruising consistent with soft tissue colliding with rocks or trees during a fall into the gully where the bodies were found.'

Stella replayed the image of the victims falling off the rocks above her and crashing into the side of the gully that she'd imagined while standing among the rocks next to their bodies. 'So, they were alive after their fall?'

'They might not have been conscious, but they would still have been alive,' said Steve. 'Anyone's guess how long they would have survived, though. There's no way either of them could have climbed out of there unaided, given the extent of their injuries.'

'Any change in your thoughts on cause of death?'

Steve shook his head. 'They were killed by someone pounding their heads in with a rock.'

Stella wondered what had motivated their killer to climb down into the gully and finish them off with a rock, and found herself thinking someone must have wanted assurance they were dead and not just left to die. She felt a shiver. She was dealing with a cold-blooded killer.

'Can we prove that?'

'He made it easy for us, Stella. The rock found near the bodies is covered in blood and brains. We've already got a match with the blood from the victims and the lab's working on a DNA analysis of the brain material.'

'What's your estimated time of death, Steve?'

'Early afternoon, Tuesday, give or take a couple of hours.'

'Nothing to identify the killer?'

'Not on the bodies,' said Steve. 'We're still running tests on the blood samples collected at the scene and on their clothing.'

'Let me know if you find anything.'

'It'll be in the report.'

Brian parked in front of the house in Seaford Rise where Robert and Wendy Washington had lived for the last twelve years. Stella looked at the neat front garden with its rose bushes and trimmed lawn.

'Someone's house proud,' said Brian.

'Or was,' said Stella, as she opened her door and got out of the car.

The front door of the house was opened by a thin, grey-haired woman standing with the aid of a walking stick.

'Mrs Washington?' said Stella.

'Yes. Are you the police?'

'Detective Sergeant Bruno,' said Stella, showing her ID, 'and this is Detective Constable Rhodes.'

'Took your time getting here,' said Mrs Washington. 'Thought you'd be here yesterday after they asked me to identify Robert.'

'We were in Melrose, yesterday,' said Stella. 'Do you think we could come in? We have a few questions we need to ask.'

Mrs Washington turned and shuffled into the sitting room with the aid of her walking stick. 'Shut the door behind you!'

Brian closed the door as they followed Mrs Washington into the sitting room, where she eased her frame into a padded recliner and indicated they should sit.

'I'm sorry about your husband's death,' said Stella. 'I know it's not an easy situation to deal with.'

'You can keep your false sympathy, thank you,' said Mrs Washington. 'What would a young lassie like you know about coping with something like this?'

'Quite a bit, actually,' said Stella. 'I've been a widow for ten years, Mrs Washington. My husband was killed on the job.'

Mrs Washington stared at Stella. 'Don't bullshit me, young lady!'

'I assure you, Mrs Washington, I'm not just saying that to

make you feel better. I know what it's like going home to an empty bed and telling a small boy his daddy is not coming home again, ever.'

There was silence. Mrs Washington looked away. Stella waited.

'I'm so sorry,' said Mrs Washington. 'That must have been horrible. I didn't mean to be rude. Can we start again?'

'Would you like me to make a cuppa?' said Brian.

'Tell us a bit about your husband,' said Stella. 'What sort of man was he?'

Mrs Washington put down her teacup. 'Bob and I became close around fifteen years ago, a couple of years after his first wife, Christine, died. We've been married for the last twelve years or so.' She looked up and smiled at Stella. 'He was a bit of a charmer, always making friends.'

'What kind of work was he involved in?' said Stella.

'He was a civil engineer before he retired. Designed roads and bridges, and things like that.'

'When did he retire?'

'About eight years ago,' said Mrs Washington. 'When I had my accident.'

'Car accident?' said Stella.

'Like your husband, Sergeant. I was hit by a drunk driver on my way home from work,' said Mrs Washington. 'Buggered up my legs. Took me months to learn to walk again.'

'So, your husband gave up his job to take care of you after the accident?'

'I think he used my accident as an excuse to leave work so he could spend more time with his camera,' said Mrs Washington.

'I take it photography was more than just a hobby for him,' said Stella.

'He and Judy had an online business selling photos of Australian landscapes. That's why they were always going places,' said Mrs Washington.

'Did you ever go with them?'

'Camping's not my thing,' said Mrs Washington, 'not even in one of those fancy caravan park cabin things they liked to stay in.'

'How long had your husband known Judy Redding?' said Stella.

'Judy's Christine's sister,' said Mrs Washington.

Interesting, thought Stella, wondering how long Washington and Redding had been sleeping together. 'Was she married?'

'She and Gerald split before I met Bob. From the little I've heard about him, I gather he was a bit of a bastard to her.'

'Gerald Redding?' said Brian.

'No, Redding is her maiden name. His name's Harmer.'

'Do you know where we can find him?' said Stella.

Mrs Washington shook her head. 'I've never met him.'

'How would you describe your husband's relationship with Judy Redding?' said Stella.

'What do you mean?'

That was defensive, thought Stella. 'Anything beyond business or friendship?'

Mrs Washington glared at Stella. 'What are you suggesting?'

'I'm not suggesting anything, Mrs Washington, but it appears they slept in the same bed in the cabin they were staying in and, according to the manager of the caravan park, it wasn't the first time they'd shared a one bedroom cabin.'

Mrs Washington looked down at her legs. 'I couldn't give

him some of the things he needed after the accident, things that Judy could do for him.' She looked up at Stella. 'We came to an arrangement.'

'Does anybody else know about this arrangement?' said Stella.

'I don't think so. It's not like we told anybody.'

'And, how did you feel about the arrangement?' said Stella, thinking she wouldn't have agreed to sharing her husband, or Shaun for that matter, with anyone.

'I would have been left on my own like this if I hadn't gone along with it,' said Mrs Washington. 'Anyway, it all worked out. We all got what we wanted and everybody was happy.'

'What was your relationship with Judy Redding like?'

'We were friends. She was good fun.' Mrs Washington smiled. 'We spent a lot of time together.'

Stella found that hard to believe. 'You weren't angry about her having sex with your husband?'

'Someone had to,' said Mrs Washington. 'I couldn't. No, she was doing me a favour.'

She obviously thinks it's still a man's world, thought Stella. 'Did Judy have any children?'

'There's a son, Darren. He went with his father when they split up.' Mrs Washington shrugged. 'He was eighteen or nineteen when they separated. He'd be in his forties, now.'

Stella wondered whether an adult son would be worried enough about his mother's relationship with his uncle to do something about it. 'Did your husband ever mention he'd been threatened?'

'Bob wasn't the sort to make enemies, Sergeant. Besides, how does someone make enemies taking photographs of trees and kangaroos?'

'Was he involved in anything else?'

'Lions,' said Mrs Washington. 'In fact, I met Bob at a Lion's function. My first husband, Tom, was a member before the cancer took him.'

'Do you have any children, Mrs Washington?'

'I have a son, Laurence. He lives in Montreal.' She smiled at Stella. 'He's married to a Canadian girl. They're coming home for Bob's funeral.'

'That's good,' said Stella. 'Did your husband have any children with his first wife?'

'Not that I know of.'

Stella wondered what else Mrs Washington didn't know about her husband's past. 'Was there any specific reason why your husband was in Melrose this week?'

'They'd bought one of those flying camera things. He was like a kid with a new toy. Wanted to use it on Mt Remarkable.'

'Ah, the missing drone,' said Stella. 'Had he used it anywhere else?'

'They took it up to the park in Belair a couple of times to get the hang of using it around trees and, before that, Bob tried it out on the oval at the high school. He reckoned it was pretty easy to use.'

Stella wondered if Washington had been observed inadvertently filming something somebody didn't want anybody else to know about. 'Where did your husband store images from his cameras?'

'Everything went onto his laptop.'

'Did he back things up?' said Brian.

'It's all in the cloud, somewhere,' said Mrs Washington. 'Dropbox, I think.'

'Do you know how to access his computer and his mobile phone?' said Stella.

'He'll have all that stuff written down somewhere in his study.'

'Do you mind if we have a look?' said Stella.

'It's that room across the hallway,' said Mrs Washington, pointing towards the doorway. 'I'm afraid I can't tell you much about what you'll find in there. That was his private domain. I wasn't even allowed in to clean. But, I know he wrote things like passwords down just in case.'

'See what you can find, Brian,' said Stella. She waited for him to get up and walk across to Washington's study. 'Can you think of any reason why anybody would want to kill your husband, Mrs Washington?'

'I'm afraid I can't help you there, Sergeant. I've never heard anyone say a bad word about him in all the time I've known him.'

Stella wondered whether Mrs Washington was painting her a glowing picture of a wonderful man because that was the truth or if it was what she wanted her to believe about him, because based on what she'd seen, her description did not align with the facts, unless someone had made a terrible mistake and killed the wrong people.

'What made you think something was wrong when he didn't call you on Tuesday night?'

'We had an agreement. He called every night at seven when he was away so I wouldn't have to worry. I knew something had to be wrong when he didn't call and I couldn't get either of them to answer their phones.'

'Did he call on the Monday?'

'Yes. Told me they were eating at the North Star and planning to take the drone up the mountain on Tuesday.' Mrs Washington smiled. 'He sounded excited.'

'Did you speak to Judy?'

'Yes. She said they were fine, and she'd let me know how they got on with the drone.'

'We'll do our best to find out who did this,' said Stella.

'I'm sure you will, Sergeant,' said Mrs Washington. 'When will I get his body for the funeral?'

'It'll be released as soon as the pathologist finishes his tests, which I'd expect to be early next week.'

Brian walked back into the room.

'Get what we need?' said Stella.

'I believe so,' said Brian, tapping his notebook.

'Do you have his laptop?' said Mrs Washington.

'Yes. It was in the cabin at the caravan park.'

'I'd like to have that.'

'Everything will be returned to you once we've finished with it,' said Stella. 'Would you like a list of what we're holding?'

Mrs Washington shook her head. 'I'm only interested in his laptop and the car.'

'We'll be in touch as soon as we know anything,' said Stella. 'I'm sorry we had to meet this way.'

CHAPTER 4

AFTER THEIR INTERVIEW with Wendy Washington, Stella and Brian drove to the apartment in Moana where Judy Redding had lived.

Stella inserted the key they'd found among Judy's belongings, turned it clockwise and pushed on the door, which opened into a short hallway that led into the main room of the apartment. She slid aside the glass door at the end of the hallway. 'Shit!'

Brian peered over Stella's shoulder at the mess on the floor. 'I'll take a look around the back.'

Stella retreated to the front porch while Brian checked the side windows and the small yard at the rear of the apartment.

'No sign of a break-in, Sarge.'

'See if any of the neighbours know anything, Brian. I'll get CSI out here.'

Stella arranged to meet the CSI team at the apartment and slipped her mobile back into her pocket. She looked up as Brian returned with an elderly gentleman wearing a dressing gown over his clothes and slippers on his feet.

'This is Mr Rogers, Sarge. He lives in number four. Says he saw her son here on Tuesday afternoon.'

'Was that unusual, Mr Rogers?' said Stella.

'Not really. He's here most weeks, at least once a week.'

'How did he get in?'

'He's got a key. Let's himself in whether Judy's here or not.'

'Have you met him?'

'Darren? Yeah, I've met him. He's a lad with a few problems.'

'Problems?' said Stella.

'Not very social,' said Mr Rogers.

Could be interesting, thought Stella. 'What sort of car does he drive?'

'One of those Hyundai things. A little red one that's seen better days.'

'See anybody else around this apartment, Mr Rogers?'

'I thought I saw a light in her front room Wednesday morning when I got up to have a pee. I thought Darren must have left it on. Now, I'm not so sure.'

'Why not?' said Stella.

'Darren left about an hour after he arrived,' said Mr Rogers, 'and, I'm pretty sure her light wasn't on when I went to bed.' He looked at Stella with what she thought was a sheepish grin. 'It's not like I spy on her, Sergeant, but I can see the front of her place from my bedroom. Anyway, I thought he must have come back but, then, there was that dreadful story on the news.'

'That's why we're here,' said Stella.

'Well, the light was off when I got up later, so I thought I must have imagined it.'

'What time was it when you saw the light?'

'Around two in the morning. That's when I usually have to get up.'

'How well did you know Judy Redding?'

'She's kept an eye on me since my wife died, so I guess you could say I know her pretty well.'

'Did you know Robert Washington?'

'Bob? Yeah, I knew Bob. He was married to Judy's sister. Spent a lot of time here after his wife died. That's when they started their online photography business. Have you seen their photos of the Flinders Ranges? Amazing!'

Stella wondered what else Judy Redding had been involved in that would explain her murder, since she couldn't imagine anyone being killed over amazing photographs of the Flinders Ranges.

'Is that all she did?' said Stella.

'She used to take wedding photos before she and Bob started their online business,' said Mr Rogers, 'but I'm pretty sure she'd given that away.'

'Did she ever say anything to you about being threatened?'

'Not to me, no.'

'Did she tell you she was going to Melrose?'

'She always told me when they were going away so I wouldn't worry about not seeing her around.'

'Ever meet Bob's new wife, Mr Rogers?'

'No. He always came around on his own.'

Stella handed Mr Rogers one of her cards. 'If you think of anything, Mr Rogers, please give me a call.'

While they waited for the CSI team to arrive, Brian searched through the case file for details of Judy Redding's next of kin.

'Her son lives in Elizabeth Downs, Sarge. We've got a mobile number. Looks like he was notified Wednesday afternoon while we were on our way to Melrose.'

'Any record of him contacting us before the search got underway?'

'Looks like the only person concerned for their where-abouts was Wendy Washington.'

'I guess that's not unusual,' said Stella, 'especially if she's had no contact with her ex and she told her son she'd be away for a week. But, I'd like to know what he was doing here while she was away. Check Registrations while you're at it.'

Brian keyed in Darren Harmer's details and waited for the search engine to display the results of his query.

'Red Hyundai i30.'

'We'll need him to tell us if anything is missing, assuming he didn't trash the place himself.'

'If our friend Rogers is right, Sarge, it's possible whoever broke in already knew they were dead.'

'Unless this is a random break-in by someone who'd worked out she was away.'

A white van pulled into the parking space outside apart-ment two. 'The boys are here,' said Brian.

'Give Darren a call. If he's available, set up a time. We need to speak to him.'

Stella got out of the car and walked over to where Sgt Barry Rice and the CSI team were unpacking their gear.

'We've got to stop meeting like this, Barry. People will start to talk.'

'People are already talking about you, Stella, and it's got nothing to do with me. How's Shaun?'

'Busy with the Hartley case.'

'That's got a couple more weeks to run from what I hear,' said Barry. 'What are we looking for?'

'Anything that will tell us who's been in this apartment. There's no obvious sign of a break in but, according to one of the neighbours, her son, who has his own key, was here Tuesday afternoon. He also thinks someone, possibly the son again, was here in the early hours of Wednesday morning.'

'Any other known visitors, Stella?'

'I expect you'll find prints from both our victims. I gather Washington was a regular visitor and you might want to get some prints from Mr Rogers in number four.'

'Okay. Do you have the key?'

'I'll get the son in so we can get his prints,' said Stella, handing Barry the key. 'Hopefully, Brian's managed to contact him, otherwise I'll get a patrol out to locate him.'

'Good luck with that. I'll get something to you as soon as I can.'

'Thanks, Barry.'

After an hour of negotiating traffic on their trip from the southern to the northern suburbs, they turned off Main North Road and headed into the depths of Elizabeth Downs. After a couple of turns, Brian parked their car in front of a new looking house with a dead front lawn and a faded red Hyundai i30 in the driveway.

'Looks like he hasn't got around to establishing the garden,' said Brian, as they walked up the driveway to the front door.

'Either that or he forgot to water it,' said Stella.

Brian rang the doorbell and they waited.

'He did say he'd be here, didn't he?' said Stella.

'He's here,' said Brian. 'Saw him watching from the front window when we pulled up.' He rang the doorbell again.

The front door opened slightly, held in place by a security chain. 'Are you the police?'

'I'm Detective Constable Rhodes, Darren. I spoke to you earlier. Can you let us in?'

'What do you want?'

'We want to talk to you about your mother,' said Brian.

'She's dead.'

'I know,' said Brian. 'We need to ask you a few questions.'

The door closed, then opened to reveal a balding man in his forties, wearing a dirty T-shirt stretched over the rotund belly overhanging the leather belt holding up his jeans.

'I'm Detective Sergeant Bruno,' said Stella, showing him her ID. 'Are you Darren Harmer?'

'Yeah.'

'Is that your car?' said Stella, pointing to the Hyundai.

Darren nodded. 'I thought you wanted to talk about Mum.'

'I do,' said Stella. 'Are you going to invite us in?'

'No,' said Darren. 'Dad says I'm not to let people into the house.'

'Does your father live here?'

'Yes, but he's not here.'

'Will he be here after work?' said Stella.

'He works at Roxby,' said Darren. 'He won't be home 'til Wednesday.'

'Does he know about your mother?'

'I told him. He said we'd work it out when he gets back.'

Obviously Judy Redding's death had not been an important enough event to bring her ex home early, thought Stella. 'When did he go up to Roxby?'

'Wednesday the week before last,' said Darren. 'He does two on and one off.'

That would put him out of the picture, if it was true, thought Stella.

'Darren, do you know your mother's neighbour, Mr Rogers?'

'Yeah.'

'He told us you visited your mother's apartment on Tuesday. Is that right?'

'Yeah. I go there every Tuesday.'

'Even when she's away?'

'She leaves food for me in the fridge.'

'Do you remember what time you were there?'

'I have to leave by three to beat the traffic coming home,' said Darren.

'You didn't go back early Wednesday morning, by any chance, did you?'

Darren crossed his arms and rested his right shoulder on the doorframe. 'Why would I do that?'

Good question, thought Stella. 'Does anybody else have a key to your mother's apartment, Darren?'

'I don't know.'

'Did your mother keep her apartment neat and tidy or was she a bit messy?'

'Mum doesn't like mess. I always have to be careful not to make a mess.'

'It looks like someone's been in her apartment, Darren. Do you think you could tell if anything was taken?'

'Maybe.'

'And, we'll need a set of your fingerprints.'

'Why?'

'We need to know which prints in your mother's apartment are yours so we can identify the ones that aren't.'

'Oh.'

'Get your coat and your keys, Darren. You need to come with us.'

It was dark by the time they got back to the apartment in Moana, after stopping off at the police station in Elizabeth to get Darren Harmer's fingerprints into the system.

'Slip these over your shoes, and don't touch anything,' said Sgt Rice, handing Darren and Brian plastic shoe covers.

'Find anything interesting?' said Stella, as Brian took Darren on a tour of the apartment.

'Looks like he got in through the roof,' said Barry. 'There's a couple of broken tiles on the back section.'

The burglar had obviously cased the place, thought Stella. 'He must have known no-one was home in these apartments.'

'The man from number four told us the adjoining apartments are holiday homes,' said Barry. 'Bloke probably could have smashed a window and nobody would have heard him.'

'Anything to identify whoever it was?'

'We've got some fibres that were caught on the rafters above the manhole and plenty of prints.'

'I've got the son's in the system for you,' said Stella.

'Thanks,' said Barry.

Brian and Darren returned from their tour of the apartment.

'The only things Darren thinks are missing are her cameras, laptop, purse and mobile phone, and we have those.'

'Did she have any jewellery?' said Stella.

'Mum wasn't into that stuff.'

'I wonder what they were looking for, then?' said Stella.

'The only things Mum collected were photographs,' said Darren, 'and her collection is still here.'

'What about the photographs she took?'

'They're all online or on her computer,' said Darren.

'Car's still in the garage,' said Sgt Rice.

'We've got the key,' said Brian.

'Did she keep any money in the house?' said Stella.

'I don't think so.'

'Maybe that's why they made such a mess,' said Sgt Rice. 'They didn't get anything for their trouble.'

'Might pay to check with the owners of the holiday apartments, Sarge,' said Brian, 'in case this has nothing to do with her death.'

'See if Mr Rogers knows who any of them are.'

CHAPTER 5

FIRST THING SATURDAY MORNING, Stella made her way to DI Williams' office.

'So, what's happening with your Melrose case, Bruno?'

'Still early days, sir. No clear leads.'

'Have you spoken with the wife?'

'Yes. Claims she was aware her husband was having sex with Redding, who happens to be the sister of his first wife.'

DI Williams raised an eyebrow.

'They'd come to an arrangement, apparently.'

'Bit unusual, don't you think?'

Stella shrugged. 'Washington wouldn't be the first bloke to have a wife and a mistress, sir, but this is the first time a wife has told me it was an agreed arrangement.'

'His first wife's sister?' said DI Williams. 'How long's he been married to his current wife?'

'Twelve years.'

'Wonder how long he'd been banging his sister-in-law.'

'It's not like we can ask her, sir, but her ex might have something to say about it. They split up around twenty years ago, according to Mrs Washington.'

'Could the wife be behind this?' said DI Williams. 'Perhaps she was getting the raw end of this arrangement.'

'If she's involved, she'd need help,' said Stella. 'She can hardly walk. There's no way she could climb Mt Remarkable, let alone go down into that gully and bash their heads in.'

'You did it, though, didn't you, Bruno?'

'I haven't been in a car crash that buggered up my legs like she has, sir. She walks with a stick.'

'Check her out, Bruno. You never know who she might be connected to.'

Suspecting the spouse was typical DI Williams, thought Stella, but having met Mrs Washington she couldn't picture her arranging for someone to murder her husband. If she had, though, it occurred to Stella she'd have known when to raise the alarm to draw attention away from herself. She decided to check Washington's call record to confirm the nightly phone call story, in case DI Williams was right.

'I had to get CSI out to Redding's apartment. There's been a break-in. But, according to her son, it appears nothing was taken.'

'Random or connected to her murder?'

'Too early to say,' said Stella. 'I'll wait and see what CSI come up with. The place was turned upside down as if they were looking for something.'

'Did CSI get anything from the place they were staying in Melrose?'

'That's a bit of a puzzle, too,' said Stella. 'There's no sign anybody's been in their cabin or Washington's car, and that's where all their expensive equipment was. The only thing that appears to be missing is his new drone, and that could still be on the mountain up some tree.'

'Maybe robbery isn't the motive, Bruno, but why would someone break into her apartment and not his house.'

'Mrs Washington was home,' said Stella, 'and she has an alarm system.'

'Or she organised the break-in.'

'Guess that's a possibility we'll need to explore,' said Stella.

DI Williams scratched the back of his head. 'Anything come through on Crime Stoppers?'

'One anonymous call from a public phone in the Elizabeth Shopping Centre about Washington getting what he deserved. We're following up with the shopping centre to see if their CCTV covers the phone booth.'

'Doesn't Redding's next of kin live out there somewhere?'

'Her son. Darren Harmer. Lives in Elizabeth Downs with his father, who works at Roxby.'

'They have alibis?'

'The son was seen at his mother's apartment early after-noon on the day they were killed by one of the neighbours,' said Stella, 'and he's told us his father has been in Roxby for the last two weeks. I'm following that up.'

'That sighting at her apartment a coincidence?'

'Apparently not. He's a regular visitor on Tuesdays. Some-thing about collecting food from his mother.'

'How old's this son?'

'Early forties.'

'Mummy's boy is he?'

Stella shrugged. 'Bit of a social isolate, I think. I wouldn't be surprised if he was on the spectrum.'

'What's he do?'

'Website design. Set up the website our victims used to sell their photographs.'

'Maybe they were taking photos of people or things they shouldn't have. You need to find out a bit more about these people, Bruno. They obviously pissed someone off.'

'That might take a while, sir. There are a lot of photos.'

'Keep me posted, Bruno, but don't be surprised if it's the wife. It usually is when there's another woman involved.'

———

Stella's mobile phone rang as she left DI William's office.

'Got a minute, Stella?'

'Sure, Barry. What's up?'

'Got a match for some of the prints from that place at Moana. A Jason White,' said Barry. 'He's got form. Last done for break and enter about eight years ago. Been out since March last year.'

'Got an address for me?'

'Christies Beach. I'll send you the details.'

'Ta.'

Stella heard the ping of Barry's email arriving as she ended the call. She opened the email and keyed White's details into the database. White had been in and out of the justice system since he'd turned fifteen, the same age as her son. She wondered what his backstory was and why he'd break into an apartment and not take anything.

'You awake, Brian?'

'Studying this phone log, Sarge.'

'That will have to wait. We've got a suspect to talk to about the break-in at Redding's.'

'Who?'

'Someone called Jason White,' said Stella. 'Wouldn't be surprised if the break-in had nothing to do with the murder, though. Looks like break and enter is his thing.'

'Give me a tick,' said Brian. 'I need a comfort stop.'

'I'll meet you downstairs in five.'

———

The backup patrol from Christies Beach was parked three houses down when Brian pulled up in front of the address they had for White.

The door was answered by a blond-headed boy Stella thought was about ten.

'Who are you?'

Stella smiled. 'The police. Is your father home?'

The boy turned back into the house. 'Mum! The police are here again!'

A woman appeared behind the boy in the doorway. 'What do you want?'

Stella held up her ID. 'Detective Sergeant Bruno. I'd like to talk to Jason. Is he home?'

The woman crossed her arms across her chest. 'Can't you lot leave him alone?'

'Is he home?' said Stella.

A slightly built man with a shaved head, wearing jeans and a loose fitting black sweatshirt, came up behind the woman standing in the doorway. 'It's alright, honey. I haven't done anything.'

'Jason White?' said Stella.

'Yeah. What do you want?'

'I'd like to ask you a few questions,' said Stella.

Jason pushed past his wife and stood on the porch with Stella and Brian. 'What's this about?'

'We're investigating a murder,' said Stella.

'A murder?'

Stella opened the image of Judy Redding on her smartphone and showed it to Jason. 'Do you know this woman?'

Jason looked at the photograph and shook his head. 'No.'

'But you know where she lived,' said Stella.

'What?'

Stella showed him a photograph of the Moana apartments

and watched Jason's eyes flick from her to Brian and then to the patrol car coming to a stop in front of the house.

'What's this got to do with me?'

'Where were you in the early hours of Wednesday morning?'

Jason looked at his wife. 'Here. In bed.'

Stella looked at the woman standing in the doorway. 'Is that right?'

The woman shrugged. 'Yeah, I suppose.'

'What does that mean?' said Stella.

'I was asleep, wasn't I?

'Why does it matter?' said Jason.

'There was a break-in at these apartments on Wednesday morning,' said Stella, 'where this woman lived, and your finger-prints are all over the place.'

Jason glanced at his wife waiting in the doorway. 'I did a job for her.'

'So, you knew her, then?'

'Judy,' said Jason. 'She takes photos.'

'What was this job you did for her?'

'I clean carpets,' said Jason. 'I did her place Thursday before last. Had to shift her furniture. Happens a lot with older women living on their own.'

'Why didn't you say so?' said Stella.

'I did something else for her,' said Jason, looking at his wife.

Stella waited.

'She took some photos of me.'

'Why would that be a problem?' said Stella.

'She asked me to take my clothes off,' said Jason.

'Why?'

'Said she'd get me some modelling work for a group she worked for,' said Jason. 'Easy way to make money.'

'Guess you'll be missing out on that,' said Stella. 'Do you have a copy of the invoice for the carpet cleaning job?'

'Sure. It'll be in my van.'

Stella waited for Brian to get in behind the wheel. 'What do you think?'

'Wonder who got him the carpet cleaning job. Perfect cover for casing a place if you ask me.'

'Maybe,' said Stella, 'but I'd like to know more about those photos he claims she took of him and who she was planning to sell them to.'

'Means we're back to square one with the break in, though, Sarge,' said Brian, easing the car out into the street.

'Yeah, well let's not write it off just yet, Brian. I'd like to find out a bit more about this carpet cleaning operation before we let him off the hook.'

'Did you see the look his wife gave him when he said she'd asked him to pose in the nude?'

Stella laughed. 'No wonder he didn't want to admit he knew her until I told him about the prints.'

CHAPTER 6

STELLA STOOD with Shaun on the sidelines at Campbelltown Memorial Oval watching Josh's soccer team, under the direction of her brother, Stefano, play in the Sunday morning competition.

'Not looking good,' said Shaun, as one of the strikers on the opposing team sent the ball into the back of the net for the second time in ten minutes.

'It's only a game,' said Stella.

'Still, I like to be with the winning side,' said Shaun.

'Don't we all?'

Shaun wrapped his arm around her shoulders. 'Making any progress with your double murder?'

'No motive and no witnesses,' said Stella, 'but one intriguing bit of information.'

'What's that?'

'Someone broke into one of the victim's homes but didn't take anything. Just trashed the place.'

'Maybe their intention was to send a message.'

Stella had to admit to herself she hadn't thought of that. 'If that's the case, there's probably no connection between the break-in and her murder.'

'Why would you think that?'

'Everything points to the break-in being in the early hours of Wednesday morning, which is well after they were killed.'

'Maybe your victims have more than one set of enemies,' said Shaun.

'That would complicate things,' said Stella.

'Could make it interesting, though.'

Stella nudged him in the ribs. 'Interesting isn't exactly what I'm looking for.'

'Any idea who did the break-in?'

'Nothing concrete. Just something that doesn't quite feel right.'

'What do you mean?'

'Her carpets were cleaned by an ex-con with a record for break and enter a few days before she left on her trip with Washington. His prints are all over the furniture.'

'What did he have to say for himself?'

'Initially, he denied knowing who she was, but I think that might have been because his wife was listening when we spoke to him,' said Stella. 'Turns out he posed for some nude photos he didn't want her to know about. Seems Redding had promised him some easy money but he had a copy of the invoice he'd given her for cleaning her carpets, and he's got an alibi for the time of the break-in.'

'Still, those photos might be worth following up.'

'Waiting for access to her computer. Boys haven't cracked the password yet.'

'What's Frank Williams think?'

'That it's the wife. That's what Frank always thinks.'

'Have to admit, that story about their arrangement is a bit weird, don't you think?'

'Don't go getting any ideas, lover boy. Frank would be right if it was me and I found out you were screwing around.'

'So, you agreeing with Frank?'

Stella leant in closer to Shaun. 'For all we know, she could have been happy with the arrangement, but that won't stop me questioning her story. Trouble is, I just don't have any evidence pointing me to anyone.'

'But, it's a possible motive, honey.'

After Monday morning's briefing with DI Williams, Stella scrolled through the call log for Robert Washington's mobile phone. She compared the lists of incoming and outgoing calls. He'd received considerably more calls than he'd made.

She sorted the incoming calls by phone number. A high percentage of them were from his wife's number. Stella made a note and sorted the outgoing calls. Washington had made more calls to Redding than he had to his wife over the last six months of his life. She looked at the location data. Most of the calls to Redding had been made from Seaford, suggesting he'd called her from home.

Stella wondered if that meant anything, given the arrangement Wendy Washington had told her about. Then she recalled Wendy claiming her husband had called her every night when he was away on his trips. She sorted Robert's outgoing calls to his wife by date, looking for a discernible pattern, before realising there was one piece of information she didn't have.

'Brian, are you into Washington's laptop?'

'Yeah.'

'Check his calendar. Is there a record of when he went on his trips?'

'Give me a minute.'

Stella waited.

'Looks like he went somewhere in the first week every second month, at least over the last twelve months.'

Stella looked at Washington's calls to his wife's number. There was nothing suggesting he'd called his wife from places outside the metropolitan area during the first week of any month over the last six months. She looked at his wife's calls to his number and narrowed her search to the first week of March. Wendy had called Robert every night at 7 pm.

'Where was he in the first week of March, Brian?'

'Port Lincoln.'

'Appears Mrs Washington was the one doing the calling when he was away.'

'Is that a problem?'

'Don't know, but it looks more like a nagging wife checking on her husband than a concerned husband calling home to reassure her he's okay.'

'Yeah, well in my book, Sarge, a concerned husband wouldn't be away screwing his girlfriend every second month even if his wife knew about it.'

'Not all husbands are blessed with a loving wife like you, Brian.'

'Trust,' said Brian. 'Makes all the difference.'

'Yeah, and not sharing yourself with your sister-in-law,' said Stella. 'Anything interesting on that laptop?'

'Dunno, yet. There's heaps of photos.'

Stella left Brian to explore the contents of Washington's laptop and turned her attention to Judy Redding's call log. Redding had called a lot more numbers over the last six months than Robert Washington and Stella wondered if they were work or social calls. She looked at the details listed next to each number. Most of the calls were to locations within the Adelaide metropolitan area, a few were to interstate contacts. There were several incoming calls from international numbers Stella recognised from having seen them on the missed calls register on her own phone. She wished someone would find a way to stop the idiots making those calls at all hours of the day and night, as she was sick of blocking them individually as they hit her phone.

She turned her attention back to her task and looked to see if she could find the number for Coast Carpet Cleaners that Jason White had given her, and found it listed in Redding's outgoing and incoming calls in the week before the date of the invoice Jason had given her. At least that part of his story checked out.

Stella looked at the numbers Redding had called and wondered how many people she'd told she was going to Melrose with Washington. Someone had to have told their killer where they'd be, otherwise she was dealing with a random event, and Stella didn't like random events.

———

Stella waited for Darren Harmer to answer his phone.

'Darren, Detective Sergeant Bruno. Do you have a minute?'

'Yeah.'

'Darren, who would have known your mother was going to be in Melrose last week?'

'Me. Mr Rogers, I guess. Mum always told him when she was going away.'

'Anybody else?'

'Well, Mrs Washington would have known,' said Darren, 'and anybody she told.'

'So, not that many people?' said Stella.

'I wouldn't say that,' said Darren. 'They usually told their subscribers where they were going for their photo shoots. Hang on, let me check their last newsletter.'

Stella waited. She could hear the sounds of Darren using a keyboard and assumed he was searching for the newsletter on his computer.

'Here it is. It went out on the twenty-sixth of April with their itinerary,' said Darren. 'It even says they were planning on using their new drone.'

'Who got that email?'

'It goes to people all over the world,' said Darren. 'There's about five thousand subscribers.'

God, half the world would have known where to find them, thought Stella. 'Do you have access to their list of subscribers?'

'I have access to all their stuff. I do the admin on their website.'

'Can you send me a copy of that list of subscribers?'

'Sure.'

'You don't happen to know the password for her computer, by any chance, do you?'

'Try rosebud57 with a capital D, 'said Darren. 'If that get's you in, you should be able to access her Mailchimp account. She used the password manager in the browser to make it easy to log in.'

'Okay, thanks,' said Stella. 'I'll let you know if that works.'

Stella hung up and called the technician working on circumventing the password on Redding's laptop. 'Try rosebud57 with a capital D.'

Stella waited while the technician tried the password.

'We're in, Sarge. I'll bring it down to you.'

CHAPTER 7

STELLA SCROLLED through the list of subscribers in the victims' Mailchimp account, wondering if it contained the killer's details and how on earth she'd know if she was looking at them.

'Why would anyone subscribe to a photographer's website, Brian?'

'To download images to use on a blog or to decorate coffee cups and T-shirts. You should see some of the stuff you can buy online,' said Brian, smiling at her over the top of Washington's laptop. 'I reckon I've seen some of these photos on Facebook. You know, those pictures people write words on.'

'People pay for those, do they? I thought there were sites where you could get that sort of thing for free.'

'Guess some people prefer to pay so their images stand out from the crowd,' said Brian.

Stella opened the victims' website from a link in Redding's favourites. It contained thousands of images curated into categories.

Every image was available for download, at prices ranging from $5 through to $50 depending on size and resolution, or through an annual membership offering unlimited downloads for $250. Stella clicked through the categories. None of them offered nudes, so she wondered what Redding had planned to do with the shots she'd taken of Jason White.

'Why would anyone want to kill a photographer?' said Stella, 'especially one specialising in Australian landscapes?'

'Check out her photos app, Sarge. See what else she was shooting. Those pictures of White have to be somewhere,' said Brian, as he opened another album on Washington's laptop. 'Looks like Washington wasn't shy about including people in his images. This lot looks like they were taken in the city.'

Stella opened the Photos app on Redding's laptop and clicked through the albums. Redding had quite a collection of images of young men standing in what looked to Stella as a standard set of poses, ranging from fully dressed to totally undressed, taken in front of a screen she recalled seeing in the studio Redding had set up in the back bedroom of her apartment.

'Take a look at these, Brian. I wonder who she was selling these to.'

Brian stood behind her and looked over her shoulder. 'Nothing like that on his computer, Sarge.'

'Perhaps she was freelancing on the side without his knowledge.'

'Maybe she just liked looking at young bodies.'

Stella leant back in her chair. 'Jason said she'd promised him money when she took these. She had to be selling them somewhere.'

'Gay porn would be my guess, Sarge.'

'You don't think women are into pornography, Brian?'

'I guess you'd know more about that than me, Sarge. I only know about the stuff blokes look at, but I hear women are more into stuff made by women for women.'

'That would figure,' said Stella, 'and we are dealing with a female photographer here.'

'What would be our motive?' said Brian.

'Maybe one of these guys had second thoughts or she didn't pay him what she'd promised.'

'What would be his motive for killing Washington?'

'Good question, Brian. And, why in the Flinders?' said Stella. 'There's something we're missing here.'

'Is there any way we can find out who these blokes are, Sarge? Talking to them or whoever she was sending their portfolios to might help us work out what's going on.'

'I wonder if she got them to sign a contract of some sort.'

'She'd need their bank details to pay them,' said Brian.

Stella turned back to Redding's laptop. 'Let's see what I can find.'

As Stella searched the contents of Redding's laptop, she noticed a clear preference for order. The photographs were catalogued and tagged. The folders and files were organised according to a logical naming system.

After reading several documents, Stella realised Redding had been operating a boutique modelling agency, placing photographs of her clients with magazines around the world and setting up appointments with fashion photographers for her models. She opened a spreadsheet named *Contact Details* in a folder named *Models* and scanned the details of the fifty-two models Redding had listed. She looked for Jason White and found his details in the last row of the list.

She opened a file named *Placements* and scanned its contents. Redding had been representing some of her models for more than ten years and had enjoyed more success placing some than she had with others.

She opened a file named *Payments*. It appeared Redding had paid thousands to a few of her models, hundreds to several others, and nothing to most of the young men she had persuaded to pose for her.

Stella read through the agency agreement Redding had used with her models. She had promised to represent them and promote them to her contacts in the industry. The wording contained no guarantee of income or success but there was a clause awarding Redding twenty percent of any income earned, which a quick online check revealed was fairly standard.

Stella turned her attention to Redding's emails, where she found a folder named for each of her models. She opened each folder and read through any recent emails Redding had saved in it. There were a few inquiries concerning recent placements, several confirmations of appointment details with a fashion photographer in the city, and some thank you notes for recent payments. There was nothing threatening.

Stella called the fashion photographer mentioned in the emails and asked him about his relationship with Redding.

'I've known Judy for years, Sergeant. In fact, back in our younger days, we did weddings together. That was before I set up my own business and she got interested in landscapes.'

'What about recently?'

'She had a stable of young male models as a side interest, I'd say. I've used a few of them but there's not that much demand for them these days.'

'Are you aware of anything that would suggest she was in trouble?'

'I can't think of a reason why anyone would want to kill her, if that's what you mean?'

'If you hear anything, you've got my number.'

Stella slipped her phone into her pocket and decided she was probably on a wild goose chase. 'Think it's time we had a coffee, Brian.'

───────

When they reached the coffee shop, Stella commandeered a table in the outside seating area while Brian placed their order. She watched the traffic in Angas Street and wondered what else her dead photographers had been mixed up in.

'I wonder if we're looking in the wrong place for a motive,' said Stella, as Brian placed the table number between them.

'I was thinking I'd look through their bank records,' said Brian.

'Why's that?'

'In case they were blackmailing someone with an incriminating photograph.'

'You'd pay cash for that, wouldn't you?'

'Probably, especially if it was a lump sum,' said Brian, 'but what if you were making a regular payment? You could make it look like a subscription or something like that.'

The waitress arrived and served their coffees.

'Do you think whoever they were blackmailing would be dumb enough to leave a trail, especially if he then decided to kill them?'

Brian shrugged. 'You never know your luck if you don't play the game, Sarge.'

Stella sipped her coffee. 'We should probably be talking to a wider circle of people who knew them.'

'Perhaps we could start with his mates in Lions,' said Brian, 'seeing he's been a member for years.'

'And let's see if we can find any members of their extended families to talk to besides his wife and Darren.'

'Any luck with locating her ex, Sarge?'

'He's in the clear. His employer's given him a solid alibi for the day of the murder.'

'What about the boys up north? They having any luck interviewing the locals?'

'Still nothing, as far as I know,' said Stella.

'Somebody must have seen something,' said Brian. 'It's not as if we're dealing with the invisible man.'

'It's a pretty small place, Brian.'

'Guess the locals have become immune to tourists, which might explain why they didn't see anything out of the ordinary,' said Brian, as he placed his empty coffee cup on the table.

'Hadn't thought of it like that, but I suppose if you see strange cars every day strange cars sort of become normal and you no longer notice them.'

'Maybe we are dealing with an invisible man, then, Sarge. Or at least someone so everyday normal nobody noticed him.'

'That would make him a local, wouldn't it?'

'Or someone familiar enough with the place to know how to blend in.'

CHAPTER 8

BRIAN PULLED into the car park of the Seaford Central Shopping Centre and found a place to park two rows back from the entrance.

'Let's hope our man's on time,' said Stella, glancing at the photograph of himself Ross Eagles had sent her.

'He's retired, isn't he?'

'That doesn't mean anything, Brian. My dad's retired but he's always got a million things on.'

They walked into the shopping mall and made their way to Gloria Jean's Coffees, where Ross Eagles was waiting for them.

'Mr Eagles?' said Stella.

'Call me Ross.'

'This is Detective Constable Rhodes,' said Stella, showing him her ID. 'Can we get you a coffee, Ross?'

'A flat white, if you don't mind,' said Ross.

'Shall we find a table?' said Stella, handing Brian a twenty dollar note.

'Sure,' said Ross, leading them to a table on the edge of the seating area.

'Come here often?' said Stella, as she pulled out a chair.

'My office away from home, you might say.' Ross smiled

and sat opposite Stella. 'I only live around the corner, a five-minute walk and, besides, they make better coffee than I'd ever make you.'

'Thanks for making the time to speak to us, I know how busy the retired life can be these days.'

'Being busy beats sitting around doing nothing, Sergeant. That's one reason I took on being Club President.'

Brian arrived with their coffees and sat down between Stella and Ross.

'How well did you know Robert Washington?' said Stella.

'Bob and I go way back, Sergeant. I was best man when he married Chris.'

'So, you'd know Judy Redding as well, then?'

'Oh, yes, I knew Judy. I wanted to marry her back then, but that was before Gerald came on the scene. And, well, you probably know what happened there.'

Stella nodded. 'Are you married, Ross?'

'Lost Georgia to that damn breast cancer not long after Chris died,' said Ross. 'Me and Bob were both on the prowl again in our fifties.' He shook his head. 'It's not the same.'

'Is that when Bob met Wendy?'

'It's a small world, Sergeant. Wendy was Tom Landy's wife. Wonderful man, Tom. Worked with me right up until the cancer got him. Terrible way to go, you know.' Ross took a sip of his coffee. 'Anyway, we'd all been in Lions for years, and a couple of years after Tom's passing, Bob and Wendy announced out of the blue they were getting married.'

'Bit of a surprise, was it?' Stella took a sip of her coffee and waited for Ross to reply.

'Was to me. I thought he'd hooked up with Judy.'

'How did you feel about that?'

'Didn't mean anything to me, Sergeant. I wasn't really looking for another relationship. I'm happy enough on my own.'

'Fair enough,' said Stella. 'Is there anything in Bob's past that might have come back to haunt him?'

'What do you mean?'

'Anything he might have been involved in that led to someone getting hurt or losing a lot of money?'

Ross leant back and took a long sip of his flat white. 'You know, Bob was a charmer. He was one of those blokes that didn't make enemies, but he did tell me once he'd been threatened a couple of times after he'd been an expert witness in a trial.'

'Oh, when was that?'

'It was before Chris died, about five years before she died, I reckon.'

'Do you remember any of the details about the trial?'

'It had to do with a construction company. They'd altered the plans for a bridge without consulting the engineer who'd designed it, and it collapsed. It was big news at the time. Bob was called in to investigate and give evidence at the trial. They went bust.'

'Do you remember the name of the company?'

Ross scratched his head. 'Wilson Construction, or something like that. It was in all the papers.'

'So, this would have been about twenty years ago?'

'That sounds about right.'

'Did Bob by any chance tell you who had made those threats after the case?'

'No, but I think he might have reported it, at least he said he was going to.'

'If that's the case, we should be able to follow that up,' said Stella. 'Is there anything else you can think of that might have triggered a desire to kill him?'

Ross shook his head. 'Not really. Bob was a people person. He didn't go around making enemies.'

'Bob not the type to play around?'

'Bob? You've got to be joking. Faithful as a dog, he was.'

Stella glanced at Brian. He was staring at the coffee cup between his hands. She could see he was doing his best not to smile.

'How would you describe his relationship with Judy?'

'That was all business after he married Wendy. At least, that's what he told me. Said the only thing they had in common was their passion for photography.'

'Do you know anything about what Judy was involved in?'

'Didn't really have all that much to do with her after she decided I wasn't the one, to be honest. She moved out of my orbit when she married Gerald, and only came back in after Chris died, when Bob brought her to functions before he teamed up with Wendy. All she ever talked to me about was photography.'

'Was Bob always into photography?'

'He took it up as a hobby when we were at uni. Used to tell me all sorts of stories about what they got up to in that darkroom.'

'You were never tempted?'

'I didn't have the patience for all that fiddling about. I didn't get into taking photos until I got one of these things.' Ross waved his smartphone in the air in front of him. 'Georgia was the one who took the photos of the kids when they were growing up.'

'Did Bob have kids?'

Ross shook his head. 'It didn't work out for him and Chris. That was one of his regrets, not having kids of his own.'

Stella finished her coffee and handed Ross one of her cards. 'Thanks for you time, Ross. If you think of anything else that might help, please give me a call.'

Stella searched the internet for Wilson Construction on her smartphone as Brian turned the car onto Commercial Road and headed back towards the city. After scrolling through several pages of hits, she came across an article covering the court case. 'Ah, here's our case.'

Stella scanned the article. 'Washington's named as the expert who confirmed the company hadn't complied with the original engineering specifications.'

'So, Eagles was right about that bit,' said Brian.

'We checked the database for Washington, didn't we?'

'There was nothing there, Sarge.'

Stella pulled the onboard computer towards her and keyed in Washington's details. 'Not even a speeding fine!' She pushed the screen away and leant back into her seat.

'Maybe he was having a lend of Eagles,' said Brian.

'People generally don't make that stuff up, Brian. More likely he didn't take it seriously.'

'Perhaps he should have.'

Stella gazed through the windscreen. The Wilson Construction case had been heard before she joined the force. 'Do you remember this case at all, Brian?'

'That would be a civil case, Sarge. I was playing in the drug taskforce back then.'

'Guess it wouldn't hurt to read the court transcripts and find out who was impacted by the decision.'

'Anyone named in that article you were reading?'

Stella reopened the article. 'It names the directors, John Anthony and David Mark Wilson.'

'Didn't we interview some Wilsons in Melrose?'

Stella opened her notes. 'The people staying in Whitby

Street. John and David, and their wives. They claimed they'd spent the day at Alligator Gorge and had the photos to prove it.'

'Those blokes were in their early sixties, weren't they?'

'Yeah, but they looked a hell of a lot fitter than you, Brian.'

'I'm working on it.'

Stella smiled. Brian was on a diet and a mandatory exercise program that saw him on the golf course every morning before he came to work. 'You'll get there, Brian.'

'Thanks for the vote of confidence, Sarge.'

Stella took in the smile in his eyes. She liked Brian, but she also enjoyed stirring him about his lack of physical fitness.

'I wonder if they're the same people,' said Brian.

'Guess we'd better find out.'

'Twenty years is a long time to wait for revenge, don't you think?'

'Some people are patient, Brian.'

'You'd think you'd get over it after all that time.'

'Twenty years of slow simmering resentment can push you over the edge if you don't let it go, Brian.'

'Yeah, so May keeps telling me.'

'I wonder what triggers someone to take that next step.'

'It's always me forgetting to do something that sets May off.'

'You better be careful then. You don't want to go pushing May over the edge. She might be tempted to find another use for those golf clubs of yours.'

'I think I'm safe, Sarge. She would have done it by now if she was going to do it.'

'I wouldn't be so sure, Brian.'

Back in the office, Stella ran background checks on the Wilson brothers while Brian scoured through the victims' bank accounts.

The brothers had declared bankruptcy following the judgement in the Wilson Construction case, and did not appear again in company records until ten years later, when they'd registered as the directors of Seaford Landscaping.

Stella reviewed the company records for Seaford Landscaping and discovered there'd been a change in ownership at the start of the year. That fitted with the Wilson brothers being retired, which was what they'd told her when she'd interviewed them in Melrose.

She keyed their details into the database. Neither brother had a criminal record. Stella knew she'd need something besides the coincidence of the brothers being in Melrose at the time of the murders to convince DI Williams they were suspects.

She sat back in her chair. They had motive: Washington's assessment that they hadn't adhered to the design specifications for the bridge had led to the court decision that destroyed their business. They had opportunity: they'd known where Washington would be on the day he was killed. But why now? Why not when their passions were hot, twenty years ago?

It just didn't seem likely to Stella. Their wives would have to be in on it, at least as far as confirming their alibi, and there was the question of Judy Redding. Why would they kill her? As far as she knew, there was no connection between Redding and the Wilsons. Was Redding simply collateral damage? That didn't fit with a revenge killing in Stella's thinking. There was something missing, and Stella didn't like it when things didn't add up. Besides, how would they have known Washington would be in Melrose?

She ran a search on the list of subscribers to the victim's

website. The three Wilsons listed were all located in the United Kingdom and none were named John or David, but that didn't necessarily mean they weren't on the list, given the way people composed email addresses and the fact they could input anything into the name fields when they subscribed.

Stella looked across at Brian. He was staring at the screen of his computer.

'Having any luck, Brian?'

Brian looked up from his monitor. 'Nothing jumping out at me, Sarge. All looks pretty routine to me.'

'Think we might have to talk to the Wilsons.'

CHAPTER 9

When John Wilson arrived at Christies Beach Police Station accompanied by Gordon Swift, his lawyer, Stella wondered whether he was simply taking precautions or if he had something to hide.

'What is the nature of your inquiries, Sergeant?' said Gordon, as they took their seats in the interview room.

'This is a murder investigation, Mr Swift. Your client is one of the last people to have seen the victims alive.'

'I understand he's already given you a statement about that, Sergeant.'

'That's correct,' said Stella, 'but a few things have come to our attention since we last spoke with Mr Wilson that I'd like to discuss with him.'

'Like what?' said John.

'You never mentioned you knew Robert Washington, Mr Wilson. Why was that?'

John Wilson smiled and leant back in his chair. 'I knew who he was, Sergeant, but I wouldn't say I knew him. I guess someone has mentioned our court case to you. Would I be right?'

'That has come up,' said Stella.

'Well, I never saw it as his fault we got done over, if that's what you're worried about?'

'Care to explain?'

'We made a mistake. We got the calculations wrong and the materials we used weren't up to the job. We were lucky no-one got hurt.'

'Perhaps you should read the court transcripts instead of wasting my client's time, Sergeant,' said Gordon.

'I've read them, Mr Swift. They don't tell me how your client felt, since they only report what was said in court, and I'm obliged to probe a little deeper than that to establish if there is a link or not. I can't do that without your client's cooperation.'

'It's okay, Gordon,' said John. 'There is no link to expose. I'd didn't have any hard feelings against the man. He was only doing his job.'

'Have you had any interactions with Mr Washington since that time?' said Stella.

'As you can imagine, we had to start again after that disaster. We lost everything, including our reputation. In fact, I had to go interstate to find work, and I didn't come back until my brother wanted to start a landscape gardening business here in Seaford. This area was booming back then. There were new houses going up everywhere.' He paused and smiled. 'Life's funny, you know. We'd only been in business for a couple of years when we got the job to landscape Bob Washington's place. That's the only time I had anything to do with him, until we bumped into him in that pub in Melrose last year.'

'Last year?' said Stella.

'We do a trip up into the Flinders most years,' said John. 'That was when he told us he was into landscape photography.'

'Have you bought any of his work?'

'My wife likes that sort of stuff,' said John. 'I think she

might have signed onto their website. I know she gets their newsletter.'

'So, you knew they'd be in Melrose again this year?'

'Maureen did mention it.'

'How did your brother react to meeting Mr Washington again?'

'That's a speculative question, Sergeant,' said Gordon.

'Oh, he wasn't fussed,' said John, waving away his lawyer's objection. 'They'd met through Lions before I came back from Victoria.'

Bloody small world, thought Stella. 'Did you know Judy Redding at all?'

John placed his elbows on the table and brought his fingertips together in front of his face. 'I hadn't expected to see her again, especially not with Washington.'

Stella felt a tingle in the back of her neck. 'Oh, why's that?'

'Her name was Harmer when she was with us. She did our accounts,' said John. 'Lost her job when we went under.'

'She was Washington's sister-in-law,' said Stella.

'Keeping it in the family, was he?'

'What do you mean?' said Stella.

'I got the impression they were a couple,' said John, 'even though David said she wasn't his wife.'

'She was his first wife's sister,' said Stella.

'Well, one doesn't like to talk badly of the dead, Sergeant, but there was definitely chemistry between those two.'

'Had you seen Ms Redding since the collapse of your construction business?'

'Not until last year,' said John.

'When will your brother be back?' said Stella. 'I'd like to talk to him as well.'

'Friday.'

'Thank you for coming in, Mr Wilson. If you think of anything that might help, please give me a call.'

'Only wish we'd accepted their invitation to join them that morning, Sergeant. Things might have worked out differently if we had.'

'Why didn't you?' said Stella.

'We'd done the summit walk the day before,' said John, 'and the girls wanted to see Alligator Gorge. We'd missed it last year because of the rain.'

Before heading back to the city, Stella decided to call in on Wendy Washington and check the landscaping story John Wilson had told them.

There was a black Toyota Rav 4 parked in the driveway when they pulled up in front of the house.

'Looks like a professional job,' said Brian, as they walked to the front door.

'I wasn't aware you'd become an expert in garden design, Brian?'

'May's having our front yard done by a couple of young blokes. It's got this sort of look to it.'

'What look's that, Brian.'

'Organised.'

Stella laughed and pushed the button for the doorbell.

A few moments later, a man with silver hair and well-defined muscles opened the door. 'Can I help you?'

'Police,' said Stella, holding out her ID. 'I'd like a word with Mrs Washington, if she's home.'

'Let them in, Dan!'

'Dan Stiles. Wendy's brother,' said the man, offering his hand.

'Detective Sergeant Bruno,' said Stella, 'and this is Detective Constable Rhodes.'

'Come in. She's in the front room.'

Wendy Washington was sitting in the same recliner they'd left her in on their last visit.

'Any news?' said Wendy.

'Not yet, I'm afraid,' said Stella, 'but I have a couple of questions I'd like to ask you, if you don't mind.'

'What about?'

'Did your husband ever mention John or David Wilson?'

'We bumped into David and Mandy at a Lions' function about ten years ago. It was a bit of a laugh, especially for the boys. Bob had to explain to me what had happened when they'd first met. Didn't seem to bother them.'

'Bob would have been well known to David Wilson, then?'

'I'd say so. We did a lot of things together for Lions before I had my accident.'

'What about David's brother, John?'

'He's not in Lions, as far as I know, but I met him when Bob had the landscaping done.'

'Were you aware Judy had worked for the Wilsons before the court case?'

'Bob never said anything about that,' said Wendy. 'Why all these questions?'

'We spoke to Ross Eagles. He told us about the court case and said Bob had told him he'd been threatened a few times after the case.'

'That was all before I got together with Bob, and he never said anything about threats to me. Besides, Ross is a bit of an old woman, if you know what I mean. Likes his gossip.'

'The other thing is the Wilsons were in Melrose at the time of your husband's death. In fact, they had dinner together in the North Star Hotel on the Monday night.'

'I thought I heard Mandy in the background,' said Wendy.

'Where were they the day Bob and Judy were killed?' said Dan.

'Alligator Gorge,' said Stella.

'That's not far from Melrose,' said Dan, 'only be a half hour drive, I reckon.'

'Know the area, do you, Mr Stiles?'

'I have a few clients up that way.'

'And what do you do, Mr Stiles, if you don't mind me asking?'

'I'm in IT, Sergeant. I help small business owners set up accounting software on their computers.'

'So, what are you suggesting?' said Stella.

'They were friends, Dan,' said Wendy.

'Bob caused them a lot of grief,' said Dan. 'I'd want revenge if he'd done that to me.'

'That's not how John Wilson sees it,' said Stella.

'Just saying,' said Dan. 'They'd be on my list of suspects.'

Stella blinked. She didn't like being told how to do her job, especially by older men.

'Do you know John or David Wilson, Mr Stiles?'

Dan shook his head. 'I only know what I've heard, Sergeant. I've never met them.'

'I take it you knew Bob?'

'Yes.'

'Dan and I have always been close, Sergeant. He was the first person I told about Bob,' said Wendy.

'Everybody who knew Bob is on my list of suspects, Mr Stiles.'

'Guess you have to look at it that way, Sergeant. No offence. I don't mean to be telling you how to do you job. You're the detective.'

'None taken, Mr Stiles. Did you know Judy?'

'Met her a few times, but I wouldn't say I knew her.'

'Thanks for confirming what John Wilson told us, Wendy. I'll be in touch if there are any developments.'

'I hope you find who killed them soon.'

'By the way, I hear we've released your husband's body,' said Stella. 'When's the funeral?'

'Monday morning. We're holding it in the Heysen Chapel at Centennial Park at ten.'

'Has your son arrived?'

'Yes, they're in the city, otherwise you could have met them.'

'Perhaps we'll meet them on Monday.'

Stella made a note of the registration number of Dan Stiles' Rav 4. Something about the way he'd spoken to her when suggesting the Wilsons be considered as suspects didn't sit right. She couldn't quite put her finger on what it was but there was something about his tone that made her feel uneasy.

'Sounds like the Wilsons are out of the frame, Sarge,' said Brian, as he started the car.

'Unless all the friendship stuff is a front,' said Stella. 'What did you make of Stiles?'

'Bit keen on fingering the Wilsons.'

'A little too keen for my liking, Brian.'

'Seemed to know a bit about the local geography.'

'Well, it is a popular tourist destination, and he did say he had clients in the area.'

'Probably wouldn't hurt to check out his story, Sarge.'

Stella gazed at the passing houses as Brian made their way back towards Commercial Road and wondered why people chose to live this far out from the centre of the city.

'We don't seem to be getting anywhere fast with this one,' said Brian.

'Someone's thought this through, Brian. Can you think of a better place to murder someone? Out of sight, half way up a mountain, on the doorstep of a town where no-one takes much notice of anyone heading to or from one of the most popular walking trails in the region. Ideal spot for a murder, I'd say.'

'Still, I find it difficult to believe no-one saw anything. Someone must have seen the killer after he came back down the mountain, unless he hiked in from Mambray Creek and then back out that way.'

'How long would that take?' said Stella, recalling what Paul Sleep had said about that option being a long shot.

'Two, maybe three, days each way.'

'If he did hike in from there, that would mean our killer would still have been on the mountain when the bodies were found, and we've been looking for him at the wrong end of the trail.'

'Perhaps we should put a call out to anyone who was camping in the Mambray Creek area over the weekend before they were killed?'

'What would we be looking for, Brian?'

'Someone who's left a vehicle unattended in the camping ground for several days or been seen coming down the trail with camping gear. It gets bloody cold up in those hills overnight at this time of the year, Sarge. There are huts you can camp in, but our killer would still need a thermal sleeping bag at the least.'

'Worth a try, I guess.'

'If our killer hiked in from Mambray Creek, that would definitely make it premeditated, Sarge.'

'Yes, and he'd have to have known in advance when they were going to be on the mountain.'

'He's either got to be on their list or connected to someone who knew where they'd be, if you ask me,' said Brian.

'If we assume our killer is not on the list, and not connected to anyone on the list, that narrows our field down to people they'd told personally, and that's not a very long list, is it?'

'Are you thinking what I'm thinking, Sarge? That DI Williams might be right after all?'

'Let's not jump to conclusions, Brian. Let's see if we get any leads from this Mambray Creek angle and join some dots before we go there.'

CHAPTER 10

FIRST THING THURSDAY MORNING, Stella called Sgt Paul Sleep at Booleroo Centre, who was coordinating ground activities in and around Melrose, to find out what he thought of the Mambray Creek option.

'I know you thought it was a bit of a long shot, Paul, but what do you think? Worth pursuing?'

'I've been looking at the walking trails, Stella. He could have come in from the Wilmington end as well, using the Heysen Trail. I've got a couple of my boys walking those trails looking for signs of recent activity at any of the huts or camp sites. They're due in Melrose sometime tomorrow.'

'Let me know if they find anything.'

'No problem, Stella,' said Paul. 'I've also spoken to the handful of campers at Mambray Creek this week, but you might want to put out a call to people who were using the campsite or were on the Heysen Trail between Melrose and Wilmington last week. More likely they'd be from down your way than up here.'

'I've got that in the works.'

'Oh, and before you go, Stella. I've got a group of Scouts

who've volunteered to search the area around the crime scene for that drone this weekend.'

'How did you swing that?'

'One of the advantages of being a local, Stella. My little brother's the Scoutmaster.'

Stella laughed. 'Be great if they find it.'

She'd only just finished talking to Paul Sleep when Barry Rice walked up to her desk.

'Been looking at the evidence we picked up from the trail made by the killer as he climbed out of that gully, Stella.'

Stella looked up. 'Killer?' The last time she'd spoken to Barry he'd been talking killers.

'Going by a comparison of the impressions we took, and our analysis of the digital record, I'm pretty certain all the footprints on that trail were made by the same pair of boots. I'd say your killer went up and down the side of that gully more than once.'

'Why would he do that?'

'My guess is he was looking for something.'

'The drone, or it's controller,' said Stella.

'I'd say he found the controller, Stella. It would have been in the vicinity of the victims or attached to one of them.'

'How far can a drone be from its controller, Barry?'

'Several kilometres, but the model they were using only has a thirty-minute max flight time.'

'So, if the battery was flat or it crashed, the killer may not have retrieved the drone, even if he had the controller?'

'Let's hope that's the case, Stella, and there's something useful on its memory card if anyone finds it.'

'Paul Sleep's just told me he's got some Scouts lined up to look for it this weekend.'

'That sounds promising.'

'And, if they don't find it, Barry, there will be people all over that mountain in a few weeks when the Fat Tyre Festival kicks off over the June long weekend. I'll get Paul to talk to the organisers if his Scouts don't find it.'

Within hours of releasing her appeal for help through the media, Stella was reading the transcript of a Crime Stoppers' call from a man who'd reported seeing a black SUV, possibly a Toyota Rav 4, left standing in the day visitors car park of the Mambray Creek Camping Ground by someone who'd gone on a longer hike. The caller, a frequent user of the camping ground, had been there with his family on the weekend before the murders and claimed he'd seen the small black SUV when they'd gone on a hike on the Saturday morning, and again when they'd returned from a second hike on the Sunday.

Unfortunately for Stella, he hadn't recorded the registration number or taken a photograph of the vehicle. When pressed, he'd told Crime Stoppers he thought the car had standard South Australian plates and that cars being left in the car park for several days was not all that unusual, since the park was a popular destination for overnight hikers. He claimed he'd only noticed the car this time because it had been the only one left in the car park that weekend.

Stella wondered how many black Toyota Rav 4s there would be in the state, and how many of them she could connect to Washington and Redding, besides the one she'd seen in Washington's driveway.

'Brian, how's that background on Stiles going?'

'Nothing out of the ordinary, Sarge. Nothing in the database and no family to speak of, besides his sister.'

'Anything to suggest he's into bushwalking?'

'Stack of photos on his Facebook timeline,' said Brian. 'Looks like he's hiked through the Mt Remarkable National Park a few times.'

'Does he go on his own or with someone?'

'Belongs to a bushwalking group called the Salisbury Saints. Looks like there's three, maybe four members.'

'Get their details. We may need to talk to them.'

'Shouldn't be too hard. What's the bushwalking connection?'

'We've got a caller saying he saw a black SUV, possibly a Rav 4, in the car park at Mambray Creek over the weekend prior to the murders.'

Brian scrolled through Stile's Facebook timeline. 'He hasn't posted anything, if it was him. Could be a coincidence, I suppose. Did they get the rego number?'

'No, but they thought the plates were local.'

'He lives in Prospect, so I guess he'd have gone up Port Wakefield Road.'

'What do you reckon his motive would be, if he's the killer?'

'Maybe he's simply the executioner, Sarge. I reckon we could be dealing with the oldest motive in the book.'

'You think the wife's behind it?'

Brian leant back in his chair and put his hands behind his head. 'I don't know about you, but I don't buy her arrangement story. When I ran it past May, she didn't think any self-respecting woman would put up with that.'

'We're going to need some evidence, Brian.'

'Let me see what traffic can tell us. There aren't that many ways to leave the city if you're heading that way.'

Stella wasn't looking forward to briefing DI Williams if they turned up any evidence confirming Stiles had been in the park at the time of the murders. She didn't like eating humble pie, especially not from Frank Williams' plate.

After several hours of watching recorded traffic from the routes Stiles could have used on his way north on the Saturday morning prior to the murders, Stella was ready for a break.

'I need a coffee, Brian. This is giving me a headache.'

'What time did our caller say he'd first spotted the SUV, Sarge?'

Stella looked at her notes from her conversation with the camper who'd called Crime Stoppers. 'Told me they'd arrived at the camping ground around ten and went for their first hike a little after eleven.'

'It's possible the SUV was there before Saturday,' said Brian.

'Guess so,' said Stella. 'After all, he is self-employed.'

'He's definitely not in any of this footage from Saturday morning.'

'Okay, let's get a coffee and start on the Friday footage when we get back.'

They took the elevator down to the coffee shop on the ground floor.

'What are we going to do if we don't find any sign of him leaving?' said Brian, as they sat down with their coffees.

Despite the niggle in the back of her mind telling her to keep looking, Stella knew hunches didn't get convictions. She needed evidence for that.

'We've got Wendy's phone records, Brian. See if she was in contact with him in the days before they were killed.'

'There's no mobile reception in those campsites, Sarge, but

I'm pretty sure there'd be some spots where he'd get a signal up on the mountain.'

'If he was smart he'd have turned his mobile off, and I suspect they put a lot of thought into planning this,' said Stella. 'I don't think you'll find any calls to him while he was up there.'

Brian took a sip of his coffee. 'How do you think he knew where they'd be on the mountain?'

'Either Wendy told him or he waited near the bottom of the trail and followed them up to where he pushed them over the edge.'

'If he's an experienced bushwalker, I wonder if Washington ever asked him for advice on where to go to get good photos.'

'That would really be premeditated, Brian.' Stella gazed at the late afternoon traffic in Angas Street. 'What do you think Stiles is getting out of it, if he's our man.'

'Maybe he's just an overly protective brother.'

'Why not encourage her to divorce him? Be a lot simpler.'

'You looked at Washington's financials?' said Brian. 'They're on his computer.'

'Not yet. What's he worth?'

'There's a two million dollar share portfolio, a few hundred thousand in cash, and the apartment where Redding was living,' said Brian. 'I'd say she wanted more than half, and this way she'd get the lot.'

'But what would he get?'

'Must be something he wanted badly enough to risk it, Sarge.'

Stella started on the traffic camera footage from the Friday afternoon prior to the murders, while Brian reviewed Wendy Washington's call record.

'This is interesting, Sarge. In the week leading up to the murders, she was talking to Stiles every day, sometimes more than once a day, right up until the Friday. Last call is Friday morning at eleven twenty-two. She doesn't call him again until the Wednesday, at ten sixteen, which is just after we told her his body had been found.'

'You'd think she would have called him on the Tuesday night when she raised the alarm,' said Stella.

'Guess she wouldn't have to if he already knew,' said Brian.

'Any calls from Stiles?'

'Not until Wednesday evening, at ten to seven.'

'He would have been back by then' said Stella. 'Get his call record and see if he's got a credit card. We need to find out where he was.'

'Okay.'

Stella turned her attention back to the footage from the camera at the intersection of Regency and Churchill Roads. A black SUV went through the intersection heading north on Churchill Road. She hit pause and zoomed in on the number plate. It was Stiles' vehicle.

She wrote down the time stamp and switched to the footage from the camera at the intersection of Bolivar Road with Port Wakefield Road. She fast forwarded until the time stamps matched, and then watched at normal speed. She was about to give up when a black SUV went through the intersection heading north on Port Wakefield Road. She hit pause and zoomed in on the number plate.

'Got him heading north on Port Wakefield Road at fourteen twenty-six,' said Stella.

'Well done, Sarge!'

'Still circumstantial,' said Stella.

'Check the Wednesday footage and see if we got him on the return journey.'

Stella looked at her watch. 'That might have to wait until Monday, Brian.'

'Probably take me longer than that to get his credit card details in any case.'

'Get the full works, Brian. Money might be his motivation.'

CHAPTER 11

Stella's phone rang as she was getting ready to leave the office for Washington's funeral service.

'Paul Sleep, Stella. We found the drone.'

'That's great, Paul. Where was it?'

'About three kilometres down from the crime scene.'

'What state is it in?

'A few scratches, but otherwise okay.'

'Anything on its memory card?'

'It's on its way to Forensics.'

The funeral was smaller than Stella had anticipated. Most of the mourners, including David Wilson and his wife, were members of the Seaford Lions Club. Stella noticed Wendy was supported by her brother and a younger couple she assessed as being in their forties.

The service, conducted by a civil celebrant, went for less than half and hour and was followed by morning tea in a room adjacent to the chapel.

'Any luck with your investigation, Sergeant?' said Ross Eagles.

'Making progress,' said Stella. 'Do you know Wendy's brother at all, Ross?'

'Dan? Met him when Wendy married Tom.' Ross laughed. 'Tom reckoned he'd got more than he bargained for when he married her. Two for the price of one.'

'Close, are they?'

Ross nodded. 'Inseparable, I hear. Understandable, I suppose. They grew up in foster care.'

'Oh, I didn't know that,' said Stella.

'Tragic really,' said Ross. 'Parents died when they were quite young.'

Stella accepted a cup of coffee from a member of the catering staff and allowed Ross Eagles to mingle.

She looked across the room, to where Brian was talking with David Wilson and his wife, and wondered what they were talking about.

Wendy Washington approached Stella, accompanied by the couple Stella assumed were Wendy's son and his wife.

'Laurence, here's someone I want you to meet. This is Detective Sergeant Bruno. She's investigating Bob's murder.'

Stella shook hands with Laurence Landy. 'Pleased to meet you, Mr Landy.'

'Any closer to working out who killed Bob?' said Laurence.

'We're making progress,' said Stella. 'How long are you staying?'

'We'll be here for a couple of weeks. We don't often get the opportunity to spend time with Mum.'

'It's such a long way from Montreal,' said the woman Stella assumed was his wife.

'Any closer?' said Wendy.

'I'll let you know as soon as we have something, Mrs Washington.'

Stella watched the trio walk across the room to where her main suspect stood chatting with a group of white-haired women.

By eleven thirty, the crowd started thinning as people said their goodbyes. Stella decided it was time to leave. She walked over to where Brian was talking to a woman old enough to be his mother.

'Mrs Redding, this is my boss, Detective Sergeant Bruno.'

'Hello, Mrs Redding,' said Stella.

'I'm Christine and Judy's mother,' said Mrs Redding.

'My condolences on the loss of your daughter, Mrs Redding.'

'Just make sure you catch the bugger, Sergeant. He's taken my daughter and my son-in-law.'

'When was the last time you saw them?' said Stella, squeezing Mrs Redding's hand.

'They dropped in to see me on their way to Melrose,' said Mrs Redding. 'I live in Clare, you see. They always dropped in when they were off on one of their expeditions into the Flinders.'

'How did they seem?'

'Happy. To be honest, I was disappointed they didn't get together after Christine died. They got on like a house on fire.'

'People often surprise us though, don't they?'

'You can say that again, Sergeant.'

'Do you know Wendy, Mrs Redding?'

'Not really. Bob only brought her up to see me a couple of times before she had that dreadful accident, and she wouldn't go places with him after that,' said Mrs Redding. 'That's when Bob starting taking Judy on his field trips.'

'What did you think about that?'

'Judy told me there was nothing to it when I asked. It's all about taking photos, Mum, were her exact words. I thought it best to mind my own business.'

'They certainly put together an impressive website, Mrs Redding. Have you seen it?'

'That's all Darren's work. He's the brains behind that business.'

'He does seem to know an awful lot about it,' said Stella.

'He does everything apart from take the photos.'

As if on cue, Darren Harmer appeared next to Mrs Redding. 'Come on, Grandma. I've got the car out the front.'

He scrubs up well in a suit, thought Stella, as she watched Darren shepherd his grandmother out to his waiting car.

Stella and Brian followed Darren and his grandmother out of the building and made their way towards their car.

'Pick up anything interesting, Brian?'

'Not really. What about you?'

'Ross Eagles told me Wendy and Dan were orphaned when they were quite young. Brought up in foster care, apparently.'

'Might be something to look into, Sarge.'

'He also said her first husband had joked with him about getting two for the price of one when he'd married Wendy.'

'Close are they?'

'Inseparable was the word Ross used.'

'Might explain why Dan has never married, I suppose.'

'He could be gay, Brian?'

'Yeah, guess so. It's not like you can always pick it'

Stella opened the door and slid into her seat while Brian got in behind the wheel. 'Let's go and see what our data tells us. That memory card should be with Forensics by now.'

CHAPTER 12

WHEN SHE ARRIVED BACK in the office, Stella was met by a technical officer from Forensics, who advised her he'd retrieved a twelve-minute recording of the slopes of Mt Remarkable from Washington's drone.

The technician inserted a USB stick into Stella's computer and opened the file containing a copy of the recording for her. Stella watched as the figures of Redding and Washington, standing on a rocky outcrop she recognised as the one on the edge of the path above the gully where their bodies had been found, got smaller and vanished as the drone rose above them and flew away from them as its pilot directed it down the gully towards the plain below.

The final moments of the flight were recorded as a blur of foliage as the drone veered and plunged towards the ground. The closing images of the recording were of a close up view of twigs and fallen leaves, obviously taken from a stationary drone at ground level.

'I'd say the battery died at that point,' said the technician, as her screen went black. 'The drone's hardly damaged and the memory card's not full.'

'I was hoping we'd get a shot of the killer,' said Stella.

'Sorry, Sarge, that's the only recording on the card, I'm afraid.'

Stella was disappointed. 'If we locate the controller, is there any way of showing it's connected to this drone?'

'They're usually paired when you buy them, so it should talk with the drone.'

'What do you mean?' said Stella.

'We should be able to get a feed from the drone's camera on the app in the controller.'

'We have the charger, don't we?'

'We've got everything except the controller, Sarge.'

Which could be anywhere, thought Stella.

On Tuesday morning, Brian waved Stella over to his desk as she returned from briefing DI Williams on their progress.

'How did it go?' said Brian.

'He thinks we're on the right path,' said Stella, 'but he's told me to pull my finger out and nail the bastard.'

'Don't let him get to you, Sarge. He'll be singing your praises when we solve this one.'

'I wouldn't be so sure about that,' said Stella. 'What have you got?'

'Take a look at this.' Brian placed his finger on the screen in front of him.

Stella peered over his shoulder and focused her attention on the line in the transaction report he was pointing out to her.

'Stiles bought petrol at the BP in Warnertown at twelve minutes past three on the Wednesday afternoon after they were murdered.'

'That adds ammunition to what we know about his movements,' said Stella.

'And, look at this,' said Brian, opening a second window on his screen. 'This is a copy of the final demand the bank sent him for payment of the arrears on his mortgage. He was about to lose his house until last Friday, when his sister transferred nine thousand dollars into his home loan account.'

'Might be time for a chat.'

'Want me to get him picked up?'

'No, let's go see him,' said Stella. 'I'll organise a search warrant.'

When Dan Stiles opened his front door and found her standing on his doorstep with Brian and three uniformed constables, Stella thought he looked somewhat confused, as if he had been expecting someone else.

'What's this?'

'We're here to search the premises and your car,' said Stella, handing him the search warrant. 'Perhaps you and I can have a chat while that's underway.'

Stiles led them through to the kitchen and handed his car keys to one of the uniformed officers.

'What are you expecting to find?' said Dan.

'I get to ask the questions,' said Stella. 'Care to tell me where you were the day Bob and Judy were killed?'

'Am I a suspect now?'

'I told you everyone who knew Bob was on my list, Mr Stiles,' said Stella, 'so, where were you?'

'I was hiking in the Flinders,' said Dan.

'The Flinders is a big place, Mr Stiles. Where in the Flinders exactly were you hiking?'

Dan leant back against the sink. 'Mambray Creek. Do you know where that is?'

Smug bastard, thought Stella. 'I've heard of it. Anyone with you or did you go hiking by yourself?'

'I needed a few days to myself,' said Dan. 'Had a few things to think about. Besides, it's a safe place to hike on your own. There are always people about, and you can get a mobile signal up on the mountain if you get into trouble.'

'See anybody?'

'Not anybody I knew,' said Dan. 'There were a few people in the camping ground when I got there Friday afternoon.'

'Speak to anyone?'

'No.'

'Where did you go within the park?'

'I did the Black Range Trek. Camped at Grays Hut on the way in and Scarfes Hut on the way out,' said Dan.

'Go all the way to Melrose?'

Dan crossed his arms on his chest. 'No. I did the summit from the Mambray Creek side and then made my way back to where I'd left the car.'

'Who knew where you were?' said Stella.

'Wendy,' said Dan. 'I always tell her when I go off on my own.'

'Close to Wendy, are you?'

'Suppose you could say that,' said Dan. 'We only had each other after our parents died.'

'Oh, I didn't know you were orphans,' said Stella. 'How old were you when that happened?'

'Eight,' said Dan. 'Wendy was twelve. She wouldn't let them separate us.'

'Who looked after you?'

'We ended up in foster care until Wendy was old enough to look after me by herself.'

'Didn't you have grandparents or relatives who could have looked after you?'

'Nobody wanted us,' said Dan.

'That must have been hard,' said Stella. She couldn't imagine Josh's grandparents or her brother abandoning him to foster care if anything happened to her.

'You get used to it,' said Dan.

'How did you get on with Bob?'

'He was alright.'

'Was he good to Wendy?'

'He was until she had her accident,' said Dan. 'Seemed to lose interest in her after that.'

'Wendy talk to you about how things were between them?'

'Yeah.'

'Did you know about the arrangement?'

'She tell you about that, did she?'

'Yes,' said Stella. 'What did you think about it?'

'I told her to cut her losses and leave him.'

'How did she react to that?'

'Said she'd think about it.'

'When was that?'

'Last Christmas,' said Dan.

One of the constables came into the kitchen. 'Got a moment, Sergeant?'

Stella left Stiles with Brian and followed the constable into the laundry. 'What have you got?'

The constable inserted his latex gloved hand into the backpack on the floor next to the washing machine and lifted out an electronic device.

'Is that what I think it is?' said Stella.

'Matches the one you asked us to look for,' said the constable.

Stella waited while the constable slipped the device into an evidence bag and then took it into the kitchen with her.

'Do you own a drone, Mr Stiles?'

Dan Stiles was sitting next to his lawyer when Stella and Brian entered the interview room at Police Headquarters. Stella placed her folder on the table between them and opened it while Brian activated the recording equipment.

'Mr Stiles, can you confirm for the record that you were within the Mt Remarkable National Park between the evening of Friday the twenty-eighth of April and the early afternoon of Wednesday the second of May?'

'Yes,' said Dan.

'And, for the record, whereabouts within the park were you during that time?'

'I hiked in from Mambray Creek to the summit and back along what's known as the Black Range Trek.'

'And, did you take the summit track down towards Melrose at all, Mr Stiles?'

'No.'

'Did you see anybody else on the tracks while you were there, Mr Stiles?'

'No.'

'You didn't happen to meet up with Bob Washington and Judy Redding on Tuesday the first, by any chance?'

'No.'

'But, you were aware they'd be entering the park from Melrose on one of their photographic field trips while you were there?'

'Why would I be?' said Dan.

'Wendy didn't tell you?'

Dan didn't answer.

Stella extracted a sheet of paper from her folder. 'This is a print of the call record of Wendy's phone, Mr Stiles. It shows you were in daily contact with her in the week leading up to your hiking trip. You didn't discuss Bob and Judy's upcoming field trip?'

'I don't recall her talking about it,' said Dan.

'When I look back over her call log, I see you and Wendy talk to each other nearly every day,' said Stella.

'Like I said, we're close. Always have been.'

'So, why didn't she call you on the Tuesday night when she couldn't contact Bob or Judy?'

'I was probably out of range,' said Dan.

'I don't think you understand my question, Mr Stiles. She didn't even try.'

Dan shrugged. 'You'll have to ask her.'

'Don't worry,' said Stella. 'I will.'

Dan smiled.

Stella extracted another sheet of paper from her folder. 'I'd like to talk about the drone controller found at your house, Mr Stiles. We couldn't find a drone during our search of your property. Why is that?'

'No comment.'

'We recovered the drone Bob was using on the day he was killed,' said Stella, turning to Brian. 'Show them the recording.'

Stella watched Stiles as he viewed the recording on the screen above her head.

'As you can see, that was taken by the drone they were using,' said Stella, when the video ended.

'Doesn't show anybody else, though,' said Dan. 'How's that going to help you prove I had anything to do with killing them?'

'We've spoken to the makers of the drone, Mr Stiles. They told us their drones are sold paired with a controller, so you can use them straight out of the box.'

'Where is this going, Sergeant?' said the lawyer.

Stella watched the colour fade in Dan's face. 'The controller we found at your client's place is paired with the drone we recovered from the crime scene, the drone that captured that footage you just watched.'

'Could be coincidental,' said the lawyer.

'I suppose it could be,' said Stella, 'but it's highly unlikely a random controller found in your client's possession would have Robert Washington's prints on it, wouldn't you agree?'

'That would certainly lower the odds of it being coincidental,' said the lawyer.

'I knew I should have left it there,' said Dan, 'but Wendy wanted proof.'

'Proof?' said Stella.

'You don't have to answer that,' said the lawyer.

'That I'd done it,' said Dan.

'Why didn't you take the drone as well?' said Stella.

'Couldn't find the bloody thing.'

'Why didn't you just take a photo of the bodies?'

'I did,' said Dan, 'but I wanted something solid to show her.'

Stella leant back in her chair. 'Why, Dan? Why did you do it?'

Dan looked down at his hands on the table. 'I needed the money. She promised me she'd get it for me if I did what she wanted.'

'Can you prove that?'

'I recorded the conversation,' said Dan. 'She doesn't know I did that, but how else was I going to make sure she'd pay up?'

CHAPTER 13

WENDY WASHINGTON SAT with her head down and her hands in her lap. Stella was relieved to see she was being represented by a different lawyer than her brother.

'Dan's confessed to killing Bob and Judy,' said Stella.

'Then, what am I doing here? I didn't kill anybody!'

'You don't actually have to pull the trigger yourself to be involved in a murder, Mrs Washington.'

'I had nothing to do with it!'

'That's not what Dan told us,' said Stella, extracting a sheet of paper from her folder and pretending to read it. 'He says you planned it together.'

'If he says he killed them, it has nothing to do with me. I certainly didn't ask him to do it.'

'Your brother didn't have anything to gain from killing them,' said Stella, 'unless you promised him something.'

'He probably did it to get back at Bob for what he'd done to me,' said Wendy. 'He's overly protective at times. I don't know why he's dragging me into it.'

'Dan says you looked after him when he was young. Is that right?'

'We had to stick together,' said Wendy. 'Nobody wanted us.'

'That must have been difficult,' said Stella.

'We survived.'

'He'd come to you if he was in trouble, wouldn't he? Say, if he needed money?'

Wendy smiled. 'All the bloody time.'

'And, did you help him out?'

'When I could.'

'Is that what you were doing when you paid nine thousand dollars into his State Bank account last Friday?'

'He was going to lose his house,' said Wendy. 'Wouldn't you help your brother keep his house?'

'And, would he do anything for his big sister?'

'He would if I asked him,' said Wendy, 'but I've never asked him for anything, not even when Tom died and left me with nothing but debts.'

'Is that why you married Bob?'

Wendy sat up. 'I married Bob because he was a decent bloke. I was back on my feet by the time I met him.'

Stella lifted the pages listing Wendy's call log from her folder. 'This is a record of calls to and from your mobile phone, Mrs Washington. It contains some interesting patterns. For example, when I compare this to Bob's calendar entries on his laptop, I can see you called your husband's mobile number every night whenever he was on a field trip with Judy.'

'That was so we'd all know everybody was okay,' said Wendy. 'That sort of thing becomes more important when you get older, Sergeant.'

Wendy obviously didn't know anything about Italian mothers, thought Stella. 'I see you spoke with your brother every day.'

'We've been doing that forever,' said Wendy. 'Despite all his shortcomings, Dan's still my best friend.'

'But you didn't call him the night you reported Bob missing, Mrs Washington. Why was that?'

'He was camping in the Flinders,' said Wendy. 'I didn't think there'd be a signal where he was.'

'You didn't even try, Mrs Washington.'

'Is that a crime?' said the lawyer.

'No, it's not,' said Stella, 'but offering your brother a share of your husband's estate for killing him is.'

'Is that what he's saying?'

'He has a recording of you making the offer on his mobile phone,' said Stella. 'Would you like to hear it?'

'The little shit,' said Wendy, 'after all I've done for him.'

CHAPTER 14

STELLA LOOKED at her brother sitting across the table from her. They'd been close all their lives and, even now, lived in each other's pockets. Stefano had taken over the father role for Josh when Rick had been killed. She loved him and he knew he loved her, as only a brother could.

'Would you kill someone for me, Stefano?'

'Depends,' said Stefano, putting down his fork.

'On what?'

'What he'd done to you.'

Stella smiled. It was typical Stefano to assume it would be a man she'd want killed.

'What if I just wanted him out of the way? Or to get at his money?'

Stefano looked at Shaun, sitting next to Stella. 'I hope you haven't gone and done something stupid, mate.'

'Why's that?' said Shaun.

'I'd hate to think I'd have to kill you.'

'It wouldn't be on purpose,' said Shaun, turning to look at Stella.

Stefano picked up his fork and resumed eating his pasta.

Stella put a hand on Shaun's knee under the table. 'It's okay, honey. There are other ways I can get my hands on your money.'

'Thank God for that.'

THE SCAM

STELLA BRUNO INVESTIGATES

For Crime Readers Group member Wanda Downs, who provided the spark that ignited this story and lent me her name for one of the characters.

A few Australian terms:

AFP abbreviation for the Australian Federal Police

ASIC abbreviation for the Australian Securities and Investments Commission, which is Australia's corporate, markets and financial services regulator.

Bloke is an informal term for man, similar to the American guy.

Boot is an enclosed space at the back of a car for carrying luggage or other goods. Equivalent to the American trunk.

Mobile and **mobile phone** are equivalent to the American cell and cell phone.

CHAPTER 1

STAN WATSON, a harvesting supervisor for ForestrySA, stopped his vehicle on the fire access track he'd taken deep into the pine plantations east of Nangwarry and climbed out next to the marker that identified this section of the forest as being Lot 1256. It had been ten years since Lot 1256 had last been thinned and Stan was there to determine if its twenty-five-year-old trees were ready for their third and final thinning prior to the clear-felling operation that would sweep through the forest in ten to fifteen years time.

He stood in the shade of the forest, which engulfed the fire access track, and looked at the trees in awe. The sight of tall pine trees towering above him on all sides always inspired a sense of wonder within him whenever he stepped out of his vehicle, even after thirty years. He looked at his watch. It was just after ten. He picked up his iPad and headed into the forest to inspect the trees in Lot 1256.

Stan had only walked a hundred metres or so into the forest, assessing trees as he went, when he spotted something he wasn't expecting to see: a white sedan parked among the trees about fifty metres off to his right. He made his way over to the vehicle, a recent model BMW 5 series covered in brown pine needles. It looked as if someone had driven the car into the forest and parked it under a tree and forgotten to come back, quite some time ago, thought Stan, looking at the depth of the layer of pine needles on the upper surfaces of the vehicle.

He walked around the car and took several photographs with his iPad before he noticed it didn't have any number plates. Probably stolen, thought Stan, as he peered into the interior of the vehicle. He couldn't see anything out of the ordinary. It didn't even look damaged, apart from not having number plates.

He reached into his back pocket and pulled out the leather gloves he wore whenever he was handling timber. He slipped them on and tried the driver's side front door. It opened, releasing a stream of trapped air tainted by the unmistakeable odour of death. Stan shut the door and reached for his mobile phone.

CHAPTER 2

'I'D LIKE you to look into this, Bruno,' said DI Williams, handing DS Stella Bruno the report he'd been reading as soon as she entered his office. 'Wanda Downs. Went missing a couple of years ago. Did a runner, by all accounts.'

'Do you want me to review the case, sir, or do we have something new?'

'There's been an update from Mt Gambier. Her car's been found in a pine forest outside Nangwarry, with a mummified body in the boot.'

This could be interesting, thought Stella. 'Is it Downs?'

'That's yet to be determined, but it's definitely the body of a woman.'

'Do we know how she died?'

'Not by natural causes would be my guess, Bruno, unless she wrapped herself in a blanket and then locked herself in the boot of her own car.'

Typical Frank Williams, thought Stella. There was no way the prick would give you a straight answer when he could find a way to make you look stupid. 'Okay, sir, I'll follow that up with the pathologist.'

'Get on to the husband before you do that, Bruno. I don't

want him finding out from someone else before we speak to him.'

'Understood, sir.'

A tall man, with the first signs of grey showing in his otherwise dark hair, strode into the reception area of Downs Construction from the yard behind the office building and extended his hand. 'Neil Downs.'

'Detective Sergeant Bruno,' said Stella, declining his offered hand. 'This is Detective Constable Rhodes.'

'Oh, sorry,' said Neil, retracting his hand. 'Still can't get used to this social distancing stuff. Is this about my wife?'

'Is there somewhere we can talk in private?' said Stella.

'Come through to the boardroom,' said Neil, opening a door. 'My office is a bit of a mess at the moment, I'm afraid. We're in the middle of pulling a project together.' He waited for them to enter the boardroom and closed the door behind him. 'Take a seat.'

They arranged themselves around one end of the table, with Neil sitting between them.

'Is this about Wanda?'

'We've located her car,' said Stella.

'Where?'

He seemed genuinely surprised as far as Stella could tell. 'In a pine forest about five kilometres east of Nangwarry.'

'Where's that?' said Neil.

'Down in the South East,' said Stella, 'between Penola and Mt Gambier.'

'I don't think I've ever been there,' said Neil. 'I spend a bit of time in the South East, though. I have a holiday house in Robe.'

'You'd go down the coast road, I suppose,' said Brian. 'Nangwarry's inland, in the middle of the pine plantations between Mt Gambier and Penola.'

'I see. Is that all?' said Neil, leaning back in his chair.

Stella thought he looked more apprehensive than disappointed. 'I'm afraid not, Mr Downs. The body of a woman was found in the boot of the car.'

Neil jerked up in his seat. 'Wanda?'

'We don't know yet,' said Stella, 'but I wanted to alert you to the possibility of it being your wife.'

Neil sank back into his chair. 'That's not what I wanted to hear.'

'What did you want to hear?' said Stella.

'That she's been found safe and well, even if she doesn't want to be found or come home.'

Stella made a mental note to hold onto that comment. 'When was the last time you saw your wife, Mr Downs?'

'You must have that on file somewhere,' said Neil. 'I made a statement.'

'I'm sure you did but this changes the circumstances somewhat, I'm afraid, Mr Downs.'

'What do you mean?'

'When you made your statement, Mr Downs, it was part of a missing person report,' said Stella. 'This is shaping up as a murder investigation.'

'Well, I haven't killed anybody,' said Neil.

Stella smiled. 'Tell me about the last time you saw your wife.'

Neil crossed his arms and leant on the table. 'It was just over two years ago. Sunday the 16th of September, 2018, to be precise. We'd spent the weekend at Robe. Drove down in her car to give it a decent run. We'd had an argument over dinner and Wanda was giving me the silent treatment in the car on the way back.' Neil shrugged. 'I stopped at the Shell in Tailem Bend to top up the tank and use the restroom. She drove off and left me there while I was paying for the petrol.'

'What time was that?' said Stella, noting he was still telling the same story as the one he'd told them when he'd reported his wife missing.

'Around nine thirty at night,' said Neil.

'How did you get home?'

'Called my brother. He lives in Murray Bridge, so I didn't have to wait half the night.'

Fortunate coincidence, thought Stella. 'Was that the first time she'd left you?'

Neil shook his head. 'She could be pretty impulsive when she was angry or when she didn't get her own way.'

'What was the argument about?'

'Wanda wanted to sell the house in Robe and buy a place on the Gold Coast. I told her I wasn't selling it. I hate the Gold Coast.'

Stella wondered what sort of person Wanda was if she'd left her husband after a dispute over the sale of a holiday house.

'How many times had she left you before?'

'Three,' said Neil, 'but she'd always come crawling back, until this time.'

Interesting choice of words, thought Stella, wondering what sort of relationship they'd had. 'Is that why you didn't report her disappearance straight away?'

'To be honest, I thought I'd find her at home when I got there. When she wasn't, I decided to give her a week, but then the federal police showed up looking for her and asking all sorts of questions. I had to report her missing then.'

'What were they interested in?' said Stella.

'Money, mostly,' said Neil. 'They said she'd scammed her clients out of their savings.'

'And, had she?' said Stella.

'Apparently,' said Neil. 'They went through her books and seized all her assets.'

'What sort of business was your wife running?'

'Financial planning, with her friend Kylie. They called it Doe Services,' said Neil. 'They specialised in self-managed superannuation funds for women.'

'I understand Kylie is missing as well,' said Stella.

'She went on a holiday to Bali the week before Wanda disappeared,' said Neil, 'but she hasn't come back. No-ones heard from her since she left.' Neil looked up. 'She was the first person I called when the police came knocking. All you get is her voicemail.'

'Did that strike you as a strange coincidence?'

'Yeah, especially when they said there was no record of her flying to Bali.'

'How much money are we talking about?'

'Somewhere between ten and twenty million dollars. No-one's sure what the actual figure is, apparently.'

'And, you had no idea?'

'I knew their business was booming. They'd bought a string of properties to reduce their tax bill but I had no idea they were ripping off their friends.'

Stella was not warming to Wanda. She was starting to sound like a nasty piece of work if her husband was telling them the truth. 'Friends?'

'Yeah, most of their clients were friends or friends of friends.'

'That must have been hard to deal with.'

'Thankfully they weren't my friends,' said Neil.

'And, were you caught up in it?'

'This business is a separate entity, Sergeant. Wanda and I had no business assets in common, but I had to buy out her half of the house. As I said, they appointed an administrator who seized her assets and took control of all her business accounts. It's still going through the courts.'

'So, it would appear she had a reason to disappear?'

'Yeah. I'm pretty sure it had nothing to do with the fight we had over Robe,' said Neil.

Stella stood. 'Would you want to see her again?'

'Not particularly,' said Neil. 'When will you know if it's her body in the car or not?'

'We'll need access to her dental records. Can you help with that?'

'I can get you those details,' said Neil. 'Her dentist sends a reminder card every six months. Think I've still got the last one.'

'And, would you still have any of your wife's hair brushes?'

Neil looked at Stella.

'DNA,' said Stella.

'Oh, guess I should have known that,' said Neil. 'I bagged up her personal items. The federal police told me to keep them, just in case.'

'Perhaps we can make a time to pick them up,' said Stella.

As they were leaving Downs Construction, Stella heard the ping of an incoming SMS message on her mobile phone. She took her mobile out of her pocket and looked at the screen. The message was from Josh's school, reporting him as being absent without an excuse.

'Give me a minute, Brian.'

She called Josh's number. The call went through to his voicemail. 'Josh, this is Mum. Call me when you get this.' She ended the call and rang her mother. That call went through to voicemail as well. 'Ma, Stella. Call me.'

'What's wrong?' said Brian.

'Josh is not at school and I can't get him or my mother on the phone.'

'What about your nephew? Doesn't he go to the same school?'

Stella blew him a kiss. 'You're a champ, Brian.'

Stella called her sister-in-law, Denise, who answered on the second ring.

'Do you know where Josh is?' said Stella. 'I just got a text from school saying he hasn't turned up.'

'I was just about to call you,' said Denise. 'There's been a bit of an accident. The boys are okay, bit shaken but not hurt. One of your colleagues has just dropped them home, but Ma's been taken to the Royal Adelaide. She got collected on the roundabout in George Street.'

'Is it serious?'

'Suspected broken arm and some bruising, apparently. Stefano's gone to the hospital from work.'

'What about Pa?'

'He's gone down to sort out what to do about the car. I'll take him to the hospital after I've taken the boys to school.'

That would be right, thought Stella. Her father was not good when it came to pain and suffering, especially when he was cast in a supporting role. 'Is Josh there? Can you put him on?'

'I'll get him.'

Stella waited.

'I'm not hurt, Mum. You know how slow Nonna drives. We were hardly moving.'

'What happened?'

'Nonna should have stopped to let the other car through the roundabout. It crashed into her door.'

'Is she badly hurt?'

'They said her arm's broken and the airbag hit her in the face,' said Josh. 'You know, Mum, I've never heard Nonna swear like that.'

Stella smiled. She'd heard it all. 'I guess she was upset, sweetheart. Are you sure going to school is a good idea?'

'Yeah, no point staying here.'

'What about Paolo?'

'We're fine, Mum.'

'How come you didn't answer your phone when I called?'

'My bag was on the floor behind Nonna's seat. It got squashed. My phone's all smashed up.'

Another unplanned expense, thought Stella. 'Okay, sweetheart, I'll see you when I get home.'

'Everything alright?' said Brian.

'My mother's been taken to the RAH. They had an accident on the way to school this morning. You'd better drop me at the hospital.'

'Is Josh okay?'

'Yeah, the boys weren't hurt.'

'Thank God for that,' said Brian, as they climbed into the car.

'I'll just let his nibs know I'm heading to the hospital instead of coming back to the office.'

'Okay. I'll follow up with Downs to collect the stuff we'll need to ID the body.'

CHAPTER 3

Two DAYS LATER, Stella's mobile rang as she was reading through the notes the Australian Federal Police had released to her on their Doe Services investigation. She looked at the caller ID: Steve Wright, the police pathologist.

'What have you got, Steve?'

'Not good news, I'm afraid, Stella. Your Nangwarry body is definitely not Wanda Downs. Dental work is all wrong. DNA profiles don't match.'

'Any idea who she is, then?'

'Thought you'd have a better idea on that than me, Stella.'

Stella felt her stomach sink towards the floor. 'What can you tell me about her, Steve?'

'Early forties, dark shoulder length hair, tattoo of a butterfly on her right shoulder, throat slit with a knife. Is that enough for you?'

'Hang on a minute.' Stella flipped through the notes she'd made while she was reviewing the initial missing person reports. 'Could be her business partner, Kylie Orchard. Her boyfriend said she had a tattoo of a butterfly on her right shoulder. I'll chase up her dental records for you.'

'Sounds like a plan, Stella.'

'Any idea how long she's been dead?'

'Hard to be precise with this one,' said Steve. 'Rate of decomposition was slowed by the way the body was wrapped but, at a guess, I'd say around the two year mark.'

'Thanks, Steve. I'll get back to you after I've spoken to the family.'

Brian parked the car in front of the impressive sandstone house located at the Prospect address they had on record for Karl and Miriam Orchard. The door was opened by a white-haired man wearing a business suit, dressed as if he was about to leave for the office.

'Karl Orchard?' said Stella.

'Yes.'

'Detective Sergeant Bruno,' said Stella, holding up her ID. 'This is Detective Constable Rhodes.'

'Are you here about Kylie, Sergeant?'

'It's not good news, I'm afraid, Mr Orchard,' said Stella. 'May we come in?'

'Oh, of course. This way.' Karl stepped back with his right hand on the door and pointed towards the sitting room, immediately off the hallway. 'Please, take a seat. I'll let my wife know you're here.'

Stella sat next to Brian on the couch and admired the display of fine china figurines on the mantle-piece above the fireplace while they waited for the Orchards.

'This is Miriam,' said Karl, as he escorted a diminutive grey-haired woman into the room.

Stella waited while they settled in the armchairs opposite the couch. 'Have you heard that we've found Wanda Downs' car in the South East?'

'We saw something on the news,' said Karl, looking at his wife.

'There was a body in the car,' said Stella.

The Orchards moved forward to the edge of their armchairs and exchanged glances. 'Wanda?' said Karl.

'I'm sorry,' said Stella, 'but we think it might be your daughter.'

'They look very much alike,' said Miriam. 'Are you sure it isn't Wanda?'

'I'm sorry,' said Stella, 'but we know it's not Wanda.'

Karl stood. Miriam slipped back into the depths of her armchair and closed her eyes.

'We thought she might be dead,' said Karl.

'Why's that?'

'She wasn't the sort of person to disappear and not keep in contact. We knew something had to have happened to her.'

'When was the last time you saw her?' said Stella, feeling sorry for the Orchards. It was never easy breaking the news to parents of a victim, especially parents who had been waiting years for news of their child's whereabouts.

'A couple of weeks before the Australian Federal Police contacted us. She came to dinner. That was when she told us she was going to Bali for a month.' Karl looked at Miriam and then turned back to face Stella. 'She'd broken up with Bruce earlier in the year and told us she wanted some time alone to get him out of her system.'

'You had no reason to doubt her story?'

Karl shook his head. 'We knew things hadn't been good between her and Bruce for some time. He hit her, you see? She'd told him to clear off.'

Stella hadn't seen that snippet of information in the file on Kylie's disappearance and wondered whether her father was embellishing the story or simply being more honest. That would be something she'd take up with Bruce Munro if she had to speak to him. 'Had she said anything to you about her business being under investigation?'

'The only thing we knew about her business was she was making plenty of money. At least she was spending plenty of money.' Karl sighed. 'But, if you've been talking to the Federal Police, I guess you know that's not what they think was happening.'

'I'm aware of their investigation,' said Stella, 'but it appears your daughter, if it is your daughter's body we have, was murdered, and that's what I'm investigating.'

'Oh,' said Miriam. 'That's dreadful. How can we help?'

'I need to make a positive identification of the body.'

'Do you need one of us to identify her remains?' said Karl.

'I'm afraid a visual identification is out of the question,' said Stella. 'We'll need to use alternative means.'

'What makes you think it's Kylie?' said Miriam.

'Dark shoulder length hair and a tattoo on the right shoulder.'

'The butterfly,' said Karl. 'Told her she'd regret it. Never thought it would help to identify her.'

'Do you know who her dentist was?' said Stella, 'or do you have any of her personal items, like a hair brush?'

'Yes, I think so,' said Miriam.

'And, do you know where we can find Bruce Munro?'

Karl shook his head. 'We haven't seen him since Kylie told him to clear off but he's probably still working at the same place.'

'We've got those details on file,' said Stella.

Late Wednesday afternoon, nearly a week after Stan Watson had stumbled across Wanda Downs' BMW in the Nangwarry pine forest, Stella made her way to DI Williams' office to break the news Steve Wright had just given her.

'We've identified the body, sir,' said Stella, when DI Williams beckoned her into his office. 'It's Kylie Orchard.'

'Kylie Orchard? What was she doing in that car?'

'I don't know,' said Stella, 'but her dental records confirm what we suspected from the description we had on file,' said Stella. 'Guess we were lucky the body was wrapped up and stored away from the elements.'

'Pathologist find anything else we can use?'

'Nothing to identify her killer,' said Stella, 'apart from the fact he used a knife and probably cut from left to right.'

'What about CSI?'

'All the prints they lifted from the car belong to Downs and her husband, and the victim, which isn't all that surprising when you think about it, sir.'

'I suppose not. How long do they think the car was in the forest?'

'A couple of years, going by the layer of pine needles on the roof and the amount of air in the tyres,' said Stella, opening the image on her phone that CSI had sent her.

DI Williams looked at the image and nodded. 'Any sign of Downs in the forest?'

'Not in the immediate area, sir, but there's a hell of a lot of pine forest down there.'

'Get her picture into the media. We need to find her if she's still out there, and you'd better liaise with the AFP, Bruno. We don't want a turf war.'

'They've already told me they'd appreciate our help finding her, sir. ASIC still want to talk to her about the millions she took from her clients, if she's still alive.'

'You don't think she's alive?'

'According to DS Ellis from the AFP, she hasn't accessed any of her bank accounts since she disappeared, and her mobile's been silent as well, even though they've kept her account open.'

'Start with the husband and the boyfriend, Bruno, then move on to their investors.'

'There's plenty of those,' said Stella. 'At least a hundred and twenty, according to the AFP'.

'Yes, I've read the report. Those investors are women, Bruno,' said DI Williams, 'and murder's not usually their game. Start with the men in their lives.'

'Right, sir.' Stella turned to leave.

'By the way, Bruno, how's your mother getting on?'

'She's home again, thank you, sir, but she's still pretty sore.'

'Anybody else hurt in that accident?'

'No, only my mother,' said Stella. 'And, from what she's said, sounds like she didn't see the other car coming.'

'Guess she was lucky, then.'

'Not according to my father,' said Stella.

DI Williams laughed and waved her out of his office.

CHAPTER 4

'I'M NOT GETTING a good feeling about this case, Sarge.'

'Oh, why's that Brian?'

'Everybody keeps disappearing. I've left three messages on Munro's voicemail, and when I rang the place he works they said he hadn't been into the office for over a week, and Uniform reckon he hasn't been seen by his neighbours for days.'

'Someone must know where he is,' said Stella. 'Does he have any family in Adelaide?'

Brian's mobile started ringing. He picked it up and pressed the accept button. 'DC Rhodes.'

Stella watched a smile spread across Brian's face as he listened to the caller.

'Thanks for returning my call, Mr Munro. We'd like to talk to you about Kylie Orchard.'

———

Bruce Munro met them at the Sturt Police Station with his lawyer, an older man who introduced himself as Alex Krimal-ski. Stella glanced at Brian and smiled. She'd finally seen someone wearing a suit more dishevelled than Brian's.

The Desk Sergeant ushered them into the room he'd booked for their interview and Brian activated the recording equipment.

'Thanks for coming in, Mr Munro,' said Stella.

'Please, call me Bruce.'

'Okay, Bruce. I'm going to have to ask you to take yourself back a couple of years or so to when you last saw Kylie Orchard.'

'Why is this important?' said Alex. 'I understand she's missing, but we've been asked all these questions before. Surely you have access to Bruce's earlier statements?'

'We know where Kylie is,' said Stella. 'She's in the police morgue with her throat slit.'

Alex looked at Bruce and then back at Stella. 'And you think my client did that?'

Stella shook her head. 'I have no idea what your client's been up to, Mr Krimalski, which is precisely why we're here.' Stella turned to Bruce. 'Tell us about the last time you saw Kylie.'

'We'd had a fight, another one,' said Bruce, 'and she told me to clear off.'

'When was this?'

'The first week of March, 2018.'

'Did you see her after that?'

'A couple of times. I think the last time I saw her was in June that year.'

'Where did you go after she asked you to leave?'

'I moved in with my mother for a couple of weeks, until I found a place to live. The place I'm in now.'

'What was the fight about?'

'Nothing important.'

'I'll be the judge of that,' said Stella. 'This is a murder investigation, Bruce. Not a friendly chat.' She waited a moment for him to get the message that she was in charge of the direction of their conversation. 'So, what was the fight about?'

Bruce looked at his lawyer. 'She's dead, right?'

'Do you want to see a picture?' said Stella.

'I want to be sure she's dead,' said Bruce.

Stella took out her phone and scrolled through the images the pathologist had sent her with the post mortem report, until she found the shot of the butterfly tattoo. She handed the phone to Bruce. 'Recognise this?'

Bruce stared at the image and then handed the phone back to Stella. 'I gave her that for her fortieth birthday.'

'So, what was the fight about?'

'Money.'

Stella waited.

'She was spending way too much money for someone managing other people's money. I asked her where it was coming from.'

'And, what was her answer?'

'She told me to mind my own business. I told her she'd go to prison if she got caught.' Bruce looked up. 'She laughed at me. Said she had no idea what I was talking about.'

'Is that when you hit her?' said Stella.

'What? I never hit her! Who told you that?'

'She told her parents, apparently,' said Stella.

'She was the hitter,' said Bruce, rubbing his chin. 'She loved slapping faces, especially this one.'

'How long were you together as a couple?'

'Three years. I met her after my divorce. Guess you could say we were a rebound couple. She'd only just come out of an abusive relationship, well abusive according to her, with a bloke she'd been married to for ten years.'

'And, who was that?'

'Stephen Downs. That's how she met Wanda. Stephen is

Wanda's brother-in-law. He's in business with his brother, Neil.'

That's something I have to follow up, thought Stella. 'And, how long had she been in business with Wanda?'

'Years,' said Bruce. 'I think they set up that business in 2006, but they'd started out as accountants before that. Anyway, they'd moved into managing other people's money by the time I met them.'

'And, what's your expertise, Bruce?'

'I'm a civil engineer, Sergeant. I'm working on the South Road upgrade.'

'And, what did you tell the AFP about your suspicions?'

'They didn't need me to tell them she was ripping off her clients. They already knew that. What they wanted to know was where she was. I told them the truth. I had no idea.'

'Have you had any contact with Wanda since Kylie disappeared?'

'No.'

'What about with her husband, Neil?'

'We touched base a couple of times, especially after the AFP started asking questions, but not really. It's not like we're friends or anything.'

'Would you be able to substantiate where you were in September and October 2018 if I wanted to know?'

'I keep a pretty extensive diary on my phone, if that helps.'

'Ever been to the South East, Bruce?'

'I'm from Mt Gambier. My sister still lives there, but my mother moved up to Edwardstown after my father died in 2000.'

'Do you visit your sister?'

'I take Mum down there for Christmas and Easter. She doesn't drive and my sister's got kids.'

'So, you would have been in the South East for Christmas in 2018?'

'Yes.'

'Ever been to Nangwarry?'

'Plenty of times. Dad worked in the sawmill there right up until the time he got lung cancer.'

'Why these questions about Mt Gambier?' said Alex.

'Kylie's body was found in Wanda's car in a pine forest outside Nangwarry.'

'Does that mean Wanda's down there somewhere as well?' said Bruce.

'I don't know,' said Stella, 'but that's something we need to consider.'

Bruce shrugged. 'Just thinking out loud.'

'Did you have a reason to kill Kylie, Bruce?'

'She might have been a bitch when she was upset, Sergeant, but no, I didn't want to kill her. In a way, her kicking me out was good for me. I've met someone else.'

'I hope that works out for you.' Stella smiled. 'Can you think of anyone who might have wanted to kill her?'

'I guess the AFP could give you a list,' said Bruce, 'and I dare say Wanda and Neil would have wanted her to keep her mouth shut.'

'You think Neil Downs knew what his wife was doing?'

'If I'd worked it out, what do you think? Neil's no fool.'

CHAPTER 5

STELLA ACTIVATED the video conferencing system and waited for DS Fraser Ellis to appear on the screen in front of her. Thirty seconds after she'd taken her seat in front of the camera, the monitor on the wall opposite her flickered into life with an image of Fraser smiling at her through the camera.

'Hi, Stella!'

He looked older than he'd sounded on the phone. 'Morning, Fraser.'

'So, who was in the car?'

'Kylie Orchard. Looks like she was killed not long after she disappeared.'

Fraser made a note on his pad. 'Anyone on your radar?'

'Bit early for that,' said Stella, 'but I'd like to talk to Wanda or at least find out where she is.'

'We've been looking for her for the last two years,' said Fraser, 'as I'm sure you know.'

'I've read the file,' said Stella.

'She's still in the country,' said Fraser, 'unless she found a way to slip out without going through passport control, and you'd need some serious connections to organise that.'

'Yeah, well money can buy a lot of things, including connections,' said Stella.

'Not wrong there, Stella, and our girl's got money,' said Fraser. 'According to ASIC, there's still a couple of million bucks unaccounted for but she hasn't accessed any of her personal or business accounts since the day she disappeared. She must be lugging around a suitcase full of hundred dollar notes.'

'Given they both disappeared around the same time,' said Stella, 'sounds like it was planned. Do you think the husband and the boyfriend were in on it?'

'It's possible Downs' husband helped her stage her disappearance, which he's denied, of course, but none of the money trails lead to him or his company.'

'What about Orchard's former boyfriend, Bruce Munro?' said Stella. 'Told me he'd suspected they were ripping off their clients.'

'We haven't traced anything to him either,' said Fraser. 'If he's involved, you're going to need another motive.'

'You're probably right,' said Stella. 'So, if Wanda's paying cash for everything, how come no-one's reported her?'

'My guess is she's using a false identity. That way she could be working or using the banking system without our knowledge, or she could have slowly deposited her cash into an account to avoid detection. She'd obviously know the cash deposit limit.'

Stella nodded. 'Well, at least we know she hasn't been passing herself off as Kylie Orchard, since no-one's reported seeing her either.'

'Perhaps she's had a facelift or some other form of cosmetic surgery,' said Fraser, 'which would mean someone out there knows what she looks like.'

'Or she's met the same fate as her partner in crime,' said

Stella, 'which would suggest they must have known about something someone else wanted kept secret, don't you think?'

'You've got a few theories to work with there, Stella. I'll get a refresh out on our search efforts in the other states. At least with the international border closed we won't have to worry about her leaving the country.'

'I'll take another look at their associates,' said Stella. 'Maybe someone will remember something now we know Kylie was murdered.'

———

Stella arranged to meet Wanda's parents, Geoffrey and Lauren Hayes, in the hope of uncovering something to help her find Wanda, which she saw as her best hope of learning what had led to Kylie's death.

Unlike Kylie's parents, the Hayes lived in a modest house adjacent to the suburban railway line in Ascot Park.

'Humble beginnings,' said Brian, as they got out of the car and walked up the driveway.

'Either that or they've moved down market,' said Stella, as she rang the doorbell.

They both turned at the sound of a horn blast and watched as a near-silent three-car train rolled past on its way into the city. 'At least they don't have to put up with the roar of the diesels anymore,' said Brian. 'Can't wait for them to electrify the line down our way.'

'You'll be retired before that happens,' said Stella, ringing the doorbell again.

'Yeah, that'd be right,' said Brian.

'At least you'll get free travel on your Seniors Card,' said Stella.

Before Brian could respond, the door was opened by a tall

woman with shoulder-length dark hair, pale skin and sparkling green eyes, an older version of the woman in the photographs of Wanda they had on file.

'Mrs Hayes?'

'Are you the police that rang?'

'Detective Sergeant Bruno,' said Stella, holding out her ID. 'This is Detective Constable Rhodes.'

'Ah, we've been expecting you.' Mrs Hayes opened the door and pointed down the short passageway between the rooms. 'Go down to the family room at the end. Geoff is waiting for us down there.'

They walked down the passageway and into an open-plan room with floor to ceiling windows that had obviously been added to the house in the last year or so.

'Hi, I'm Geoff,' said Mr Hayes. 'Can I get you a coffee? Flat white? Short black?'

Stella looked at the plate of cupcakes on the table. 'Flat white, no sugar, thanks.'

'And, what about you, young man?'

'The same, thank you.'

Stella looked at Brian and smiled.

'What?' said Brian.

Mrs Hayes joined them. 'Please. Sit down.'

'Nice room,' said Stella, as Mrs Hayes sat opposite her at the table.

'We had it done when Geoff retired last year,' said Mrs Hayes. 'He got a nice redundancy package for retiring early.'

Stella heard the sound of a coffee machine and turned to admire the kitchen.

'Yes. We put in a new kitchen as well,' said Mrs Hayes. 'Don't know how I coped all those years with the old one.'

Mr Hayes served their coffees and sat next to his wife.

'Wanda your only child?' said Stella.

'No, she has two sisters and a brother,' said Mrs Hayes, 'but she's our eldest.'

'As I mentioned on the phone, we've located her car and, no doubt, you've seen or heard our renewed calls for help in finding her,' said Stella.

'We thought she'd have contacted us by now,' said Mr Hayes. 'We don't know what to think.'

'What hasn't been released publicly yet is we've located her business partner,' said Stella.

'Yes, Neil told us,' said Mrs Hayes. 'Dreadful.'

'How do you think we can help you, Sergeant?' said Mr Hayes, putting down his coffee cup and offering them the plate of cupcakes.

Stella took a cupcake and pulled back the paper before biting into it.

'We're trying to figure out where she may be hiding,' said Brian. 'Anything you can tell us about places she liked to visit would be helpful.'

'I guess you've looked at Robe,' said Mr Hayes.

'What about places you visited when she was growing up?' said Brian.

'We didn't have much money in those days,' said Mrs Hayes. 'Catching the train to Brighton for a day on the beach was about as good as it got, I'm afraid.'

'Wanda had left home before I got my big break at work,' said Mr Hayes, 'but she made up for it once she'd finished uni and married Neil. They've been all over the world and bought their holiday home down in Robe.'

'Even we like the place at Robe,' said Mrs Hayes. 'Neil still lets us use it when he's not down there.'

'So, you've been to Robe since Wanda disappeared?' said Stella.

'We hoped she might turn up down there,' said Mrs Hayes, 'but she hasn't.'

Stella decided to shift their focus. 'When was the last time you saw her?'

'On the Thursday night before she left poor Neil stranded in Tailem Bend,' said Mrs Hayes. 'They came for tea.'

'How did they seem?' said Stella.

Mr Hayes looked at his wife. 'Tell them.'

'There was a bit of tension in the air,' said Mrs Hayes. 'Wanda wanted Neil to sell the place in Robe and buy an apartment on the Gold Coast but he didn't want to. She tried to rope us into the discussion but I'm afraid we sided with Neil.'

'Oh, why was that?' said Brian.

'We don't like holidaying on the Gold Coast either,' said Mr Hayes. 'Too many people.'

'I can understand that,' said Stella. 'What was their relationship like in general?'

'They'd had a couple of rough patches but they always seemed to get over them quickly enough.' Mrs Hayes glanced at her husband. 'She'd left him a couple times before the night she abandoned him in Tailem Bend, but only for a week or so.'

'Do you know if she's made contact with any of her siblings?'

Mrs Hayes shook her head. 'No, but Tiffany's the one she's closest to. They were always keeping secrets from the others. Thick as thieves they were. If Wanda was going to call anybody, it would be Tiffany.'

'Perhaps you could give me Tiffany's contact details,' said Stella. 'That would be helpful.'

'By all means,' said Mr Hayes. 'Anything to help you find her, Sergeant.' He smiled. 'We can forgive her for what's she's supposed to have done. We all make mistakes, don't we? We just want to know she's okay.'

As they were getting into the car to drive back to the office from Ascot Park, Stella's mobile rang. She looked at the caller ID and answered the call from DI Williams.

'Morning, sir.'

'Where are you, Bruno?'

'Ascot Park,' said Stella. 'We're just heading back to the office.'

'Do you have an address for Bruce Munro?'

Stella wondered why he hadn't looked it up himself. It was on the case file. 'I've got an address in Shearing Street, Oaklands Park.'

'Change of plans, I'm afraid, Bruno. Munro's cleaner found his body this morning. Sturt have a patrol on location securing the scene. Best you get yourself over there.'

A small crowd of onlookers was standing in front yards and on the footpath opposite the house cordoned off with crime scene tape when they arrived. Brian parked behind the patrol car at the end of the line of vehicles on the northern side of the street.

They retrieved their crime scene gear from the boot of the car and made their way to the house at the centre of attention, where a constable signed them into the crime scene.

'The pathologist has only just arrived, Sergeant,' said the constable. 'Dr Wright.'

'Where's the body?' said Stella.

'On the kitchen floor, at the back of the house.'

'You first on scene?'

'Yes, Sergeant.'

'Where's the cleaning lady that called it in?'

'In there,' said the constable, pointing to the silver Mitsubishi Lancer parked in the driveway.

'Have you taken a statement?'

'Yes, Sergeant, but I think she may still be in shock.'

'Okay, I'll have a word with her while we're waiting for Dr Wright to do his thing.'

Before she could approach the cleaner's car, a white van pulled up across the driveway and Sgt Barry Rice and his CSI team climbed out and started unloading their equipment.

'You're here early,' said Barry.

'We were in the neighbourhood,' said Stella. 'I'll just have a word with the lady that found the body and get her to move her car for you.'

'Okay.'

Stella opened the passenger side door and slipped in beside the cleaning lady. 'Hi, I'm Detective Sergeant Bruno.'

'Annette Hughes.' She turned to face Stella. 'When will I be able to leave? I've got another house to clean.'

'You going to be okay, Annette?' said Stella, thinking Annette didn't sound much like a woman in shock.

'I need the money,' said Annette.

Stella took a slow breath. 'Okay, just talk me through what you found when you arrived this morning.'

'I got here just after nine-thirty. I'm usually here for three hours Monday mornings to clean and do his laundry, and I come back after I've done my other Monday place to take his clothes off the line and iron his shirts. He's never here. I've got my own key.'

'And, this morning?'

'I let myself in and went down to the kitchen to open the back door to let some fresh air into the place, and there he was, on the kitchen floor in a pool of blood.'

'Did you touch anything?' said Stella.

Annette shook her head. 'Came straight back out to the car and called triple zero. I only had to wait ten minutes.'

'How long have you been cleaning for Mr Munro?'

'Eighteen months or so. I come every week. He likes everything to be kept clean.'

'Talk to him much?'

'I've only seen him a couple of times before this morning. I let myself in, do what I have to do, and he leaves me an envelope.'

'And, was there an envelope for you this morning?'

'No,' said Annette. 'He usually leaves it on the kitchen table.'

'I see,' said Stella, understanding Annette's need to get to her next job. 'Have you given your contact details to the constable who spoke to you?'

'Yes. He said he'd type up my statement and come and see me so I could sign it.'

'Are you sure you're going to be okay?'

'I'll be alright,' said Annette, 'once I get away from here.'

'I'll get the CSI boys to move their van so you can leave,' said Stella, opening the door to get out of the car. 'Thank you for waiting.'

Stella found Brian inside talking to Steve Wright and watching the CSI photographer make a digital record of the crime scene.

'We were only talking to this guy on Friday,' said Brian, as Stella joined them.

'At least you know who he is, then,' said Steve, flashing a smile at Stella.

'Hello, Steve,' said Stella, studying the fully dressed body of Bruce Munro, lying face up in a sea of dark blood on the floor at their feet. 'Stabbed, I see.'

'Several times,' said Steve, 'with that.' He pointed to the blood stained carving knife on the floor under the kitchen table. We might get prints if we're lucky. It doesn't look like it's been wiped clean.'

'This blood looks like it's been here for a while,' said Stella.

'I'd say he was killed some time Saturday,' said Steve. 'Lucky it wasn't hot yesterday.'

'Any signs of a struggle?'

'Nothing under his fingernails, if that's what you mean.'

Stella glanced around the kitchen at the shiny new appliances, the knife block next to the toaster missing one of its knives, and the dirty dishes in the sink, and wondered why the dishes were in the sink and not the dishwasher. She walked over to the sink. There were two plates, two bowls, and two wine glasses. There was dried food caked onto the plates, but there were no dirty saucepans on the stove or in the dishwasher. She guessed Munro and his killer had shared a takeaway meal.

Sgt Rice came into the room.

'Any sign of forced entry, Barry?' said Stella.

'No, but those dishes in the sink suggest he might have been

killed by someone he knew well enough to share a meal with,'
said Barry.'

'Takeaway would be my guess,' said Stella. 'Can't see any
saucepans. Any idea where the food came from?'

Barry opened the cupboard under the sink and lifted an
empty wine bottle and a plastic bag from the rubbish bin. He
opened the bag and extracted a large paper bag with a piece of
paper attached to it. 'The Indian place around the corner on
Morphett Road. Order number 659, for pick up at seven-thirty
Saturday night.'

Stella snapped a photo of the order sheet. 'I'll touch base
with you later, Barry.'

She turned to leave. 'Have a chat with the neighbours,
Brian. See if anyone recalls seeing Munro's dinner guest arrive
sometime after seven-thirty on Saturday night. I'll just pop
around and see if anyone at the restaurant remembers who
picked up this order.'

Stella drove around to the Indian restaurant on Morphett Road
and showed the woman behind the counter her copy of
order 659.

'I'd like to know who placed this order on Saturday.'

'Just a minute.' The woman flicked back through the order
book. 'That was a cash pick up.'

'Were you here?'

'I'm always here, Sergeant. There is no-one else.'

'Do you remember the customer?' said Stella.

'A woman. A tall woman. Not many people pay cash. It's
all cards now'

'Do you remember what she looked like?'

'No, but,' she pointed to the CCTV camera above the door,

'we should have a picture of her.' The woman smiled. 'I'll get my son to show you the recording from Saturday night.'

'Thank you,' said Stella.

'Come through. Come through. My son is studying out the back.'

Stella followed the woman through an aroma filled kitchen, where two men and a woman were preparing food, to a small office at the rear of the building where a young man sat in front of a laptop computer.

'Divit, show us the recording from the security camera for Saturday night. This lady is from the police.'

'What time are you interested in?' said Divit.

'Around seven-thirty.'

Divit closed his laptop, logged onto the desktop computer on the table and scrolled through the file holding the recording they wanted to see. 'Here you go.'

They watched as a steady trickle of people walked into and out of the takeaway section of the restaurant. 'There,' said the woman. 'That's her.'

'Can you make me a copy from when she walks in to when she walks out?' said Stella, handing Divit the USB stick she kept attached to her keys.

'Do you know who she is?' said the woman.

'Not yet, but I intend to find out,' said Stella. 'The man she shared this meal with was found dead this morning.'

'I hope it wasn't our food that killed him,' said the woman. 'That would be bad for business.'

Stella smiled. 'You won't need to worry about that. I can assure you it wasn't your food that killed him.'

Divit handed her the USB stick with the copy of the recording he'd made for her. 'Do you want me to keep this recording?'

'That would be a good idea,' said Stella.

CHAPTER 7

THE BRIEFING ROOM WAS CROWDED. DI Williams had brought in several extra detectives to work on the case. Stella plugged her USB stick into the laptop connected to the room's light projector and opened the file Divit had given her.

She played the short clip several times and then froze it on a view showing the woman's face. 'This is the woman who picked up the meal Munro shared with someone on the night he was killed,' said Stella.

'Anyone recognise her?' said DI Williams.

'She looks a bit like Kylie Orchard,' said one of the detectives.

'Or that other woman we're looking for,' said another. 'Wanda Downs.'

'Yes, Orchard and Downs look similar in the photos we have of them,' said DI Williams, 'but we know Orchard's dead. So, it can't be her.'

'Downs has been missing since the middle of September, 2018,' said Stella. 'If this is her, it's the first sighting of her since that time.'

'Anybody see her arrive or leave Munro's place?' said DI Williams.

'No-one saw her,' said Brian, 'but one of the neighbours reported seeing a grey Mitsubishi Lancer parked in Munro's driveway around eight-thirty, when he arrived home from the movies with his kids. Claims he heard it leave about ten minutes or so after he got home.'

'Get the number?' said DI Williams.

'No,' said Brian, 'but he said he'd seen the car there before.'

'Munro's cleaning lady drives a silver Mitsubishi Lancer,' said Stella. 'I spoke to her. She doesn't look anything like this woman.'

'Check out what she was doing Saturday night, and find out where her car was,' said DI Williams. 'Anything from CSI?'

'They've lifted several prints that don't belong to Munro or his cleaning lady,' said Stella, 'but we don't know who they belong to at this stage.'

'Do we have prints for this Downs woman on file?'

'Yes,' said Stella.

'Get on to Traffic, Sergeant. I want a review of any footage from roads she could have used to get to and from Shearing Street, and get that security camera recording out to the media. I want that woman found this time.'

Stella and Brian caught up with Neil Downs at a building site in Dover Gardens.

'What can I do for you, Sergeant?'

'Take a look at this,' said Stella, showing him the video clip from the Indian restaurant.

'Can I see that again?' said Neil.

Stella handed him her phone.

'Where is this?'

'A restaurant in Oaklands Park.'

Neil moved out of the sunshine into the shade and watched the video again. 'When was this taken?'

'Last Saturday.'

Neil handed Stella's mobile back to her. 'Can't be sure, but it looks like Wanda, doesn't it?'

'I've only seen a couple of photos of Wanda, Mr Downs,' said Stella, 'but I've met her mother.'

'She looks like her mother,' said Neil, 'and her sister, Tiffany.' He scratched his chin. 'That could be Tiffany, if it's not Wanda.'

'What sort of car does Tiffany drive?' said Stella.

'She's got one of those Mitsubishi coupe things. A little grey one.'

'A Lancer?' said Stella.

'Yeah, a Lancer,' said Neil. 'Why is this important?'

We're going to have to talk to Tiffany when we're through here, thought Stella. 'Whoever this is,' said Stella, tapping the screen of her mobile, 'she picked up a takeaway meal from an Indian restaurant in Oaklands Park and took it around to Bruce Munro's last Saturday night.'

'Are you telling me Bruce knows where Wanda is?'

Stella shook her head. 'I wish I was, believe me. What I am telling you, though, is this woman is probably the last person to see Bruce alive before he was stabbed to death.'

'What?'

'Bruce has been murdered, Mr Downs, and your wife, or someone who looks like her...'

'You can't be serious? Wanda's not that sort of person.'

'What sort of person is she, Mr Downs?'

Neil stared at Stella and then dropped his gaze to the ground. 'She was fun when she wasn't being a bitch. I didn't think she'd leave me but she did. But, I don't think she'd kill anybody, though, especially not Bruce. But, who knows? Maybe you're right.'

'Why wouldn't she want to kill Bruce?'

Neil crossed his arms. 'Wanda was having an affair with him. That's what the argument was about the night she left me.'

Stella glanced at Brian, who was writing in his notebook. 'Did Kylie know about the affair?'

Neil put his hands in his pockets. 'She was the one who told me.'

Interesting group of friends, thought Stella. 'And you confronted Wanda?'

Neil nodded.

'What did she say?'

'She denied it.'

'But, you didn't believe her, did you?'

'How could I? Kylie had photos of her with Bruce.'

'Do you still have those photos?'

'She only ever showed them to me,' said Neil. 'She never gave me a copy.'

Convenient, thought Stella. That meant she wouldn't be able to verify his story unless they found Kylie's mobile phone. She stared at Neil and wondered if he was spinning her a yarn or unwittingly incriminating himself. 'I think you'd better call a lawyer, Mr Downs.'

'Why? I haven't done anything wrong?'

'Lying to police isn't exactly not doing anything wrong, Mr Downs,' said Stella. 'I think it's time you came clean with what you know, and you'll want a lawyer for that interview.'

The Desk Sergeant beckoned to Stella as she walked into the lobby. 'There's a Tiffany Hayes waiting to see you, Stella. I've put her in interview room three.'

Stella turned to Brian. 'Did you make an appointment?'

'I haven't made the call yet,' said Brian.

'Did she say what she wanted to see me about?'

'No, but she looks like the woman in that video you released yesterday,' said the Desk Sergeant. 'I've put someone with her.'

'Okay, Bob. I've got a Neil Downs and his lawyer coming in at two. Can you put them in room five?'

Stella walked over to the interview suite with Brian and opened the door to room three. A tall, slim woman of about forty, with shoulder-length black hair, pale skin and green eyes, who reminded Stella of both Wanda Downs and her mother, stood looking at them from across the room. Stella waited for the constable in the room to exit and take up her position outside the door.

'Tiffany Hayes?'

'Yes.'

'Detective Sergeant Bruno. This is Detective Constable Rhodes. You asked to see me?'

'That's me in the video on the news. I bought takeaway Indian from that place last Saturday night,' said Tiffany. 'Why do you want to talk to me?'

'Let's sit down,' said Stella, pointing to the chairs around the interview table. 'Do you have any ID with you?'

'My driver's licence,' said Tiffany, opening her handbag and extracting her licence from a purse.

Stella looked at the licence and handed it to Brian, who photographed it with the camera in his phone and handed it back to Tiffany.

'Bruce Munro was found dead on Monday morning,' said

Stella. 'We're investigating his murder, and we found a bag with your order number on it in his kitchen.'

Tiffany rested her elbows on the table, held her head in her hands and took several deep breaths.

Stella waited.

Tiffany looked up, eyes wide open. 'Murdered? When?'

'Saturday night,' said Stella.

'He was alive when I left him,' said Tiffany. 'You can't think I had anything to do with it?'

'You're going to have to make a statement on the record,' said Stella. 'Do you want to call a lawyer?'

'I'm a lawyer,' said Tiffany. 'I know I don't have to say anything, but I've got nothing to hide. I didn't kill him, if that's what you think.'

'Criminal law?' said Stella.

'Family,' said Tiffany, 'but the general rules of engagement are the same.'

Stella smiled. She liked Tiffany's pluck. She was either innocent or convinced she could bluff her way through an interview.

She waited for Brian to switch on the recording devices and step them through the formal start to the interview. 'Tell us about your Saturday night with Bruce.'

'Bruce called and asked me to come over. He wanted to talk about Kylie. That was around five,' said Tiffany. 'I said I'd pick up some Indian and be there at seven-thirty.'

'Are you the new woman in Bruce's life?'

'No, that's Roz. She lives in Mt Gambier. She's a friend of Bruce's sister.'

'So, why did Bruce want to talk to you about Kylie?'

'We've been looking for her and Wanda ever since they went missing. Didn't he tell you?'

'No,' said Stella, thinking Tiffany was very relaxed for

someone who had committed murder. 'So, what happened after you picked up the Indian food at seven-thirty?'

'I drove around to Bruce's and we talked about Kylie. He was pretty upset about her being dead all this time when we thought she was still alive.'

'Did he say who he thought might have killed her?'

'No, but it comes down to two people in my opinion.' Tiffany looked straight at Stella. 'My sister or her weasel of a husband.'

Stella raised an eyebrow. That was the first disparaging remark she'd heard about Neil Downs. 'What makes you think that?'

'Kylie knew too much,' said Tiffany. 'Bruce told me she'd worked out what Wanda was doing and threatened to expose her if she didn't cut her in. That's when she and Bruce split up. He didn't want her to get involved but she was greedy. She told Bruce if he didn't want to know about it, then he'd better piss off, which is what he did.' Tiffany smiled. 'He's the one who reported them to ASIC.'

'Who knew about that?' said Stella.

'About what?'

'Bruce telling ASIC what they were doing with the money?'

'He only told me about that on Saturday,' said Tiffany. 'I don't know if he'd told anybody else apart from ASIC.'

Stella looked at Brian. She was sure there was no mention of Bruce being their informant in the files they'd received from the AFP. Brian shook his head. An almost imperceptible movement, but one which told her it was news to him as well.

'What was your reaction to Bruce telling you that?'

'I knew about the scam. I was one of their clients, for God's sake, but I didn't know it was Bruce who'd told ASIC.' Tiffany leant back in her chair. 'I was grateful they'd been stopped but I was pissed off he hadn't trusted me enough to tell me earlier.'

Stella thought she'd have been pissed off too, but wondered whether Tiffany would have been angry enough to kill him over the disclosure.

'What makes you think Neil might have killed Kylie?'

'Poor love-sick Neil. He'd do anything for Wanda.'

'Even help her disappear?'

'I wouldn't put it past him. I reckon he's in it up to here.' Tiffany raised her right hand up over her head.

'How would you describe your relationship with Neil?'

'What relationship? I haven't spoken to him since he claimed my sister left him standing at that petrol station in Tailem Bend.'

'What did Bruce think of Neil? He ever tell you?'

'Bruce never talked about Neil. We only ever talked about Kylie and Wanda.'

'Do you think Bruce and Wanda might have been having an affair before she disappeared?'

Tiffany looked at Stella. 'Who told you that?'

'Neil, actually,' said Stella.

'I was the one screwing Bruce after he'd split with Kylie,' said Tiffany. 'It was fun while it lasted, but we weren't meant to be a couple.'

'Are you aware Kylie had photos of you and Bruce, and she'd shown them to Neil, claiming you were Wanda?'

'Bitch!' said Tiffany. 'Why would she do that?'

'If she did,' said Stella. 'I only have Neil's word for it.' Stella smiled. 'Tell me, did you bring the wine on Saturday night?'

'No, I don't drink.'

'Was Bruce drinking wine?'

'Not while I was there. We had mineral water.'

'What sort of car do you drive, Tiffany?'

'An ancient two-door Lancer. A silver one. Is that important?'

'One of the neighbours told us he'd seen a car like yours in Bruce's driveway that night. Did you see anyone when you arrived?'

'No.'

'Now, you said Bruce was alive when you left. What time was that?' said Stella.

'He wanted an early night. I left around nine.'

'Where did you go after you left Bruce's place?'

'I dropped in on my parents, in Ascot Park. It's only about ten minutes from Bruce's. Then I went home. Got home around ten-thirty,' said Tiffany. 'What happens now?'

'We'll get a record of this interview typed up for you to sign and we'll need to take your fingerprints, seeing you were in Bruce's house on the night of his murder,' said Stella. 'And, I suggest you get yourself a lawyer.'

'You can't possibly think I had anything to do with his death?' said Tiffany.

'Doesn't matter what I think,' said Stella. 'You're the last person known to have been with Bruce before his body was found. Until we have evidence to the contrary, I suggest you prepare yourself for being charged with his murder.'

'But I didn't kill him!'

'Then your fingerprints won't be on the knife, will they?'

CHAPTER 8

STELLA LET Brian open the door to interview room five before they entered and sat opposite Neil Downs and his lawyer, Lachlan McNamara, at the table in the centre of the room.

'Is my client being arrested?' said Lachlan.

'No,' said Stella.

'Then, why are we here, Sergeant?'

'I'm giving your client an opportunity to correct his statement about the circumstances of his wife's disappearance and to tell me where he was last Saturday evening.'

'Correct his statement?' said Lachlan.

'A few anomalies have come to my attention,' said Stella, 'and, in light of recent events, I think we should get things straight. Do you have a problem with that?'

'What recent events are you referring to, Sergeant?'

Stella looked Lachlan McNamara in the face. She'd never liked him. As far as she was concerned, he was a smug little prick who thought lawyers were in charge of the justice system.

'The death of Bruce Munro.'

Lachlan didn't even flinch. 'And, what's that got to do with my client?'

'Perhaps you could repeat what you told me earlier, Mr Downs, for the benefit of your lawyer.'

Neil turned to Lachlan McNamara. 'Sorry, mate, but I haven't been completely honest about why Wanda left me. I told everyone we'd been fighting over selling the house at Robe, but that wasn't true. Truth is, I'd found out she'd been having an affair with Bruce.'

Lachlan raised his eyebrows.

'And, how had you learnt about the affair?' said Stella.

'Kylie told me. She had photos of them together on her phone. She showed me the photos.'

'And, you confronted Wanda about it?' said Stella.

'In the car on the way back from Robe,' said Neil. 'She denied it.'

'And, you didn't believe her?'

'How could I? I'd seen the photos.'

'And, that's why she left you standing at the Shell Service Station in Tailem Bend?'

'Yeah.'

'Why did you believe Kylie and not Wanda?' said Stella.

Lachlan shifted in his seat.

'Wanda had lied to me before,' said Neil. 'Bruce wasn't the first bloke she'd had an affair with.'

'Is that why she'd left you on previous occasions?'

'Yeah, but she always came back, until this time.'

Stella wondered what sort of man welcomed his wife back after she'd had an affair with someone else. She knew there was no way she'd be doing that if Shaun ever cheated on her. 'Is there anything else in your earlier statement you need to clarify, Mr Downs?'

'Look, I was embarrassed, that's all,' said Neil. 'It was bad enough she'd left me like that. I just couldn't face having to tell the world she'd been screwing around as well. I'm sorry.'

Stella closed her folder.

'Where were you last Saturday night, say between the hours of seven-thirty and midnight?' said Brian.

'Home,' said Neil.

'Can anybody verify that?' said Brian.

'I live alone,' said Neil.

'Perhaps some of the neighbours?' said Lachlan.

'We'll check,' said Stella.

'Is my client under suspicion here?' said Lachlan.

'Given what he's just told us,' said Stella, 'he's a person of interest but, for the moment, he's free to go.'

'Thanks,' said Neil.

'Oh, and by the way,' said Stella. 'Wanda wasn't having an affair with Bruce.'

Neil looked at her. 'How could you possibly know that?'

'I talked to Tiffany. She told me she was the one having an affair with Bruce after he split up with Kylie.'

'Are you sure?'

'Perhaps you should talk to her,' said Stella. 'Sounds like Kylie was the one lying to you.'

'Why would she do that?' said Neil.

'I have no idea,' said Stella, 'and, it's not like we can ask her, is it?'

'Wanda would have known that,' said Neil. 'She was close to Tiffany. They were always on the phone to each other. I wonder why she didn't just tell me it was Tiffany?'

'Maybe Wanda wanted you to think she'd left you over the affair,' said Stella. 'Maybe she'd planned to disappear all along because someone had reported her to ASIC.'

'But,' Neil glanced at Lachlan, 'she didn't know ASIC were coming after her when she left me?'

'Are you sure about that?'

'She didn't say anything.'

Stella opened her folder again. 'ASIC sent her a letter at the end of August.' She slid a copy of the letter across the table to him. 'They'd given her twenty eight days to explain a series of transactions in her trust account.'

Neil looked at the letter and pushed it back across the table. 'Guess that explains why they turned up when they did.'

'Are you saying you had no idea what she was up to?'

'I think we're finished,' said Lachlan. 'My client's answer to that question is already on the record.'

Stella smiled. 'Just wondered whether that was something else Mr Downs feels he'd like to correct while we're here.'

'No,' said Neil. 'I've got nothing else to correct.'

'This whole thing sounds fishy to me, Sarge,' said Brian, as they waited for the lift.

'It's certainly starting to sound a little more complicated than someone doing a runner to avoid facing the music,' said Stella.

'Why do you think Kylie told him Wanda was having an affair with Bruce when she would have known it was Tiffany?'

The lift came to a halt and the doors opened onto their floor. 'What if it was part of their plan?' said Stella. 'What if they'd planned the whole going missing thing together and Tiffany and Bruce were just convenient props?'

'I wonder what went wrong, then,' said Brian. 'How come Kylie ended up dead in the boot of Wanda's car?'

'A falling out between thieves,' said Stella. 'It wouldn't be the first time.'

'You know, Sarge. I'm not sure I buy Downs' story. I think we should speak to his brother and see if we can trace his movements around the time Wanda supposedly left him standing at that service station in Tailem Bend.'

'What are you suggesting, Brian?'

'I think Downs knows more than he's letting on, and he's got motive if he thought she was having an affair with Bruce. This might not be about money after all.'

Stella dropped her folder onto her desk. 'Do we have the CCTV from that service station on file?'

'I'll have a look.'

'You do that while I write up these interviews.'

CHAPTER 9

BRIAN RETRIEVED the USB thumb drive, used to store a copy of the recording made by the security camera overlooking the forecourt of the Shell Service Station in Tailem Bend on the night Wanda Downs disappeared, from the evidence archive and plugged it into his computer. The note stored with the thumb drive told him the recording had been obtained by one of the local constables after the AFP had asked for assistance in locating Wanda Downs, and Neil Downs had described how he'd been abandoned by his wife in Tailem Bend.

He located the file on the thumb drive. Its size suggested he'd be spending some time viewing its contents. He opened the file. The recording started at 21:00:00 on 18/09/2018. Brian sipped his coffee as he watched the black and white image of the forecourt. The camera didn't capture any record of vehicles passing on the highway except for the flash of their headlights as they sped past on their way into the night.

At 21:23:13, a white BMW sedan pulled into the forecourt from right of screen and parked next to the fuel pumps. Brian stopped the recording and backed it up to get a clear image of the number plate as the BMW approached the pumps. When he had a clear image, he wrote down the registration number:

S685BNH. He checked the information in the case file and confirmed he was looking at the BMW registered to Wanda Downs.

Brian pressed play and watched a man he recognised as Neil Downs exit the vehicle from the driver's side and proceed to use the nearest pump to refuel the vehicle. When he'd returned the nozzle to its cradle on the pump, the man walked towards the camera and disappeared from view.

Thirty seconds after the man had disappeared from view, the BMW moved away from the pumps in the direction of the highway. Two minutes later, the man ran out onto the forecourt followed by another man, who appeared to be the attendant, and looked in the direction the car had taken. After a brief discussion, both men turned and walked back towards the camera and disappeared.

Brian rewound the recording and played through the sequence in slow motion. He tried freeze framing and zooming in on the BMW to see if he could identify who was sitting in the front passenger's seat. The best he could do was establish that the person inside the vehicle had long dark hair, as the person travelling with Neil did not get out of the vehicle to slip behind the wheel before driving off when he went in to pay the attendant.

Could be anybody, thought Brian. We only have Neil's word for it that it was Wanda. Could have been Kylie or Tiffany or anyone with long dark hair known to Neil. He pressed play to see why they'd copied the rest of the recording.

At 22:07:56, a white BMW sedan with registration number S685BNI drove onto the forecourt and stopped. Neil Downs walked back into view, opened the passenger side door of the BMW and climbed in. At 22:08:04, the vehicle moved across the forecourt towards the same exit to the highway Wanda's BMW had taken around half an hour earlier.

Brian keyed the registration number of the second BMW into Registrations and discovered it was registered to Stephen Downs. At least that part of Neil's story seemed to hold up.

After ejecting the thumb drive, Brian opened the report Mt Gambier had sent through on the BMW discovered in the Nangwarry pine forest. He'd recalled reading something about the number plates when he'd first read the report, and there it was. They'd had to use the vehicle identification number attached to the body of the vehicle to trace its owner, since the number plates had been removed.

Brian smiled and wondered what other mistakes Kylie's killer had made.

As Brian briefed her on what he'd seen in the security camera footage recorded at the Shell in Tailem Bend on the night Wanda Downs had supposedly disappeared, Stella wondered if Neil Downs had been lying to them all along.

'So, it could have been anybody in that car, and we only have Downs' word for it that it was Wanda?'

'Looks that way.'

'What about the statements?'

'We spoke to the attendant working at the service station,' said Brian. 'He told us he didn't see who was in the car but he did confirm Downs had called his brother and asked him to pick him up.'

'Was that confirmed?'

'There's a call log for Neil's mobile in the file that lists that call.'

'What's the date of the log?' Stella wondered what else it might tell them when examined in the context of a murder investigation.

Brian found the log. 'Lists all his calls for September 2018.'

'That might be worth another look,' said Stella. 'Did we take statements from anyone living near their holiday house in Robe?'

'A few,' said Brian, 'but not from anyone who actually remembered speaking to Wanda that weekend.' He searched through the case file and extracted a sheet of paper. 'Here, look at this one.' He handed the statement to Stella. 'This is from their closest neighbour, a woman called Helen White. Says she remembered seeing them that weekend but claims they'd kept to themselves, which wasn't all that unusual, apparently.'

Stella leant back in her chair. 'Everyone's assumed Wanda was alive that weekend, Brian, but what if she wasn't? What if her disappearance has nothing to do with ASIC investigating her firm?'

'What are you suggesting, Sarge?'

'Doesn't it strike you as odd that Kylie Orchard, who looks a lot like Wanda, disappeared a week before she did?'

Brian sat on the edge of his desk. 'Not if they'd planned to disappear because they'd defrauded their clients.'

'But what if that wasn't the case? What if she was in cahoots with whoever wanted Wanda out of the way for some other reason? Think about it. She was the one, according to Neil, who told him Wanda was having an affair with Bruce.'

'I wonder if Kylie was having an affair with Neil,' said Brian. 'Might explain why she lied to him about Wanda and Bruce.'

'Surely Neil would have seen through that, eventually,' said Stella. 'All he had to do was confront Wanda, like he told us he had.'

'Unless he acted impulsively, Sarge. Might explain why Kylie's dead.'

Stella stared at the ceiling. 'Wanda's parents told us they'd seen her on the Thursday night before she and Neil supposedly went down to Robe for the weekend. Do we know if anyone apart from Helen White saw her or spoke to her after Thursday night?

Brian put the case file on her desk and they read through the statements collected by the officers who had conducted the initial search for Wanda at the request of the AFP.

'Doesn't look like it, Sarge,' said Brian, holding up the statement given by a Meg Horton. 'According to their office manager, Wanda worked from home that Friday and Kylie had been on leave since the close of business on the previous Friday.'

'Does she say whether she'd spoken to Wanda that day?'

Brian read through the statement. 'Doesn't look like she was asked that question, Sarge.'

'See if you can jog her memory while I have a chat with his nibs.'

DI Williams listened in silence as Stella outlined her suspicions about Neil Downs' involvement in his wife's disappearance.

'You think she's dead, Bruno?'

'We don't have any evidence she's alive,' said Stella, 'unless we assume she's adopted another identity and managed to stay out of view for the last two years. But, it's not like she's a plain Jane most people wouldn't notice, is it?'

'She has access to money, though, doesn't she?'

'Only if she'd stashed away a considerable amount of cash,' said Stella. 'She hasn't accessed any of her known accounts according to the AFP.'

DI Williams looked at the photographs of Wanda Downs

and Kylie Orchard on the case board. 'I see what you mean, Bruno. They could be sisters, couldn't they?'

'Or easily mistaken for each other at a distance.'

'You think he killed them both, then?'

'It's a possibility worth pursuing, sir, don't you think?'

DI Williams stroked his chin. 'Is there anything linking him to the body found at Nangwarry?'

'His prints are all over the inside of the car, except for the steering wheel. That's been wiped clean.'

'Any smart lawyer would demolish that, Bruno.'

Especially Lachlan bloody McNamara, thought Stella. 'I know, sir, but that doesn't mean we should ignore it, does it?'

'Alright, let's get everyone together and see what we can find to flesh this out.'

***

At the end of the meeting, Stella was assigned the investigation into the murder of Kylie Orchard, DS Matt Edwards was tasked with finding Wanda Downs, and DS Dominic Francese scored the job of tracking down the killer of Bruce Munro.

After work, Stella went to Shaun's apartment in Rowlands Place. She hadn't spent any significant time with him since her mother's accident, and she missed being with him. Besides, he was always a good listener when she needed to ruminate on one of her cases.

She let herself in. Sarah, Shaun's daughter, was in her room with a pile of books.

'How's the study going?' said Stella, poking her head into Sarah's room.

'Oh, hi, Stella. Be glad when this assignment is finished. I've been working on it all semester. How's Nonna?'

'Think she's enjoying all the being fussed over,' said Stella. 'But, don't ask her about her driving.'

'The boys giving her a hard time?'

'Not the boys. They think it's hilarious. No, my father, and it's not like he's never been involved in an accident. But, it's different when it's him.'

Sarah laughed. 'Dad called. Said he'd be here at six.'

'Great, that will give me time to freshen up.'

'Where are you going?' said Sarah.

'Just across to Gaucho's. We shouldn't be late.'

Stella went into the master bedroom, had a shower and slipped into a fresh set of clothes. She was putting the finishing touches to her face when Shaun arrived.

'You look gorgeous,' said Shaun.

'And you smell like the courthouse.'

Shaun took off his suit and disappeared into the bathroom. 'Give me ten minutes.'

'Yeah, right,' said Stella. 'The reservation's not until six-thirty.'

Much later that night, Stella lay in bed alongside Shaun. He was asleep. She was working through the puzzle of her case and wondering how Neil Downs had managed to pull off a deception and a double murder.

The three glasses of red she'd had with dinner weren't making it easy for her to concentrate, as she sought the connections she'd need to explain how he did it. Sleep eventually had its way with her, and she slipped into the world of dreams with her puzzle unsolved.

CHAPTER 10

NEXT MORNING, Stella reviewed the missing person file on Kylie Orchard, who hadn't been reported missing until the eighth of October, 2018, when she had failed to turn up for work as expected and couldn't be contacted. The file contained statements from her parents, Bruce Munro, and Meg Horton, the office manager at Doe Services who had reported her missing.

The statements by Kylie's parents and Bruce Munro aligned with what they'd told Stella in person when she'd interviewed them after her body had been found.

Stella wondered where Kylie had been between the time she'd left work on the evening of the seventh of September and when she'd been killed sometime after Wanda had disappeared.

The file also contained a note from the investigating officer stating there was no record of her flying to Bali and that the white BMW sedan registered in her name had been found in her parking space in the basement garage of the apartment building where she'd lived.

Stella checked the file notes she'd received from the AFP. The apartment and car had both been seized by the adminis-

trator appointed by ASIC to wind up Doe Services and liqui-
date Wanda and Kylie's assets to repay their clients. She looked
up from the case file. 'Brian, if Orchard's car was in her parking
space when she was reported missing, how do you think she got
herself down to Nangwarry?'

'Qantas and Rex both fly to Mt Gambier,' said Brian. 'or
perhaps she got a lift with someone else.'

'Guess she could have taken the Stateliner bus,' said Stella,
'but why would someone with a car take any of those options?'

'What sort of car did she have?' said Brian.

'A white BMW,' said Stella. 'Must have been their corporate image. What do you think?'

'Do you have the rego number?'

'No, but I've got the address.'

Brian keyed in the details as Stella read them out and
waited for the database to respond. 'It's the same model as
Wanda's and Stephen Downs'.'

'What does Neil drive?'

Brian keyed in Neil's details. 'The same. They were all
driving white, 2016 BMW 5 series sedans.'

'Hmm. That opens up some possibilities,' said Stella.
'Come on, grab your coat. We need to see if we can find some
of Kylie's neighbours to talk to.'

The apartment building Kylie Orchard had called home was
located in a leafy street in Norwood, east of the city centre.
Kylie had lived in apartment six, one of twelve apartments in a
two-storey block with an underground garage for residents'
cars.

Stella pushed the button for apartment five on the intercom
board.

'Yes?' said an elderly female voice.

'Police,' said Stella.

'Do you have any ID?' said the voice.

'Yes,' said Stella.

'Can you hold it in front of the camera so I can see it? Above the buttons.'

Stella looked for the camera and held up her ID.

'What do you want?'

'We'd like to ask you a few questions about the woman that used to live in number six,' said Stella. 'Kylie Orchard.'

'Oh,' said the voice. 'Just a minute. I'll come down.'

Two minutes later, a woman with a streak of pink through her grey hair appeared on the other side of the glass door blocking the entrance and pushed a button on the wall. The door swung open and she stepped out into the foyer to join them.

'I'm Detective Sergeant Bruno and this is Detective Constable Rhodes,' said Stella. 'And you are?'

'Carol Moore.'

'Have you lived here long?' said Stella.

'We've been here for eight years,' said Carol. 'Moved in when we retired.'

'Did you know Kylie Orchard?'

'Oh, yes. She was very friendly,' said Carol. 'I saw that story about her in the paper. Dreadful.'

'Yes,' said Stella. 'We're investigating her death.'

'How can I help you?'

'Were you here during September, 2018, around the time Kylie went missing?'

'I think so,' said Carol, 'but why don't you come in and let me check my diary. I'm sure my husband will know. His memory is better than mine.'

They followed Carol through the entrance and down a

hallway to her apartment, where she let them into a spacious living area with a view out to a garden courtyard.

'Make yourself comfortable,' said Carol. 'I'll just get my husband.'

She disappeared through a doorway and came back a few moments later with a tall white-haired man carrying a mobile phone. 'This is Harold.'

'Pleased to meet you, Mr Moore,' said Stella.

Harold smiled. 'I understand you want to know if we were here in September, 2018.'

'Yes,' said Stella.

Harold opened the calendar on his mobile and scrolled through the entries.

Stella waited. Brian opened his notepad.

'We got back from the Gold Coast on the twenty-first of August and didn't go to Melbourne until the fourth of November,' said Harold, looking up. 'We always go for the Melbourne Cup.'

'And, do you have a car?' said Stella.

'It's parked downstairs,' said Harold.

'And, would I be correct in assuming your parking space is next to the space for apartment six?'

'Yes.'

'Do you remember the last time you either saw or spoke to Kylie Orchard from apartment six?'

'I remember her saying she was going to Bali,' said Harold. 'That was probably a few days after we got back from Queensland, so around the end of August.' He shrugged and looked at his wife.

'I had coffee with her the day before she left,' said Carol. 'She was looking forward to having a break from work. I told her about all the places we'd been to in Bali.'

'Did either of you see her leave?'

'No,' said Harold. 'We had the grandkids that weekend.' He smiled. 'They keep us on our toes.'

'How old are they?' said Stella.

'Ten and eight,' said Carol. 'Both boys.'

'I can see how that would keep you occupied,' said Stella. 'Now, I want you to think about when you used your car in the days after Kylie left to go to Bali. Do you remember seeing her car parked downstairs next to yours?'

'That's been bothering me since we heard she'd been found dead,' said Harold. 'You see, we saw her boyfriend, Bruce, driving her car into the garage a couple of weeks after we thought she'd gone to Bali.'

'Was the car here before you saw him returning it?'

'No, she said she'd be leaving it in the long-term carpark at the airport,' said Harold.

'Did you speak to Bruce?'

'No, he was driving in when we were driving out. He wasn't here when we got back.'

'Were you surprised to see him?' said Stella.

'Not really,' said Carol. 'He was here all the time, even after she'd told me they'd broken up.'

'What did you think of him?'

'Seemed like a nice bloke,' said Harold.

'I thought they were getting married,' said Carol. 'I was really surprised when she told me they'd broken up.'

'Did you see Bruce at any time after that?' said Stella.

'No,' said Harold. 'We haven't seen him since that night.'

'Anybody else been here trying to get into her apartment?'

'Only some lawyer who's winding up her business,' said Harold. 'They're trying to sell it. Never thought she be caught up in something like that.'

'I hope you hadn't invested any money with her,' said Stella.

Harold chuckled. 'I guess we were lucky, Sergeant. We'd retired before we met her.'

Stella waited for Brian to get in behind the wheel. 'What did you make of that?'

'Can of worms,' said Brian. 'Too bad Munro's not around to answer a few questions, though.'

'Hmm. Might explain why he isn't,' said Stella. 'I wonder how much of what he told us was true.'

'Wonder if anybody has told us the truth, Sarge.'

'Well, we know the story Neil told us about being left stranded in Tailem Bend is true. The security camera video confirms that.'

'Yeah, but we don't really know anything about what led up to that point or what happened after it, do we? Neil's given us two versions so far, hasn't he?'

Stella drummed her fingers on the dashboard. 'Let's have a chat with Stephen Downs. He was married to Kylie. Perhaps he can tell us a bit more about her.'

'Did you read the statement he made after she'd been reported missing?' said Brian. 'Said he hadn't seen her since their divorce.'

'Yeah, well Munro told us he hadn't seen her for months before she disappeared too, didn't he?'

'Might be time to chase up some phone records, Sarge. See if we can track Munro's movements.'

'He's not the only one I'd like to track, but let's talk to Stephen Downs first.' Stella slipped her mobile out of her pocket and called Downs Construction.

Stephen Downs agreed to meet them in his office.

CHAPTER 11

'I was wondering when you'd want to speak to me,' said Stephen, as he led Stella and Brian into the design studio that served as his office.

'Investigations have a life of their own, Mr Downs,' said Stella, as she took a seat at the circular table next to Stephen's drawing desk. 'We can't always control the timeline.'

'You mentioned you were investigating Kylie's death. I'm not sure I can be of much assistance with that.'

'We're trying to determine her movements in the weeks leading up to her death, and I was wondering if you had any idea where she might have gone when she was supposedly in Bali,' said Stella.

'I didn't even know she was supposed to be in Bali until I was interviewed by the federal police,' said Stephen. 'She hadn't been all that keen on Bali when we were married.'

'She'd been to Bali before, then?'

'We went there after her second miscarriage. Thought it might help her get over it.' Stephen shrugged. 'Don't think it did, though. We seemed to drift apart after that.'

'When was that?' said Stella.

'Couple of years before we split up.'

'Have you ever wondered where she went when she disappeared?' said Stella.

Stephen leant back in his chair. 'Plenty of times, but I never thought she'd end up down in the South East. She was such a city girl. Never liked living in Murray Bridge. She was always in the city. Guess that's why she set up with Wanda in Norwood. She liked being close to the action.'

'Did you ever meet Bruce Munro?'

Stephen shook his head. 'To be honest, we didn't have much to do with each other after the divorce. I wanted to move on with my life and let her get on with hers.'

Stella thought that sounded reasonable. 'Did you have much to do with Wanda?'

'Family gatherings and the like,' said Stephen. 'She and Neil moved in their own social circle down here in the city. I only come down for work. My social life has always been in Murray Bridge. Neil's the one who moved away when he married Wanda.'

'When was the last time you saw Wanda?' said Stella.

Stephen stroked his chin with his right hand. 'Couple of weeks before she disappeared. She dropped into the office to see Neil but he wasn't here.'

'How did she seem?'

'Same old bubbly Wanda as far as I could tell.'

'Were you aware of your brother's marital problems?' said Stella.

'We'd talked about them,' said Stephen. 'I tried to talk him in to leaving her but...' Stephen shrugged. 'He didn't see it that way.'

'Tell us about the night Neil called you from Tailem Bend.'

'Not much to tell, really. He called when she left him stranded. I drove over to Tailem Bend to pick him up.'

'Did he go home that night?'

Stephen shook his head. 'Stayed overnight with me. I took him home in the morning on the way to work.'

'He wasn't keen to find out if Wanda had gone home after she'd left him at that service station?'

'He tried calling her. She wouldn't answer, so we decided it might be best to give her time to cool down.'

'Neil tell you why she'd driven off?'

'They'd had a fight, apparently. He'd confronted her about some photographs he'd seen of her with Bruce.'

So, he'd told his brother the same reason he'd now given them, thought Stella. 'Did he tell you who'd shown him those photos?'

Stephen looked down at his hands resting in his lap. 'Kylie.'

'Do you think Kylie knew about their marital issues?' said Stella.

'I don't think there were too many secrets between Kylie and Wanda, to be honest.'

'Why do you think Kylie showed those photos to Neil?'

Stephen crossed his arms on his chest. 'Neil and I have had lots of conversations about that. My best guess is they were setting him up to see how he'd react. Wanda was like that. She was always pulling his chain.'

'Has he told you it was Tiffany in the photos?'

'Tiffany? I thought she was gay.'

'Apparently she had an affair with Bruce after he'd broken up with Kylie,' said Stella.

'Are you sure?'

'She told us herself,' said Stella.

'If you say so,' said Stephen.

'What did Neil do when Wanda didn't come back or make contact?'

'Wanda's office manager called him on the Monday. Apparently some people from ASIC had turned up at the office and wanted to know where she was. He waited a week, then reported her missing. We thought she might have panicked and done something stupid.'

'Like killing herself?'

'Yeah, but when her body didn't turn up we thought she'd probably left the country through some backdoor.'

'And, when did you realise Kylie had disappeared as well?'

'Not until the federal police came to see me in early October.'

'Do you think they'd planned their disappearance?'

'Seemed like it when I found out what they were supposedly doing with their clients' money.'

'What do you think now?'

'Now, I'm not so sure, especially since Kylie's body was found in Wanda's car.' Stephen looked up. 'I mean, where's Wanda? Did she kill Kylie?'

Good question, thought Stella. 'Is there any reason why all four of you were driving the same model BMW?'

'That was Wanda's idea. She had a contact in the industry. We got a special price for buying four at the same time.'

'Any idea who might have wanted to kill Kylie besides Wanda?'

'I guess there'd be a lot of people with a motive, Sergeant, but I really have no idea. It's not like Kylie went out of her way to make enemies. She was a people person, not a homebody like me.'

Stella thought he was making them sound like a mismatch from the start. 'How did you meet?'

'At uni. Guess I was a little more exciting in those days. You know, big dreams, wanted to change the world.'

'What happened?'

'Life, Sergeant.' Stephen swept an arm around his office. 'Dreams get drowned by the responsibilities of making a living.'

'I guess we all have that problem,' said Stella. 'If you think of anything else, Mr Downs, please give me a call.'

CHAPTER 12

WHEN SHE RETURNED to the office, Stella joined DS Matt Edwards, who was leading the search for Wanda Downs, and DS Dominic Francese, the lead on the Munro murder case, in DI Williams' office for their afternoon briefing, but the inspector was not in his office when they arrived.

'Making any progress, Dominic?' said Stella.

'Still early,' said Dominic, 'but the pathologist's estimated time of death could be a problem for Tiffany Hayes.'

'Why's that?'

'According to her statement, she left Munro's place around nine. I spoke with her parents, who confirmed she'd arrived at their place around nine fifteen, but with a time of death between nine and eleven, she could have killed him before she left.'

'Any prints on the knife?' said Stella.

'Couple of partials we still haven't matched, but her prints are on the plates and glasses found in the sink.'

'What about the wine bottle?'

'It's only got Munro's prints on it but they're still working through the prints they lifted from other parts of the house.'

DI Williams walked in and shut the door. His face was so red Stella thought he was about to explode.

'Are you okay, Frank?' said Matt Edwards. 'We can do this later if you like.'

'Some little bastard's torched my wife's car,' said DI Williams. 'Is she okay?' said Stella.

The inspector sank into the chair behind his desk and took several deep breaths. 'She's fine, thank you, Bruno. Her car was stolen last night. Traffic's just found what's left of it in Camp-belltown.'

'Hope you had it insured, Frank,' said Matt.

'It's insured, Matt, but I'd still like to wring their bloody necks, little shits!' The inspector sighed. 'Now, what have you lot got to report?'

'I'll start,' said Stella. 'I spoke to the people that lived next door to Orchard. According to them, Munro was a frequent visitor even after he and Orchard had split up, but he told us he hadn't seen her since their break up. And, they claim they saw him returning her car to her parking spot two weeks after they thought she'd gone to Bali.'

'I guess that would imply he knew where she was,' said Dominic.

'Or at least where she'd left her car,' said DI Williams. 'Anything else, Bruno?'

'Her car's a white BMW. Same model as Wanda's. Same model as both the Downs brothers drive.'

'Oh, I see where this is going,' said Matt. 'They could have played musical chairs with the cars.'

'Munro told us he'd worked out what Kylie and Wanda were up to,' said Stella. 'He told Tiffany Hayes, at least according to her, he'd reported them to ASIC, but there's nothing in the file I got from the AFP confirming that.'

'That might have given him a reason to blackmail them,' said DI Williams, 'but what would he gain from killing Orchard?'

'My guess is whoever killed Orchard killed Munro,' said Stella. 'I'd say he'd become a liability once Orchard's body turned up simply because he knew too much.'

'So, we're back to the husband,' said DI Williams.

'Or Wanda,' said Matt.

'What makes you think she's still alive?' said Stella.

'There's no body,' said Matt.

'Plenty of places out there to hide a body, Matt,' said Dominic.

'You have to wonder why Orchard's body was left in Wanda's car,' said Stella.

'I think someone wanted us to find it,' said DI Williams. 'Someone who doesn't want us to find Wanda.'

'I'm going to pull the phone records of Munro and both the Downs brothers from mid 2018 onwards,' said Stella. 'We need to know where they've been and who they've been talking to.'

'Do it,' said DI Williams. 'You have anything, Dominic?'

Stella wondered what she'd have to do for him to use her first name but decided she wasn't going to lose any sleep over it. She'd worked for Frank for years and, for whatever reason, he'd called her Bruno right from the start.

'Tiffany Hayes looks like our most likely suspect, sir,' said Dominic.

'What would be her motive?' said Stella.

'Bring her in and see if she sticks to the story she told Bruno,' said DI Williams. 'What about you, Matt?'

'I'm working with Mt Gambier. We've got a renewed appeal for sightings of Wanda up and running.'

'Okay, keep me posted.'

CHAPTER 13

NEIL DOWNS SAT on the outside deck of his holiday home
listening to the sound of the waves pounding the nearby beach.
He enjoyed being in Robe and came down from the city as
often as he could. He poured himself a second glass of
Cabernet Sauvignon, one of the signature wines of the Coon-
awarra region located inland from the coast, and wondered if
he'd done the right thing telling the police about the fight he'd
had with Wanda over the photos Kylie had shown him. He'd
said it to deflect their focus from Wanda but wondered if he'd
inadvertently implicated himself in Bruce's death. Perhaps not,
he thought, since they hadn't moved to arrest him after he'd
blurted it out.

He took a long sip of wine and watched the sun sink into
the sea on the horizon. As the clouds changed from orange and
pink to grey and, finally, black, he hoped his luck would hold,
despite the mistake he'd made.

He wondered where Wanda was and why she'd killed
Kylie. The last time he'd seen her was on the Sunday morning
she had driven off from Robe to pick up Kylie in Mt Gambier,
with the intention of heading to Melbourne to start over.

Bruce had driven Kylie to Mt Gambier the day she'd told everybody she was flying to Bali and helped him pull off the ruse at Tailem Bend. But he'd wanted to spill the beans when Kylie turned up dead.

Neil hadn't intended to kill Bruce. He hadn't even taken a weapon with him when he'd gone to see him. He'd only wanted to make sure Bruce was going to keep to his part of the bargain. He'd even offered him more money but Bruce hadn't been interested. He'd told Neil he couldn't live with the guilt and deception any longer and wanted to come clean.

Neil hadn't counted on Bruce reneging on their agreement, and there was no way he could have let him tell the truth; he'd promised Wanda he'd wait until it was safe to join her in Melbourne. As it transpired, there'd only been one way to ensure Bruce would keep his silence, and Neil had taken it.

He took another sip of his wine and wondered if killing Bruce had also been a mistake. Then he sat up with a start. What if it hadn't been the deception of the disappearances Bruce had been feeling guilty about?

Neil realised he didn't know what Bruce had been doing the day Wanda had driven off from Robe. He'd always assumed Bruce had stayed at his sister's in Mt Gambier until it had been time for him to come to Robe. But what if he hadn't? What if he'd murdered the girls instead of helping them on their way?

Shit, thought Neil. That would certainly explain why he hadn't heard from Wanda despite her promises.

'You bastard, Bruce!'

He looked around. No-one had heard him. The surrounding holiday homes sat in darkness. At this time of the year, they were empty. Their owners working day jobs elsewhere and dreaming about their next beachside getaway weekend.

Neil got up and paced around the decking. What was he going to do now if Bruce had killed Wanda as well? It wasn't like he could tell anyone, unless he wanted to go to prison for killing Bruce.

CHAPTER 14

BRIAN SCROLLED through the data he'd received in response to his request for the mobile phone records of Bruce Munro and the Downs brothers.

He checked the location data listed in Stephen Downs' record for the weekend Wanda had disappeared. Stephen had clearly been in Murray Bridge that weekend and there was a record of his brother's call from Tailem Bend.

Next, he checked Neil's record for the same weekend. It confirmed he'd travelled from Adelaide to Robe on the Friday, but much earlier than Brian had expected, and spent the weekend in Robe at one location before travelling back to Tailem Bend and then to Murray Bridge, after he'd called his brother from Tailem Bend on the Sunday night at 21:34.

Brian scrolled through the location data in Neil's record for the weeks following his wife's disappearance. He'd stayed in the Adelaide metropolitan area. It certainly didn't look as if he'd made any effort to find her apart from calling her number on several occasions.

He turned his attention to the call log on Neil's number for the week leading up to her disappearance. There were multiple daily calls from Wanda's number and several from Bruce

Munro's number. Brian made a note and wished he'd paid more attention to Neil's incoming calls when he'd initially reviewed the copy of Neil's telephone log in the missing person file on Wanda.

For someone who'd told them he wasn't friends with Neil Downs, Bruce Munro had certainly called him a few times that week. Brian wondered if they'd been organising something and added a comment to his note.

As they already knew Wanda hadn't used her mobile phone after she'd left Neil standing on the forecourt of the service station in Tailem Bend, Brian turned his attention to Bruce Munro's call log. It looked like Bruce had spent the weekend in and around Mt Gambier, but he'd travelled to the area on the weekend before and spent several days in Robe before going to Mt Gambier, where it looked like he'd spent most of his time in Suttontown, on the western edge of the city.

However, Munro had travelled from Suttontown into the vicinity of Nangwarry and back on the morning of the 16th before travelling to Robe in the late afternoon, where it appeared he'd turned off his phone, since the next location record was dated the 17th of September, the day after Wanda had disappeared. Brian made another note and decided it was time to update DS Bruno.

'What does his statement say about his whereabouts that weekend?' said Stella.

'He wasn't asked,' said Brian. 'The focus was on Neil Downs, and the story was Bruce and Kylie had broken up back in March. Seems nobody thought there was a connection between Bruce and Wanda's disappearance, and nobody knew where Kylie was from after the 8th of September. Her phone hasn't been connected to the network since that date.'

Stella called the CSI unit and asked them to check Wanda Downs' car for any indicators showing Bruce Munro had been in the vehicle.

'That could take them a while,' said Brian.

'We need to get Neil Downs back in here,' said Stella. 'I don't think he's been honest with us about his relationship with Bruce.'

'I'll get Uniform on to it,' said Brian.

'Think I'll have a word with DS Francese.'

CHAPTER 15

DS MATT EDWARDS came into the squad room and approached Stella's desk. 'Just had a call from Mt Gambier, Stella. They've found a skeleton about a kilometre from where Wanda's car was found. Early indicators are it's probably her.'

'Well, at least I was right about one thing,' said Stella.

'What's that?' said Matt.

'She's dead, and she's no doubt been dead since she supposedly disappeared.'

'Guess whoever killed Orchard must have killed her as well,' said Matt.

'Yeah, and the phone data suggests Munro was in the area at the time,' said Stella. 'I've got CSI double checking for any signs of him being in the car.'

'Shame he's in the morgue,' said Matt.

'Well, we haven't pinned it on him yet.'

'What about the husband?'

'Brian's bringing him in. He's got some interesting telephone calls to explain,' said Stella. 'Seems he and Munro were a lot closer than either of them let on.'

'Perhaps they were in on it together,' said Matt. 'At least as far as helping Wanda and Kylie to disappear.'

If looks could kill, thought Stella, as she walked into the interview room with Dominic Francese, the expression on Lachlan McNamara's face would be deadly.

'This is Detective Sergeant Francese,' said Stella. 'He's looking into the murder of Bruce Munro.'

'Is that why we're here?' said Lachlan.

'We're here to establish the exact nature of the relationship between Mr Downs and Bruce Munro,' said Stella.

'I thought that was already clearly established,' said Lachlan.

Stella made a show of reading her notes. 'Bruce told us he hardly knew you, Mr Downs, and that he'd only spoken to you a few times since Wanda and Kylie had gone missing. That sound right to you?'

'Pretty much,' said Neil. 'We'd only met a few times socially through my wife's business when he was with Kylie. He dropped off the radar when she broke up with him.'

'You didn't confront him about the affair you thought he was having with your wife?'

'You don't have to answer that,' said Lachlan.

'I only confronted Wanda,' said Neil. 'I wasn't interested in Bruce.'

'Mr Downs, are you aware of the Telecommunications Interception and Access Act?'

Neil looked at Lachlan. 'What's she talking about?'

'That's the law that requires your mobile phone provider to store data on your calls for at least two years.'

'Law enforcement agencies can access that data without a warrant as long as they follow due process,' said Stella.

'What are you saying?' said Neil.

'That data includes details of who you speak to and where your phone was at the time,' said Stella.

'Where are we going with this?' said Lachlan. 'It's not like my client hasn't told you where he was when his wife disappeared or the night Bruce Munro was killed.'

Stella took another piece of paper out of her folder. 'The location data for your mobile phone over the weekend starting Friday, the 14th of September, 2018, confirms your claim that you spent the weekend in Robe. At least, it confirms the location of your phone, and your location if we assume it was on your person at the time. It also shows you were in Tailem Bend at the time you said you were and the call record shows you called your brother when you said you had.' Stella looked up. 'And, we have independent confirmation of that from the security camera recording from the Shell Service Station in Tailem Bend.'

Neil shrugged.

Lachlan looked at Stella as if he was about to say something. Stella held up her hand.

'I've stated the obvious,' said Stella, 'so you'd know we have your phone records, Mr Downs, but I haven't told you what's in these records that I want to know about, nor have I told you what we know about Bruce's movements that same weekend.'

Beads of perspiration appeared on Neil's forehead.

'You know where Bruce was, don't you, Mr Downs?'

'No comment,' said Lachlan.

'That won't help him,' said Stella. 'Bruce was in Robe on the afternoon of the 16th of September, and his phone was pinged by the same tower that pinged your client's phone before it was turned off.'

Neil leant backed in his chair and blew out a long breath.

'Want to tell us how you and Bruce helped Wanda and Kylie disappear, Neil? Because that's what happened, isn't it?'

'Can I have a moment with my client?' said Lachlan.

When the interview resumed, Stella thought Neil looked as if he'd aged ten years.

'My client's willing to admit he helped his wife disappear,' said Lachlan, 'but nothing beyond that.'

'Tell us about it,' said Stella.

Neil looked up. 'It was Wanda's idea. Wanda always got what she wanted. If she'd been happy with the life we had, none of this would have happened. But, she always wanted more. When people started trusting her with their money, she couldn't help herself. And, then Kylie found out what she was doing and wanted a slice of the action. I should have listened to Bruce when he came to me, but it was too late by then, they were in too deep to get themselves out.'

'So, what was the plan?' said Stella.

'We came up with the Bali trip so Kylie could disappear and then the service station idea so Wanda could join her.'

'Where were they going?'

'The idea was they'd go to Melbourne and start something else. They had plenty of money.'

'Cash?' said Stella.

'Yeah, a suitcase full of the stuff.'

'What was in it for you?' said Stella.

Neil looked at his hands. 'For me? There was nothing in it for me. I hadn't used any of her money. I made sure she had nothing to do with my business.'

'So, why help her get away with it?'

'I loved her,' said Neil. 'I'm still waiting for her to let me know where she is.'

'You don't really expect her to call, though, do you?'

Neil shook his head. 'Not since Kylie turned up dead. She was supposed to be with Wanda.'

Stella waited while he wiped his eyes with the back of his hand. 'When was the last time you saw Wanda?'

'On the Sunday morning. She was going to Mt Gambier to pick up Kylie and then head off to Melbourne.'

'Where was Kylie staying in Mt Gambier?'

'At Bruce's sister's place in Suttontown.'

'Was Bruce with her?'

'Yeah.'

'And he was the one driving the car at Tailem Bend?'

'Yeah.'

'And that was Kylie's car with Wanda's number plates on it?'

'Yeah. Bruce knocked up a fake set.'

'Are you sure they were fake?'

'No reason to think otherwise,' said Neil.

'What was in it for Bruce?'

'Money,' said Neil. 'The girls paid him in cash.'

'So, they paid him off with stolen money,' said Stella.

'I suppose you could say that.'

'What do you think happened to them?'

Neil shrugged.

'I think you know,' said Stella.

'That would be speculation,' said Lachlan.

'What if I told you Bruce's mobile phone travelled to Nangwarry on the morning of the 16th?'

'Still speculation,' said Lachlan, 'and, it's not as if we can confirm that with Bruce, is it?'

Stella turned to Dominic. 'Over to you.'

'Want to tell me about where you were on the night Bruce Munro was stabbed to death, Mr Downs?' said Dominic, opening his folder on the table in front of him.

'We've already been over that,' said Lachlan.

'Well, Mr McNamara, a few things have come to light that seem to contradict your client's previous statement,' said Dominic.

Neil closed his eyes.

'Like what?' said Lachlan.

Dominic slipped a photograph of a white BMW sedan out of his folder. 'This is an image from the traffic camera on the intersection of Marion and Oaklands Roads in Park Holme.' He pointed to the time stamp. 'It was taken at 21:13 on the night Bruce Munro was murdered.' He pulled out a second photograph of the same white BMW sedan. 'This is the same car going through that intersection in the opposite direction at 23:09. This car is registered in the name of your client, Mr McNamara, and, as far as I know, it hasn't been reported stolen.'

'So, I went for a drive,' said Neil.

'Long way from Norwood,' said Dominic, 'but, not all that far from Bruce Munro's.'

'Circumstantial,' said Lachlan.

'You could be right,' said Dominic, 'but a direct contradiction of your client's previous statement.'

'So, I made a mistake,' said Neil.

'Yes, you certainly, did,' said Dominic, taking another sheet of paper from his folder. 'You wiped everything down you thought you'd touched inside Bruce's house except for the knob on the inside of the toilet door, and you weren't as thorough as you thought you'd been when you wiped the handle of the knife.'

'What?' said Neil.

'Your prints are on the knob of the toilet door.' Dominic slid the image across the table for him to examine. 'And, we have a partial match with your right thumb from the handle of the knife you left on the kitchen floor.' Dominic looked straight at Neil. 'Want to tell us what happened?'

'No comment,' said Lachlan.

'Are you sure, Mr Downs?' said Dominic.

'No comment,' said Neil.

'Neil Downs, I'm arresting you for the murder of Bruce Munro and for assisting your wife to fake her disappearance.'

CHAPTER 16

STELLA SAT NEXT to Matt Edwards in DI Williams' office waiting for the inspector to get off the telephone.

'That was Steve Wright,' said DI Williams, as he placed the handset back into its cradle on his desk. 'He's identified the skeletal remains retrieved from Nangwarry as Wanda Downs.'

'Any idea how she died?' said Matt.

'Blunt force trauma to the back of the head. Probably with something like a hammer was Steve's guess.'

'Time of death?' said Stella.

'Around the same time as she disappeared,' said DI Williams.

'Well, if it was Munro who killed them,' said Matt, 'he'd have to have had an accomplice. Nangwarry's about thirty ks from Mt Gambier. Someone had to have driven him back going by his mobile phone data.'

'Think we need to speak with his sister,' said Stella.

'I'll get Mt Gambier to bring her in,' said DI Williams, 'and, I want you two down there to wrap this up before the media gets hold of the gory details.'

Linda Munro was a thin woman of thirty-five with long strawberry blond hair tied back in a pony tail. She glared at Stella and Matt as they walked into the interview room, resentment at having been held in the police cells overnight written all over her face.

'I'm Detective Sergeant Bruno,' said Stella, 'and this is Detective Sergeant Edwards. We're investigating the deaths of Wanda Downs and Kylie Orchard.'

'Is that why I've been kept here overnight away from my kids?' said Linda.

'Yes,' said Stella, opening her folder and taking out the search warrant she'd brought with her. 'This is a search warrant authorising a search of your house, Ms Munro. That search is going on as we speak. Is there anything you want to tell us about what we might find?'

Linda looked at the duty lawyer who had been called in to represent her. 'Can they do that?'

The lawyer skimmed the search warrant. 'I'm afraid so.'

'What exactly are you looking for?' said Linda.

'A suitcase full of money, a hammer, a knife,' said Stella, 'and anything that might have belonged to Wanda and Kylie.'

'Oh,' said Linda, dropping her head to gaze at the top of the table.

'Want to tell us about the weekend of the 15th and 16th of September, 2018?' said Stella.

'What do you want to know?' said Linda. 'That's a couple of years ago.'

'Was your brother staying with you that weekend?'

'Could have been. He was always coming down to see the kids.'

'He would have had Kylie Orchard with him,' said Stella.

'Yeah, I remember that weekend,' said Linda. 'The

weekend of the great escape.' She looked up, eyes filled with defiance. 'Didn't go to plan, though, did it?'

'What happened?' said Stella.

'They had a fight. Kylie threatened Bruce with a knife in the kitchen. It got out of hand. She ended up dead on the floor. Shit, there was blood everywhere. Took us ages to clean up the mess. Lucky the kids were asleep. They didn't hear a thing.'

'What did you do with the body?'

'Wrapped it in a blanket and put it in the boot of her car, which was around behind the house.'

'What happened next?'

'Bruce told me about the money. He said they had about a million bucks cash in a suitcase.' Linda laughed, but there was no humour in her laugh. 'We decided we could keep the money if we killed Wanda when she turned up to collect Kylie. It was too easy. Bruce hit her over the head with the hammer as she got out of her car. Didn't even make much of a mess.'

'How did the bodies end up near Nangwarry?' said Stella.

'We put them in Wanda's car. Wrapped her in a blanket on the back seat and put Kylie in the boot. I put the kids in Kylie's car and followed Bruce. He knew where to go. I made sure the kids didn't see what he was doing.'

'How old are your kids?' said Stella, wondering what impact the events would have on them.

'Four and six,' said Linda. 'It's not like they could tell anybody but I didn't want them knowing what was going on. I didn't want them having nightmares.'

Poor kids would probably be having nightmares after today, thought Stella. 'What happened to the money?'

'I bought some things for the kids. Bruce took some. We paid off Mum's mortgage. I got some new stuff for the house. I've still got most of it.' Linda smiled. 'It's not like I wanted to attract attention to myself. I just wanted to give my kids a good start in life. It's hard being a single mother and not having a job.'

Stella looked at Matt.

'Linda Munro, I'm arresting you for being an accessory to the murder of Wanda Downs and Kylie Orchard and for receiving stolen goods.'

'What will happen to my kids?' said Linda.

'We'll find someone to take care of them,' said Stella.

'Can you call my mother?' said Linda. 'She'll look after them.'

CHAPTER 17

As they sat around the outside table under the pergola connecting the houses in her family compound waiting for lunch to be served, Stella listened as Shaun teased her mother over the summons she'd received to appear in the Adelaide Magistrates Court.

'Don't listen to him, Ma,' said Stella. 'They'll probably only fine you and give you some demerit points.'

'Should take away her licence,' said Mr Bruno, winking at Shaun.

'I'll see what I can do,' said Shaun.

'You'll do no such bloody thing,' said Denise, placing a bowl of hot pasta in front of him. 'And, Pa, you should be ashamed of yourself.'

'Only joking,' said Mr Bruno. 'She's a good driver.'

'And, don't you forget it,' said Mrs Bruno.

'He's only worried about paying the fine,' said Stella. 'I'll pay it if it makes you feel better, Pa. After all, she was taking Josh to school.'

'No, I'll pay it,' said Mr Bruno, sprinkling grated cheese over his pasta.

There was silence for a few moments as everyone started eating.

'I've got a month off,' said Stella.

'What are you going to do?' said Denise.

'As little as possible,' said Stella. 'Thought I'd spend some time with Ma and be here for Josh.'

'That would be a change,' said Josh.

'Go easy, mate,' said Shaun. 'Your mum's been working hard to make this a safe town to live in.'

'And, I'll drive you to school for a change while Nonna is recovering.'

'Mum, school finishes next week.'

'Does it?'

'Just as well Zio was around to help me pick my subjects for year twelve,' said Josh.

'Oh, sorry, sweetheart. Perhaps you and I can spend a few days away together so I can make it up to you.'

'That would be good, Mum.'

Stella looked at Shaun. 'I'll see if I can fit you in for a few days before I go back to work.'

'Make the most of it,' said Shaun, laughing. 'He's not going to want to go on holidays with his mother for much longer.'

DECEPTION

STELLA BRUNO INVESTIGATES

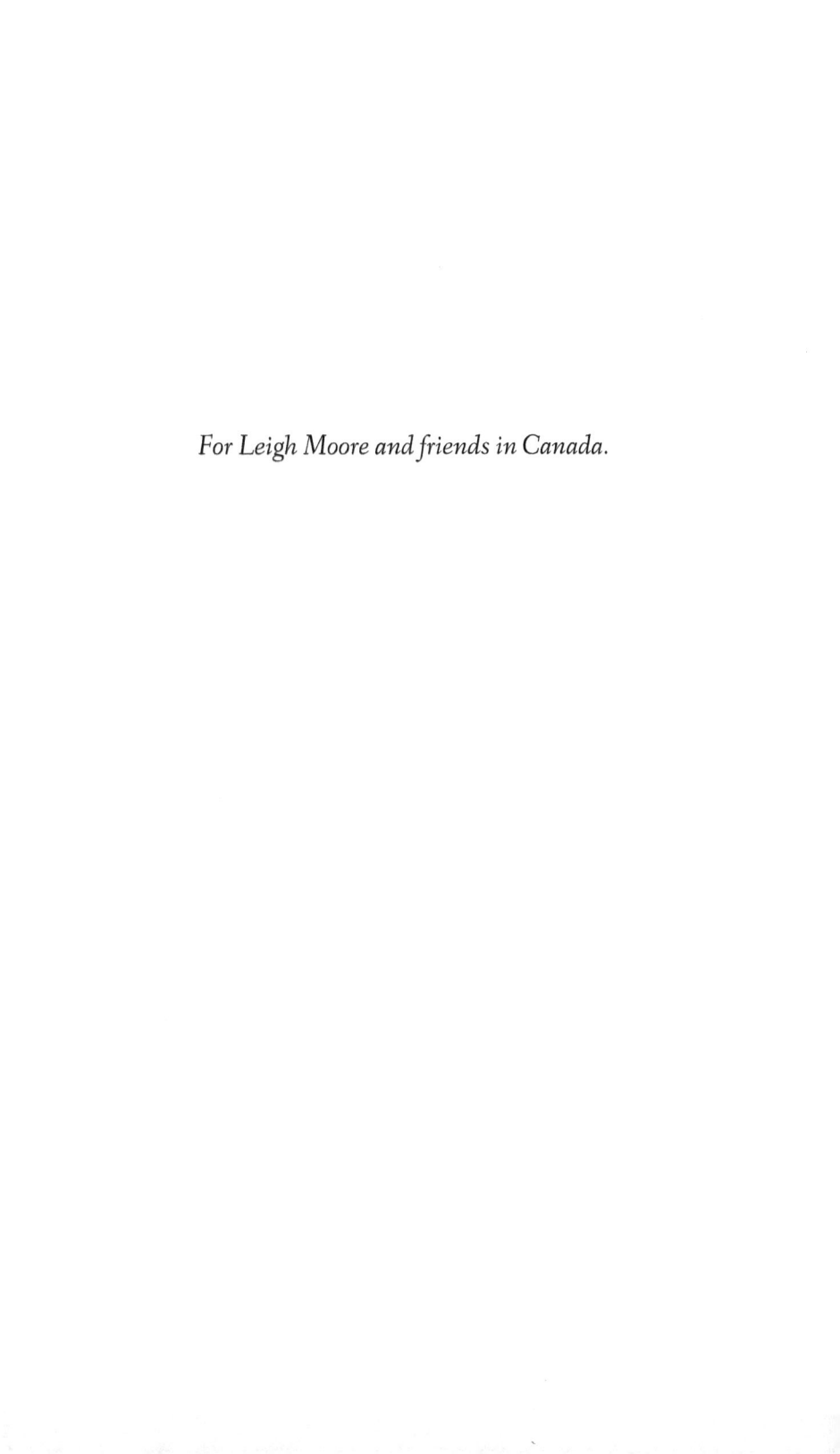

For Leigh Moore and friends in Canada.

CHAPTER 1

Brighton Beach was where people went to play in the water during the heat of summer or walked along the sand in the wind at other times of the year. Neither pursuit, however, was the reason Detective Sergeant Stella Bruno and Detective Constable Brian Rhodes descended the steps from the Esplanade on a cold Tuesday morning in early June.

Waves crashed onto the beach and rushed towards their shoes, only to recede back into the roiling sea, as they made their way along the wet sand to the group of people standing under the jetty.

Stella surveyed the turbulent waters of Gulf St Vincent. 'Hope the tide's going out, Brian. Don't fancy getting my feet wet.'

'It's going out,' said Brian, doing up his coat in an effort to stop the wind from slicing him in two. 'Doubt we'll be here long.'

'Well come on, let's get this over with before those clouds out there rain on us.'

They joined Sgt Barry Rice and his team of crime scene investigators underneath the jetty, where Dr Steve Wright, the pathologist, was examining the contents of a partially open large black plastic bag.

Despite the wind, the smell told Stella the body had been in the bag for some time. 'What do we have, Steve?'

'Male, possibly early forties. No head, no hands, no clothes,' said Steve. 'Probably been in this bag for a week, maybe longer.'

'Obviously not killed here,' said Barry. 'Bag was in the water when we arrived.'

'Who found it?' said Stella.

'Old bloke walking his dog,' said Barry. 'He's given us a statement. Walks along here every morning.'

'So, it's floated in, then?'

Barry nodded. 'I've got the dive team coming to search the area in case the rest of him is here someplace, but a body like this could have been dumped anywhere along the coast south of here or over the side of a boat out there somewhere.'

Stella looked out to sea. The storm clouds appeared closer and ready to dump their payload. 'Think we should wrap it up here, Barry, before we get drenched.'

'Get onto Missing Persons, Brian. See if they have anyone who could be our man.'

'What if he's not a local?' said Brian.

'Let's cross that bridge when we get there.'

'What if no-one's reported him missing, Sarge? I mean, decapitation is not your garden style murder, is it?'

Stella stared out at the ocean and watched the storm clouds sweep in and blot out the little sunlight there was. She was glad they'd made it back to the car before the rain arrived. 'We'll have to see what Steve says about the cause of death, Brian.

Removing his head and hands could have been a post mortem effort to hide his identity.'

'Still says organised crime,' said Brian. 'We could be pushing shit uphill on this one.'

'Be nice to have a crime scene,' said Stella. 'At least that would give us something to go on.'

Brian started the car. 'Glad I'm not on the dive team. Don't think they're going to be having much fun down here today.'

'Still, it's got to be done,' said Stella.

CHAPTER 2

STELLA FOUND OBSERVING an autopsy unsettling enough at the best of times, but the experience took on a somewhat surreal aspect when the body on the table was headless. She focused on Steve Wright as he examined the remains of their unknown victim and recorded his observations.

'There are no wounds on the body apart from the obvious ones where the head and hands were removed, and they're definitely post mortem.'

'What do you think they used?'

'Meat cleaver would be my guess,' said Steve. 'Clean cuts, especially on the wrists.'

Stella pictured her local butcher cutting up a side of lamb and shivered. 'Any identifying marks?'

'No tattoos, no surgical scars. An unusual birth mark on the left shoulder, though.' He pointed to a white spot resembling the shape of a strawberry. 'That might help in identifying him if someone comes forward,' said Steve.

'Better send me a shot of that in your report then,' said Stella, making a note.

'And, these marks here,' said Steve, pointing to faint bruising on the arms and across the chest. 'They're definitely post mortem. Probably made by something tied around the bag holding the body. They look like pressure marks from a rope, but they haven't broken the skin, which is what makes me think the rope was tied around the bag, not the body.'

'They must have tied a weight around the bag before dumping it,' said Stella.

'That would be consistent with these marks,' said Steve, 'but they obviously didn't do a very good job of it though, did they?'

Stella nodded her agreement. 'How long do you think he's been dead?'

'No more than a week.'

'No-one in his age range has been reported missing in that timeframe,' said Stella.

'Surely somebody will report him missing,' said Steve. 'With a height around 180 centimetres and weighing somewhere around 95 kilograms, I'd say this bloke was in good physical condition before someone did this to him.' Steve looked at Stella. 'I mean, it's not like he'd have been living on the street. Too healthy for that. Someone's going to miss him.'

'I hope you're right, Steve, otherwise I've got nothing to go on. I don't know who he was, how he was killed, or where.'

'Obviously we're shot for prints,' said Steve, 'but we'll have a DNA profile for you. Should at least let you match any other body parts.'

'If we find any,' said Stella.

Steve shrugged. 'I'll let you know if anything comes back in the toxicology report.'

'Thanks, Steve.'

Stella pulled off her protective clothing and made her way back to the squad room to update DI Williams.

'We're going to need a breakthrough to solve this one, sir.'

'Nothing from the post mortem then?'

'All we have is a fit looking bloke of about forty, around 180 centimetres tall, with a white birthmark shaped like a strawberry on his left shoulder. Getting anyone to identify him based on that description has to be a long shot, especially since we have no face.'

DI Williams stroked his chin. 'Start with that and see where it goes. You never know, it might be enough to trigger someone's memory.'

'Anything from Uniform at Glenelg, sir?'

'No other sightings. Best guess is someone either dumped the bag under the jetty or it came in on the tide. Divers didn't find anything either.'

'That's not surprising, sir. Ocean's a big place.'

'The rest of him could be anywhere, I suppose,' said DI Williams. 'I'm leaving this with you, Bruno, until we get something to go on.'

'Let's hope he doesn't end up like Somerton Man,' said Stella. 'He was found on the beach in 1948. We still don't know who he was, and he had a face.'

'Let's hope our victim is a local.'

'And, someone's prepared to talk,' said Stella.

On the Friday morning after she had released a description of the victim to the media, Stella sat at her desk without having received a response to her plea for help in identifying the body. She wondered whether that meant nobody missed him, which could mean he wasn't a local, or if it meant nobody was prepared to come forward and talk about him, which could mean any number of things. Frustrated, she decided it was time for a coffee and was about to suggest going for one to Brian when Barry Rice called.

'We have a hit for the DNA from the Brighton body, Stella.'

'Someone we know then?'

'Jordan Banks. You might remember the case. He played footy for Central Districts. Got fifteen years for rape. Released in May, year before last.'

Stella did a quick calculation in her head. 'Can't say I recall the case, Barry. Reckon I might have been on maternity leave around that time.'

'Oh, yeah. Forgot about that. I'll send you the details.'

Stella put down her phone and turned to Brian. 'We've got a name. Jordan Banks. He's on the sexual offenders' database.'

'Played for Central Districts. Got fifteen years,' said Brian. 'It was the first case I worked with DI Williams when he was my sergeant.'

'See if you can find some next of kin details while I let his nibs know we have a name.'

CHAPTER 3

BRIAN PARKED the car in front of the modest single storey house in Davoren Park where Jordan Banks had lived with his parents until the morning he'd been arrested for raping seventeen-year-old Chloe Randel.

'Place hasn't changed much,' said Brian.

'Our reason for visiting sure has,' said Stella.

'They were good people,' said Brian. 'I'm surprised they're still living here. The trial was pretty rough on them.'

Stella rang the doorbell. The door was opened by a woman with grey hair and an easy smile.

'Mrs Banks?'

'Yes.'

Stella held out her ID. 'Detective Sergeant Bruno.'

'Are you here about Jordan? Mandy's only just told me she's reported him missing.'

Stella glanced at Brian. 'We're here about Jordan, Mrs Banks, but I'm afraid we have bad news. Can we come in?'

Mrs Banks looked at Stella and then at Brian. 'I know you. You've been here before.'

'You have a good memory, Mrs Banks,' said Brian. 'I interviewed you the morning your son was arrested.'

'I'm not sure I want you in my house.'

'I'd rather not be here delivering this news, but I understand,' said Brian. 'I'll wait outside if you want me to.'

Mrs Banks stared at Brian for what seemed like ages to Stella.

'It's alright. It wasn't your fault. You were just doing your job.' Mrs Bank stepped back and let them into the sitting room at the front of the house.

'Is your husband home?' said Stella.

'He's at work, love.'

'Does he work nearby?'

'Drives a forklift for Woollies in their big warehouse over at Gepps Cross.'

Stella realised they'd driven past the Woolworths Distribution Centre on their way to the house. 'You might want to give him a call and ask him to come home.'

'Why's that?' said Mrs Banks.

'We're here to inform you that Jordan's been murdered, Mrs Banks. I'm sorry.'

Mrs Banks sank back into the armchair she was sitting in. Ashen-faced, she stared at Stella.

'I'll make a cuppa,' said Brian, moving across the room to the door leading into the kitchen.

Stella waited. She was in no hurry to share the gory details of Jordan's death with his mother.

'When?'

'We don't know yet,' said Stella. 'His body was found on the beach at Brighton on Tuesday morning.'

'That was on the telly,' said Mrs Banks. 'They said you didn't know who it was.'

'We do now,' said Stella.

'I thought they said the body didn't have a head or any hands?'

'We have Jordan's DNA on file.'

'Oh. Of course.'

Brian came back with three cups of tea on a tray and gave the one he'd laced with sugar to Mrs Banks. They sipped their tea in silence and waited for Mrs Banks to recover from her initial shock.

'Who's Mandy?' said Stella.

'Jordan's girlfriend. She's seven months pregnant.'

Stella wondered why Mandy hadn't reported Jordan missing until this morning. 'Do they live together?'

'Yes, but Jordan drives a truck interstate. He's away for weeks at a time.'

'Would you like us to call your husband?' said Brian.

Mrs Banks pulled her mobile phone out of her pocket and scrolled through her contacts. She handed the phone to Brian. 'That's the number.'

Brian walked out to the kitchen to make the call.

'When was the last time you saw Jordan?' said Stella.

'He was home for a few days a couple of weeks back. They were here for a barbecue that weekend. To be honest, we haven't seen much of him since he got out of prison. I think it's Mandy making the effort to keep him connected with us.'

'I guess it must be difficult all round,' said Stella.

'He made a stupid mistake, like a lot of his mates. Only he didn't get away with it, did he?' Mrs Banks looked up. 'He paid for what he did. We all did. We've done our best to forgive him, but I think he thinks he let us down.'

Brian came back into the sitting room. 'He's on his way.'

'Thanks for doing that,' said Mrs Banks.

'Do you have a number for Mandy?' said Stella.

It took Stella and Brian twenty minutes to drive from Davoren Park to the address in Enfield that Mandy Webster had given them. The house, located at the end of a street of recently subdivided blocks filled with new dwellings, had seen better days. Brian pulled up behind the patrol car the Community Liaison officer had parked in front of the house.

'Looks like a rental to me,' said Brian, as they got out of the car, 'but that's a fairly flash car there.' He pointed to the recent model Mazda 6 parked in the driveway.

'Perhaps that's her car,' said Stella, thinking Jordan wouldn't have had time to earn the money to buy a new car since he'd been released from prison, 'or she has a visitor.'

Brian noted the registration number while Stella rang the doorbell.

The voice on the phone had sounded young, younger than Stella had expected to hear when she'd called to get the address, so she was a little surprised when Mandy turned out to be in her mid-thirties.

'I'm sorry we have to meet in these circumstances,' said Stella, 'but we need to ask you some questions.'

'I understand,' said Mandy, 'but it's all a bit of a shock.'

'Why did you wait until today to report him missing?'

'What do you mean?'

'His body was found on Tuesday,' said Stella.

'He was supposed to get back on Tuesday, but he sent me a text saying he'd broken down outside Broken Hill and had to wait for a part.'

Stella looked at Brian. Jordan had been dead for a week by Tuesday, according to Steve Wright. 'When was the last time you saw him?'

'The morning of the Monday of the week before. That would have been the first of the month. He was doing a run up to some place in Queensland but he had to go to Melbourne first.'

'Was that usual?'

'Yeah, he did that trip a couple of times every month.'

'Who did Jordan work for?'

Mandy looked at her hands. 'I don't really know, to be honest. I never asked and he never said.'

That sounded like a red flag response to Stella. 'Can you tell us anything about the truck he was driving?'

Mandy shook her head. 'I've never seen it.'

'How did he get to work? Did you drive him?'

'He rode his bike or caught the bus,' said Mandy.

'Motorbike?'

'No. Mountain bike. He wanted to keep fit.'

Stella wondered whether Mandy was purposely being vague or whether Jordan had gone out of his way to keep the details of his employment from her. 'So, you only have his word for it that he was driving a truck and making those interstate trips?'

'I suppose,' said Mandy, 'but someone was paying him good money to do something, and it's not like he would lie to me, and he was away a lot.'

'Cash?' said Stella, not feeling as confident as Mandy that Jordan hadn't lied to her about what he had been doing. 'Was he paid in cash?'

'Is there anything wrong with that?'

'That depends,' said Stella, 'on why he was being paid in cash.'

'What do you mean?'

'Some people use cash to avoid paying tax,' said Stella. 'Others use it to make it hard to trace their payments.'

'Oh,' said Mandy, 'like people who don't tell Centrelink about their income so they can keep their pension?'

'A bit like that,' said Stella. 'Did Jordan have a bank account?'

Mandy shook her head. 'We used my account. I got a second card but he hardly ever used it.'

Stella thought Jordan sounded like someone trying to stay hidden, at least from official eyes. 'Did he put all his cash into your account or keep some in the house?'

'He only ever kept a couple of hundred dollars spending money,' said Mandy. 'The rest went into my account.'

'How much?'

Mandy crossed her arms. 'Four of five grand every time he came home.'

'And, you never asked where it came from?'

Mandy shrugged. 'He always said it was his pay for driving the truck. What was I supposed to do? I'd been surviving on the parenting payment until Jordan moved in.'

'And, when was that?'

'About eighteen months ago.'

Stella looked around the room and nodded to the Community Liaison officer standing in the doorway to the kitchen. The furniture was new. There was a big screen TV on the wall. It appeared Jordan hadn't been shy about spending money on Mandy.

'I gather Jordan had a mobile phone. Was that on a plan or prepaid?'

'Don't know. It was his work phone.'

'Can you give me the number and show me the text message he sent you on Tuesday?'

Mandy picked up her phone and scrolled through her contacts. Brian wrote down Jordan's number. Then she opened the text message she'd received. Brian wrote down the details and took a photo of her screen.

'Did he have a computer?'

'He used my laptop if he needed to go online.'

'We're going to need access to that and your banking records,' said Stella.

'I need my laptop. I've got assignments to finish before this one's born.'

'We'll take a copy of the hard drive and get it back to you as soon as possible,' said Stella. 'Should only take a day or so.'

Mandy looked at the Community Liaison officer.

'I'll chase it up for you. They're usually pretty good with this sort of thing,' said the Community Liaison officer.

Stella hoped Barry Rice's people wouldn't be snowed under when she asked them to work on the laptop. 'Did Jordan have many friends?'

'Not really,' said Mandy. 'His mates from before didn't want to know him when he got out. Anyway, he wasn't around much. He was always away. The only blokes he ever talked about were ones he'd met inside.'

'Any names stand out?'

'He never used what you'd call proper names,' said Mandy. 'They all had nicknames.'

Stella thought she'd probably have more luck starting with his prison records and decided not to push Mandy for the names.

'How did you meet Jordan?'

'He was in Mobilong with my cousin, Dan Zimmerman. I met him at the party the family had for Dan when he got out.'

Stella wondered whether Jordan had been working with people he'd met inside and if Dan would know more about that than Mandy. 'Do you have Dan's contact details?'

Stella waited while Brian recorded Dan Zimmerman's contact details.

'You mentioned you were on the parenting payment,' said

Stella, wondering if there was another man in Mandy's life besides Jordan.

'I have a daughter, Hayley. She's eight.'

Two on her own would be a handful, thought Stella. 'Is Hayley's father still around?'

Mandy snorted. 'Pete's never been around. Haven't seen him since the day I told him I was pregnant.'

'What was Jordan's reaction to finding out you were pregnant?'

'It was his idea. He was looking forward to being a dad. He was good with Hayley. She's going to be devastated when I tell her.'

Stella waited until Mandy regained her composure. 'Did Jordan ever mention anything about being in danger? Or feeling threatened?'

Mandy shook her head. 'We were happy. He was just trying to get enough money together so we could buy a place of our own. I don't know why anybody would want to kill him.'

'What about the reason he went to prison?'

'That was all media talk when he was released,' said Mandy. 'No-one's ever said anything to us, to our face.'

Stella smiled, but she had no intention of eliminating the family of the girl Jordan had raped from her list of potential suspects just yet. She'd come across people who'd kept grudges alive for a lot longer than seventeen years, and was aware there were people out there who didn't think rapists should ever be released.

'Do you have a recent photo of Jordan you can give me? We'll need something to use when we ask people if they've seen him.'

'Bit late for that, isn't it?'

'If we're going to find out who killed him, Mandy, we'll

need to trace his movements since you last saw him, and the only way we can do that is to ask the public for help.'

Mandy scrolled through the photos on her phone. 'Will this one be okay?' She handed the phone to Stella.

'That will be fine. Can you send it to me?' Stella handed her a business card with her email address and waited until she heard the ping of the incoming email notification before checking the image. 'Thanks. That's fine.'

'What will happen with his body?'

'We'll let you know when you can arrange for a funeral director to collect it.'

'Will I be able to see it?'

'If you want to,' said Stella, 'but you might want to think about that. A headless body is not a pretty sight.'

'I just want to know for sure.'

'The DNA profile is a perfect match. I'm sorry, but I don't think there's any room for doubt.'

After spending the day with Banks' mother and girlfriend, Stella needed someone to talk to. She called Shaun, who said he'd cook her dinner. Stella put away her phone and smiled to herself. Shaun always found time for her, which was one of the reasons she loved him.

Just after six, Stella let herself into Shaun's apartment in Rowlands Place. He was cooking the meal he'd promised her in the kitchen. It smelt good. She walked up behind him and lent her head on his shoulder.

'Can I have a hug?'

Shaun turned and embraced her. 'That bad, hey?'

Stella released him from her embrace and slipped off her shoes. 'I need a drink.'

'There's Chardonnay in the fridge.' Shaun turned back to the pan on the cooktop.

'What are you making?'

'Beef stir-fry. Nearly ready.'

Stella poured the wine and sat at the table to watch him. She enjoyed watching Shaun in the kitchen. It meant she wasn't the one standing at the stove.

Shaun joined her at the table with their plates.

'Found out who our headless body was today,' said Stella, 'an ex-con named Jordan Banks.'

Shaun picked up his fork. 'Some standover merchant who finally got his comeuppance?'

Stella realised Shaun would have no idea who Banks was, since he'd been working as a prosecutor in Melbourne at the time of Banks' conviction. She sipped her wine and smiled across the table at him. 'No, a rapist. Served his full fifteen year sentence.'

'Some people never forgive them, you know.'

'Spoke with his mother and his girlfriend. She's pregnant. Sounded like he was getting his life together but I'm not sure I'm getting the truth about that.' Stella forked some of the stir-fry into her mouth. 'Mmm, this is good.'

'Did you expect anything else?'

They ate in silence for a few minutes.

'So, what's his story?'

'Supposedly he was driving a truck interstate but the girl-friend claims she doesn't know who he was working for.'

'How long have they been together?'

'Eighteen months according to the girlfriend,' said Stella, 'and get this. The girlfriend's a cousin of a bloke he did time with at Mobilong.'

'Small world,' said Shaun. 'How'd they meet?'

'At a party her cousin's family had when he was released.'

Shaun picked up his glass. 'You'd think she'd know who he worked for after eighteen months, wouldn't you?'

Stella nodded. 'And, he was being paid in cash.'

'Maybe he just didn't want her to know what he was doing. After all, decapitation and dumping the body at sea has an organised crime feel, wouldn't you agree?'

'Can't argue with that, especially after she told us she got a text message from him around twelve hours after we'd pulled what was left of him out of the ocean.'

'Sick bastards as well,' said Shaun. 'Want a top up?'

Stella passed him her glass. 'I better call Josh and let him know not to expect me.'

'Just as well he practically lives with your parents.'

Stella smiled. 'Consider that an added benefit, Mr Porter.'

CHAPTER 4

Stella looked up Dan Zimmerman's prison file. He'd served five years of a seven year sentence for embezzlement in Mobilong Prison, before being released early on parole. He'd been housed in the same unit at Mobilong as Jordan Banks for the last two years of Jordan's incarceration and released three weeks after him.

Stella ran his name through the cases database. There were no active cases associated with his name, which told her he'd stayed out of trouble since his release. She pulled up the notes on the case linked to his conviction. He'd been working as the office manager of a freight forwarding operation in Lonsdale and misappropriating funds to feed a gambling habit at the time of his arrest.

The personal details described him as married with one child. She cross-checked the address on the record with the one Mandy had given her. It looked like he'd returned home after he'd served his time.

She called the number Mandy had given her for Dan. The call went through to voicemail. She left a message and turned her attention to preparing the media release she wanted to issue in time for the evening news bulletins.

Fifteen minutes later her phone rang.

'Is that Detective Sergeant Bruno?'

'Speaking.'

'It's Dan Zimmerman. You asked me to call about Jordan.'

'Can we make a time to meet?' said Stella. 'Jordan's been murdered.'

'I know. Mandy told me, but I don't know if I can help you much.'

'I'd like to talk to you, Dan. You spent time with him in Mobilong. You might remember something that could help me work out where to start looking. Where's the best place to meet?'

'Here, I suppose. I'm home most days.'

'I can be there in around thirty minutes. Will that work for you?'

'As long as I can pick up the kids by three fifteen.'

Stella looked at her watch. 'I'm on my way.' She ended the call and slipped the phone into her pocket. 'Come on, Brian. Dan Zimmerman's agreed to talk to us.'

———

'Where are we headed, Sarge?

'Dover Gardens.'

Brian eased the car out into the traffic, turned right onto Pulteney Street, and headed towards Greenhill Road.

'Making any progress with that mobile phone number his girlfriend gave us?'

'Don't know why she thinks it's a work phone,' said Brian. 'It's in his name.'

'Perhaps that's what he told her,' said Stella. 'What else?'

'It was nowhere near Broken Hill last Tuesday, and it hasn't been to Queensland recently either, although it's been to Melbourne a lot over the last six months.'

'Where was it the night that text message was sent?'

'Brighton. In the vicinity of the Esplanade Hotel.'

Probably in a car parked overlooking the jetty, thought Stella. 'Someone's definitely jerking our chain, Brian. Any idea where it is now?'

'No signal after that message was sent. I'd say whoever has it sent that text to Mandy and then turned it off.'

'What about the call log?'

'Looks like he only ever used it to communicate with Mandy and his mother.'

'That's not going to be much help, is it?'

Brian turned onto Greenhill Road and headed west towards Anzac Highway. 'Tells us he lied to his girlfriend about where he was, Sarge. That's got to be something.'

'Did he have a licence to drive a truck?'

'That bit's true at least,' said Brian. 'He was driving trucks before he went to prison.'

Stella watched the traffic and wondered what Jordan had been up to.

'How much money is in her account?'

'About forty grand, but he's put close to two hundred grand through that account over the last eighteen months.'

'No wonder the girlfriend has a new car and all that new furniture in her house,' said Stella. 'Find any accounts in his name?'

'One with the ANZ, but it's only been used to pay his mobile phone account since he started putting money into his girlfriend's account. It's got just under twenty grand in it.'

'Cash deposits?'

'Yeah, but not as high. Around three grand a month for the six months after he got out.'

'So, whatever he was doing, looks like it started as soon as he was released.'

'That'd be my guess, Sarge.'

Stella wondered if Jordan had discussed any of his plans with Dan Zimmerman or if Dan was involved.

The Zimmerman residence, one of the few remaining older houses in Shinnick Street, was overshadowed by an enormous gum tree that looked as if it had been there longer than the house.

They crunched their way through the gumnuts and dried leaves covering the front garden and climbed the two wooden steps leading up to the front porch, where Brian pushed the button for the doorbell.

Dan Zimmerman led them through the house to a small dining area at the rear with a view out over a vegetable garden that took up most of the backyard.

'Your handiwork?' said Stella, pointing through the window.

'Bloke's got to do something,' said Dan. 'No bastard will give me a job.'

'How does that work?' said Stella. 'Jordan had a job. I thought he would have had more trouble finding a job than you.'

'Nobody trusts me around money,' said Dan. 'Not even my wife.' He smiled at Stella. 'Gambling's an addiction. Makes you do stupid things.'

'I've read your file,' said Stella. 'How come you didn't lose your house?'

'This is my mother's house,' said Dan. 'She wouldn't let me

take out a mortgage over it. That's why I ended up doing what I did. I owed money to some pretty unsavoury types.'

That made sense to Stella. 'Your wife work?'

'She's the finance officer at Seaview High.'

Stella thought Dan was lucky his wife had stood by him. She wasn't sure she'd have done the same but they weren't there to judge his living arrangements. 'We're trying to trace Jordan's movements before he was killed. When was the last time you saw him or heard from him?'

'About three weeks ago. They were here for lunch.'

'How was he?'

'What do you mean?'

'Was he worried about anything?'

'Seemed his normal self.'

'Do you know where he worked?'

'Didn't Mandy tell you?'

'She said she didn't know,' said Stella, glancing at Brian. 'All she could tell us was he drove a truck interstate and was away a lot.'

'Yeah, he was driving a truck alright. It was all he ever talked about inside.' Dan smiled. 'Freedom of the road. Jordan couldn't wait to get out and get back on the road.'

'Do you know who he was driving for?'

'Scott Ridley Freighters.'

That sounded familiar to Stella. 'Isn't that the company you used to work for?'

'Yeah. They were desperate for drivers. Scott probably would have given me a job if I'd had a heavy vehicle licence.'

Stella stood to leave.

'Do you have a mobile number for Jordan?' said Brian.

'Sure.' Dan pulled his phone out of his pocket and gave Brian the number.

'Thanks,' said Brian, as he slipped his notebook back inside his coat.

———

As they walked out to their car, Brian showed Stella the number Dan had given him. 'It's not the same as the one Mandy gave us, Sarge.'

'Trace it when we get back,' said Stella, opening the door on her side of the car. 'Let's go and have a chat with whoever's running Scott Ridley Freighters down in Lonsdale.'

CHAPTER 5

TWENTY-FIVE MINUTES LATER, Brian pulled into the car park of Scott Ridley Freighters, located off Sherriffs Road, Lonsdale. They walked past several trucks with red and white livery backed into the loading bays of the warehouse occupying most of the site as they made their way to the office.

'Can I help you?' said the woman sitting at reception.

'Police,' said Stella, showing her ID. 'I'd like to talk to whoever's in charge about one of your drivers.'

'Which driver would that be?' said the receptionist.

'Jordan Banks.'

'Let me check for you but I'm not sure we have a driver by that name.'

Stella glanced at Brian while the receptionist queried their driver database.

'We don't have a Jordan Banks, I'm afraid.'

Stella pulled out her phone and opened the photo of Jordan that Mandy had sent her and showed it to the receptionist. 'Do you recognise this man?'

The receptionist nodded. 'That's Ronnie Edwards. He was terminated a couple of weeks back.'

Stella glanced at Brian and raised an eyebrow. She

wondered how the receptionist would react when she told her the news about Ronnie's final termination. 'Oh, why was that?'

'Failed the drug test, according to this. That's instant dismissal. All the drivers know the policy.'

'How long had this Ronnie been working here?' said Stella.

The receptionist consulted her screen. 'About two years.'

'Do you by any chance have a record of his driver's licence on file?'

The receptionist looked at her computer and scrolled through her records. 'Doesn't look like it, but he would have had to show it to Mr Ridley to get the job.'

'Is Mr Ridley available?'

'He's in the warehouse.'

'Can you call him for me,' said Stella. 'You see, this is Jordan Banks, and we're investigating his death.'

Scott Ridley, a man in his fifties with short steel grey hair, invited them into his office and shut the door. 'You wanted to talk about Ronnie Edwards?'

'Actually, I want to talk about this man,' said Stella, showing him the photograph of Jordan on her phone.

'That's Ronnie.'

'Not according to his DNA,' said Stella. 'This is Jordan Banks.'

'Told me his name was Ronnie Edwards,' said Scott.

'Do you require your drivers to have a heavy vehicle licence?' said Brian.

'I guess you'd know the law, mate,' said Scott.

'Ronnie show you his licence before you employed him?' said Brian.

'I wouldn't have given him the job if he hadn't.'

'But, it didn't have the name Ronnie Edwards on it, did it?' said Stella.

Scott looked at his hands. 'Look, the bloke was fresh out of jail. I needed a driver. He had the right licence. We came to an arrangement.'

'Did that include paying him in cash?'

Scott glared at Stella.

'We're not the Tax Office, Mr Ridley, but we can call them in, if you like.'

'He got paid electronically like everybody else, straight into his bank account.'

'Got those account details?'

Scott picked up the phone on his desk. 'Beckie, bring me the bank account details we used for paying Ronnie.'

Stella heard a printer operating outside the office door, and then the receptionist came in with a sheet of paper.

'Give it to her,' said Scott, pointing at Stella. 'The banks don't check the account name. It's all about the numbers.'

'Where did Jordan go when he was driving for you?' said Stella.

'Most of our work is overnight interstate deliveries but Jordan did a regular run from here to Brisbane via Melbourne a couple times a month. He was basically two weeks on at the start of the month and then two weeks off.'

'Delivering what?'

'General merchandise on the way up. Fruit and veg on the way back. Always came back through Broken Hill.'

'When was the last time you saw him,' said Stella.

'What's today? Monday. Three weeks, today. He turned up under the influence. I sacked him on the spot.'

'Have any other issues with him?'

'No, but I have a zero tolerance policy when it comes to drugs. Too many people get killed on the roads as it is.'

'Anybody here witness his dismissal?' said Stella.

Ridley shook his head. 'Depot's not always this busy. Beckie processed the paperwork when she got back from lunch.'

'Do you keep a record of your drug tests, Mr Ridley?'

'Only the results,' said Scott. 'We use a breathalyser.'

Stella looked at Brian. 'Anything else we need to know?'

'How did he get here?' said Brian. 'This is quite a trip from Enfield.'

'Enfield? He was living in Reynella. I guaranteed the lease for the first six months. He usually walked.'

'Do you have the address?' said Stella.

'Ask Beckie on your way out.'

Brian parked in front of the house at the address they'd been given for Ronnie Edwards. There was an early model Ford Falcon XR6 with faded paintwork parked under the carport.

Stella surveyed the overgrown front yard and wondered how long it had been since anyone had cut the lawn or pruned the rose bushes. Brian knocked on the front door. There was no response.

They made their way around to the rear of the house, where a covered patio separated the house from an extensive vegetable garden growing more weeds than vegetables. Stella peered through the large windows that opened onto the patio from a living area. The furniture was upturned in disarray. Brian tried the back door. It opened.

'Better take a look at this, Sarge.'

Stella joined him and looked at the dark tread marks some-one's boots had left on the tiled floor of the laundry.

'Looks like dried blood to me, Sarge.'

'We might have our crime scene,' said Stella. 'See if you can rustle up any of the neighbours while I get on to Forensics.'

Christies Beach sent a patrol to secure the house while they waited for Sgt Rice and his crime scene investigators to arrive.

'How did you get on with the neighbours, Brian?'

'Lady across the road recognised Jordan as Ronnie and said she hadn't seen him for a few weeks. But she reckoned that wasn't anything unusual.' Brian ran his hand through what was left of his hair. 'She remembered him having a couple visitors the last time he was here. Apparently there'd been a bit of yelling when they arrived, and she hasn't seen Jordan since they left.' Brian looked up from his notes. 'She thought he must have gone with them.'

'Did she get a look at them?'

'Couple of big blokes driving a white van. One with a beard.'

'She didn't happen to get the rego, did she?'

'No. But she said it wasn't the first time she'd see them here.'

'What time of day was it?'

'Mid-afternoon, three Mondays ago. That would make it the first.'

That aligned with what Mandy and Scott Ridley had told them, thought Stella. 'Anybody else home?'

'Not at the moment. We'll have to get Uniform to follow up after hours if this turns out to be where he was killed.'

'Run a check on the rego of that vehicle in the carport, Brian. Let's see who owns it, and then see if you can find out who owns this place.'

While Brian was running a query on the Registrations database using the computer in their car, a white van with police markings pulled into the driveway. Sgt Rice and his team of crime scene investigators climbed out and looked at the storm clouds gathering above them.

'Nice place, Stella. Can't you afford a gardener?'

'We're going for the wilderness look, Barry. You should see the progress we've made out the back.'

'Where do you want me to start?'

'Back door's open. Those shots I sent you are from the laundry floor.'

'Okay. Give me a minute and I'll let you know if this is a crime scene or if you've called me out on a wild goose chase.'

Stella waited while Barry and one of his officers suited up and then disappeared around the back of the house. Five minutes later, the front door opened and Barry called her over.

'Think you have a crime scene, Stella. That's definitely human blood in the kitchen.'

CHAPTER 6

On TUESDAY MORNING, Stella sat at her desk reading Barry Rice's report on the Reynella crime scene. Jordan's killers hadn't made much of an effort to clean up after themselves, and from the pattern of the blood splatter they'd left on the kitchen wall, it looked as if Jordan's throat had been cut while he'd been sitting at the kitchen table. As there was no mention of his head and hands, she assumed the killers had dumped them separately, perhaps in a bag with a more effectively attached weight, since no-one had reported finding them washed up along the suburban coast.

She moved to the page listing the inventory of items found in the house. There was no record for either of Jordan's mobile phones but the personal items the team had found in the house clearly suggested he'd been the sole occupant. She noted that the Ford Falcon XR6 parked in the carport had first been registered in the victim's name two years before he'd been sent to prison.

'Traced that bank account, Brian?'

'It's with People's Choice Credit Union. There are regular payments from Scott Ridley Freighters. Doubt his girlfriend knows about it. He's been using it to cover the rent on the place in Reynella and for his living expenses on the road.' Brian chuckled. 'He must have eaten at every roadhouse between here and Brisbane. I'm surprised he wasn't overweight.'

'What about that second mobile number?'

'It's got a call log as long as your arm, Sarge.'

'Anything stand out?'

'A lot of calls to and from Scott Ridley, and a monthly call from a payphone located in the Port Adelaide Plaza Shopping Centre. Last one on the morning we think he was killed.'

Stella wondered if there was a connection between that phone call and his visitors, who she was assuming were his killers.

'Have you found out who owns the house?'

'It's managed by LJ Hooker Reynella,' said Brian. 'The owners live on the Gold Coast. They're a retired couple in their eighties, according to the agent.'

Stella leant back in her chair. 'Why was he leading a double life, Brian? What was he up to?'

'What I want to know, Sarge, is where the money he was putting into his girlfriend's account was coming from. I reckon if we can find the source, that'll lead us to whoever killed him.'

Stella drummed her fingers on her desk. She could think of several places the money could have come from but wasn't sure they'd find its source until they'd identified Jordan's killers.

'See if you can find out how those payphone calls were paid for, Brian.'

'You can still use cash in a payphone, Sarge.'

'You never know your luck, Brian. Even the bad guys stuff up some times.'

'Yeah,' said Brian.'You have to wonder why they didn't clean up the mess they left for us?'

'Tells me they're confident they'll get away with it, Brian.'

'Obviously they don't know about us, Sarge.'

Stella hoped Brian wasn't making the same mistake she thought the killers had.

———

Stella read through the statements Uniform had taken from the people living around the Reynella house. They all told a similar story.

It appeared Banks had rented the property shortly after he'd been released from Mobilong. He'd turned up in the Ford Falcon XR6 which, according to his neighbours, he hardly ever drove, and introduced himself as Ronnie Edwards. Wearing a backpack and riding a mountain bike, or walking, was how they reported seeing him leaving or returning to the house. Stella checked the notes of their interview with Mandy Webster. She'd told them he either caught the bus or rode his mountain bike. Stella wondered about the mountain bike. It wasn't listed in the inventory of items found in the house at Reynella. She made a note to check if he'd left it at the Enfield house.

She turned her attention back to the statements. Some of Jordan's neighbours had reported he'd occasionally parked a Scott Ridley Freighters' prime mover in the street outside the house. Others complained he hadn't taken care of the place, but no-one seemed to have known much about him or the people who visited him, apart from the woman who lived across the road from him. She didn't work during the day and was the only neighbour to report seeing the white van and his visitors.

She opened the statement from the property manager and read that he'd agreed to let the property to Ronnie Edwards on the recommendation of Scott Ridley, who had guaranteed the initial six month lease. The agent reported he'd had no problems with Ronnie as a tenant and that he'd paid his rent on time every fortnight since he'd signed the lease.

Stella wondered if the property manager had ever inspected the property or if he'd simply taken advantage of the situation to let out a sub-standard property with no questions asked. Stella realised he obviously hadn't confirmed Ronnie's identity, which made her suspect there was probably something about his relationship with Scott Ridley that might be worth looking into.

She was about to suggest following that up to Brian when her mobile phone rang.

'Is that Detective Sergeant Bruno?' said a woman's voice.

'Speaking' said Stella.

'My name's Mary Cummings. I'm calling from Enfield Primary School.'

'How can I help you, Mary?'

'Do you know a Mandy Webster?'

'Yes,' said Stella, wondering why someone from Enfield Primary School would want to know.

'She hasn't turned up this afternoon to collect her daughter,' said Mary, 'and Hayley had your business card in her bag. Are you a family friend?'

'Not exactly. I met her through a case I'm working on.'

'I've been trying to contact her since three fifteen. She's always here early to pick up Hayley. I'm worried something has happened to her. She's pregnant.'

'Don't you have a number to contact in emergencies?' said Stella, recalling she'd given her mother's number to her son's school.

'She's not answering either.'

Stella glanced at her watch. It was nearly four o'clock. A few things worse than going into early labour passed through her mind, given what had happened to Mandy's partner, and it occurred to her that if Mandy had gone into labour, she would have called an ambulance and the school. She didn't think Mandy was the type to abandon her daughter or to put a detective's business card in her school bag unless she'd been spooked by something. She hoped Mandy wasn't in danger and that they'd get to her in time if she was.

'I'll send someone from Community Liaison to collect Hayley. Can you look after her until they arrive?'

'I'll keep her with me in the front office.'

Stella hung up and placed a call to Operations to arrange for a Community Liaison officer to go to Enfield Primary School and for a patrol to attend Mandy Webster's house.

'Get your coat, Brian. Something's happened to Mandy Webster.'

The patrol dispatched to Mandy Webster's house reported they'd found her alive but unconscious, tied to a chair in her kitchen. By the time Stella and Brian arrived, there were several patrol cars parked outside the house and Mandy was being loaded into an ambulance.

Stella introduced herself to Sergeant Alan Wilson, who had taken charge of the crime scene.

'She's the partner of a murder victim I'm investigating,' said Stella.

'You think this could be connected, then?' said Alan.

'Possibly,' said Stella. 'My victim was bringing home thousands in cash from somewhere.'

'Whoever did this was looking for something in my opinion. This place has been turned upside down.'

'At least she's still alive' said Stella, 'so there's a chance she'll be able to tell us who did this.'

'I wouldn't count on that, Stella. The ambo's weren't that

sure she'd make it. They reckon she's been injected with something, and there was no heartbeat for her baby.'

Stella took a deep breath. 'What sort of bastards do that?'

'Didn't they decapitate your murder victim?'

Stella nodded. 'Let's hope somebody saw them coming or going.'

'I've got my people knocking on doors but,' he waved his hand around, 'half these houses are empty.'

'Be interested if anyone's seen two men, one with a beard, driving a white van,' said Stella.

'That's pretty vague,' said Alan.

'I know, but it would connect this to my murder.'

CHAPTER 7

WHEN SHE ARRIVED for work on Wednesday morning, DI Williams called Stella into his office.

'Mandy Webster died overnight, Bruno. Insulin overdose, according to the hospital. We'll have to see what the post mortem tells us.'

'Someone obviously wanted her dead,' said Stella. 'They tied her to a chair to administer the stuff.'

'These people are depraved, Bruno. She was seven months pregnant for God's sake! They need to be stopped!'

Stella nodded. She hadn't seen Frank Williams so worked up since the day someone had torched his wife's new car. 'We haven't got much to go on, sir.'

'Keep looking, Bruno.'

'I could use some help, sir.'

'I'll call in Francese. He's got capacity.'

Stella liked working with Dominic Francese. He was thorough, and had a good team of detectives under him. 'Thank you, sir.'

Stella stood in front of the whiteboard covered with crime scene photos in the incident room, waiting for Detective Sergeant Dominic Francese and his team to settle.

She jabbed her finger at the photo of Jordan Banks on the whiteboard. 'Jordan Banks. Body, minus head and hands, washed up or dumped on the beach at Brighton, Tuesday morning last week. Identified from DNA, thanks to a previous conviction for sexual assault, for which he served fifteen years. Clean since his release two years ago.' She tapped on the photo of the Reynella house. 'This is where he was living, and where we believe he was murdered before his body was mutilated.'

'Any witnesses?' said DS Francese.

'One of the neighbours reported seeing two men, one with a beard, arrive at the house in a white van on the Monday we think he was killed. She didn't get the rego but claims she heard them arguing with her neighbour, who she knew as Ronnie Edwards, shortly after they arrived. She didn't see them leave, and because she hadn't seen Banks after they'd left, she assumed he'd gone with them.'

'Ronnie Edwards?' said DS Francese. 'He was using an alias?'

'He got a job driving for Scott Ridley Freighters and moved into the house in Reynella about six weeks after his release. According to Ridley, he wanted a fresh start with a new name,' said Stella.

'Scott Ridley Freighters rings a bell,' said DC Lyon. 'I reckon we did one of their drivers a couple of years back. Part of a gang moving stolen booze out of a warehouse at Port Adelaide.'

'Follow that up, Ken,' said DS Francese.

'On the surface, his employment looks above board, apart from working under an alias, which Ridley told us he was aware of,' said Stella.

'Cash payments?' said DS Francese.

'No. His pay went into an account at People's Choice, but that wasn't all the money he was bringing home.'

'What do you mean?' said DS Francese.

Stella pointed to the photo of Mandy Webster on the whiteboard. 'Jordan was in a relationship with this woman, Mandy Webster, under his real name, supposedly living with her in a house in Enfield when he wasn't driving interstate and, according to her, putting four to five thousand dollars a month into her account in cash, which he'd told her was his pay for driving the truck. We've confirmed her story with her bank and uncovered an account Jordan had with the ANZ, which he appears to have used for storing his cash payments before he moved in with Mandy.'

'So, he must have been doing something other than driving a truck,' said DS Francese. 'Did the girlfriend know what he was doing besides driving for Scott Ridley?'

'No,' said Stella, 'she didn't seem to know much about his work situation. At least, she claimed she didn't.'

'How did he meet her?' said DS Francese. 'Enfield's not exactly close to Reynella.'

'She told us she was Dan Zimmerman's cousin,' said Stella. 'He was in Mobilong at the same time as Banks, doing time for embezzling Scott Ridley. Apparently he was the one who suggested Banks take the job with Ridley.'

'Bloody small world,' said DS Francese. 'Weren't you involved in that case, Helen?'

'Zimmerman confessed,' said DC Aplin. 'Gambling addict, if I remember.'

'That's the one,' said Stella.

'Something's not kosher there,' said DC Lyon. 'Why would Ridley take on someone who'd been in jail with Zimmerman, and let him work under an alias?'

'What are you suggesting, Ken?' said DS Francese.

'We need to probe that connection, Sarge.'

'What's this Zimmerman doing now?' said DS Francese.

'Growing veggies in his backyard,' said Stella. 'Claims no-one will give him a second chance.'

'Can I make a suggestion?' said Brian.

'Go on,' said Stella.

'I don't think our killers were after the money. I think they might be looking for something Jordan must have taken.'

'What makes you think that?' said Stella.

'He'd been banking cash for nearly two years on a fairly regular basis, which suggests it was a payment for doing something.'

'Or selling something,' said DC Lyon.

'Point is. I can understand why Banks might have held out if it was about the money, but why didn't Mandy just tell them where the cash was or give it to them?' Brian looked at Stella and then around the room. 'I reckon they were after something else, and she didn't know where it was hidden, so they threatened to hurt her baby but she still couldn't tell them.'

'That's one hypothesis we can work with,' said DS Francese, 'but I think we need to find out who else he spent time with while he was inside. I doubt he did all his time in Mobilong.'

'Did his first ten years in Yatala,' said Stella. 'We've only talked to Zimmerman so far, and only because he introduced Banks to his cousin.'

'Do the crime scene reports give us anything linking these deaths to the same killers?' said DS Francese. 'I mean, we're dealing with two very different modes of execution here.'

'It's still early days' said Stella, 'and, you're right. The only connection might be that the victims knew each other.'

'Anything else we should know about?' said DS Francese.

'Banks had two mobile numbers,' said Stella. 'One for communicating with his parents and his girlfriend and another for everyone else.'

'Was one a work phone?' said DC Aplin.

'They were both in his name,' said Brian, 'but someone sent a text to his girlfriend from his family phone on the day his body was found at Brighton, someone who knew his routine.'

'Who would that be apart from his employer?' said DS Francese.

'That might depend on which employer we're talking about,' said Brian. 'Ridley or whoever was paying him in cash.'

'That sounds like a connection,' said DC Lyon. 'Suggests how they might have found her.'

'Possibly,' said Stella, 'but we don't know yet if they called her again, or if they knew where she lived,' said Stella. 'Can you follow that up, Brian?'

'Okay,' said DS Francese. 'Let's pull all the case files we have on these people and get a list of the people now out in the community that Banks spent time with in either Yatala or Mobilong.'

'And we need to have a chat with the family of Chloe Randel,' said Stella. 'Her brothers were pretty vocal about making him pay when Banks was released.'

Stella opened the Randel case file and looked for the contact details of the members of Chloe's family who had been interviewed during the investigation. The details were eighteen years old, and although she knew people often lived in the same house for long periods, she decided to cross check their details with the Registrations database before attempting to contact them. As she was reading the details recorded for Tom and Ben

Randel, she noticed they'd both given their place of work as Randel & Sons Butchers. She did an internet search. The business was still operating from the same address in Salisbury. Her phone rang before she could write down the address.

'Stella, it's Steve. I've got the toxicology on Jordan Banks.'

Given what Scott Ridley had told her, Stella was interested to hear what they'd found. 'Anything exotic? His boss said he'd dismissed him for being under the influence the day we think he was killed.'

'There's no trace of ingested alcohol in his system but that's not conclusive, given the amount of time the body spent in the water.'

'What about anything else?'

'Nothing illicit, Stella.'

'Thanks, Steve.' Stella leant back in her chair. It was possible Scott Ridley had lied to her about sacking Banks so he'd have an excuse for not reporting him missing. She drummed her fingers on her desk and wondered why he'd do that. She made a note and then wrote down the address of Randel & Sons Butchers.

'Brian, did you speak with Chloe Randel's brothers when you were working on her case?'

'She was out with her brothers the night Banks raped her. They felt as guilty as hell they'd let their little sister go off with Banks, but he was everybody's hero that night. He'd kicked the winning goal against Sturt.'

'Remember anything else about them?'

'Oh, shit,' said Brian. 'They were apprentice butchers, and built like brick shithouses.'

'And,' said Stella, pointing to a press clipping she'd found in the file, 'I gather they weren't happy about Banks being released, at least that's what it says here.'

'I vaguely recall seeing that on the news,' said Brian. 'I

thought it was nothing more than them letting off steam. They didn't strike me as dangerous when we interviewed them. It was more like they were scared of their father and wanted to sound off to impress him.'

Men, thought Stella, I'll never understand them. 'All the same, I think we should pay them a visit.'

THE SHOP WAS empty when Stella followed Brian through the doors of Randel & Sons Butchers at 9.35 on Thursday morning. A large man in his fifties, wearing a blue and white apron and a white hat, appeared from a backroom at the sound of the bell triggered by the door.

'Jack Randel?' said Stella.

'Aye. And who'd you be? You don't look like customers to me.'

'Detective Sergeant Bruno,' said Stella, holding up her ID.

'And, I reckon I know ya mate.' Jack crossed his arms. 'What brings you out here?'

'Jordan Banks,' said Stella.

'I heard on the radio someone had done him in. What's it got to do with us?'

'Your sons still work here?' said Stella.

'They do.'

'Are they in? I'd like a word with them.'

'Why's that?'

'They made some provocative threats against Jordan when he was released,' said Stella.

'They were just words.'

'I hope so,' said Stella, 'but we're obliged to follow these things up when the subject of a public threat turns up dead. So, are they here?'

Jack turned and disappeared into the backroom. Moments later, two tall, well built men in their late thirties, one sporting a dark beard, wearing butchers' aprons and caps came into the shop from the backroom.

Stella glanced at Brian. His right hand moved to undo his coat button. She looked back at the men behind the counter and the knives on their belts. 'Which one of you is Tom?'

'I'm Tom,' said the man with the beard. 'What do you want to know?'

Stella thought his smile was genuine and felt a little more comfortable in his presence. 'I take it you're aware Jordan Banks has been murdered?'

'Got nothing to do with us,' said Ben.

That sounded defensive to Stella. 'You did threaten to kill him.'

'That was more than two years ago,' said Tom. 'Besides, that reporter wanted something outrageous from us for his story. We were just showing off for the cameras.'

'Mind telling me where you were on the afternoon of Monday, the first of June?'

'Monday's a slow day,' said Tom. 'Dad looks after the shop on his own. We usually play golf in the afternoon.'

'What about the first of June? Play golf that day?'

'What's that? Three Monday's ago?' Tom looked at Ben. 'Did we?'

'Yeah, we went to Sandy Creek. Remember, it rained.'

'Now I remember. Not my best game. He always beats me when it rains.'

'Anyone who can verify that?' said Stella.

'I paid the green fees with my credit card,' said Ben. 'You have to book and sign in when you get there.'

'Got the card on you?' said Brian.

Ben pulled his wallet out of his back pocket and extracted a BankSA credit card. 'I used this one.' He handed the card to Brian, who took a photo of the card with his phone.

'Have any contact with Jordan Banks after his release?' said Stella.

'Why would we?' said Ben. 'It's not like we were ever friends.'

Stella took that as a no. 'And where were you between nine in the morning and four in the afternoon on Tuesday this week?'

'What's Tuesday this week got to do with Jordan Banks?' said Tom. 'Wasn't his body found the week before?'

'Just tell me where you were,' said Stella.

'I was here with Dad,' said Tom.

'I was here in the morning, and then did the delivery run after lunch,' said Ben. 'I would have been back by three, though.'

'What sort of vehicle do you drive?' said Stella.

'The business has a Mitsubishi van,' said Ben.

'And, privately?' said Stella.

'Toyota Camry,' said Tom, 'and Ben drives a Mazda CX5. They're parked out the back if you want a look.'

'Do you have a delivery list for Tuesday?' said Stella.

'It'd be in the office where Dad does the books,' said Ben.

They waited while Ben went to retrieve the delivery list.

'How's your sister coping with the media coverage of Jordan's death, Tom? It can't be easy having it all bought up again.'

Tom shrugged. 'She went back to the UK after the trial. She didn't want to stay here after all that media attention made her feel like she was the one on trial, and not Jordan. It's not something we talk about when she calls.'

———

Stella read through the delivery list Ben had given her while she waited for Brian, who'd gone around to the car park at the rear of the shop with Tom to record the registration details of their vehicles.

'They'd hardly have used that van if they're the ones who killed Banks,' said Brian. 'It's got their name plastered all over it.' He handed her his phone with the photo of the van he'd taken.

'They'd have the skills and the equipment, though,' said Stella.

'And, the opportunity, unless their golf outing checks out.'

'How far is Sandy Creek from here?'

'About half an hour.'

'We can check a couple of the addresses on this list on the way,' said Stella. 'May as well wrap it up and eliminate them if we can.'

———

Fifty minutes later, after two elderly women had confirmed that Ben Randel had delivered their meat orders on Tuesday afternoon, Stella walked into the Sandy Creek Golf Club while Brian took a look around the car park.

'I'd like to confirm a booking made for the first of June,' said Stella, showing the receptionist her ID.

'What name?' said the receptionist.

'Ben Randel.'

The receptionist tapped on her keyboard. 'There's a

booking for two at 13.30 but there doesn't appear to be a record of them signing in.' She moved her mouse. 'Ah, they cancelled and rebooked for the following Monday.' She looked up. 'It was pretty wild and wet here that Monday. We had a lot of cancellations.'

'Did it rain here on the following Monday, the eighth?' said Stella.

'Yes, we had a few showers that afternoon but,' she glanced at her screen, 'it looks like the Randel booking went ahead.'

'Can you print out the details of both those bookings for me?' said Stella.

'Of course.'

Stella joined Brian in the car. 'We have a problem.'

'What's that?'

'They weren't here on the first. They cancelled due to the weather and came on the eighth.'

'That shreds their alibi for the first,' said Brian. 'Want to go back?'

'They had their chance,' said Stella. 'Time they paid us a visit.'

'What about the father?'

'We'll leave him out of it for the moment. I'll get Uniform to confirm whether he was in the shop or not on the first.'

'He might not be involved,' said Brian. 'Our witness at Reynella only saw two men.'

'And the brothers certainly fit her description,' said Stella, 'but who knows? The father may be the instigator.'

'He was pretty pissed off at the time,' said Brian. 'It was a brutal rape. No seventeen-year-old deserved what he did to her.'

'Guess that's why he got fifteen years.'

'Bastard should have got life!' said Brian.

Stella looked at him. 'We don't get to set the sentence, Brian.'

'I know,' said Brian, looking into the distance. 'But, sometimes they get it wrong.'

Stella shared his sense of frustration but knew they couldn't let it derail their resolve to track down Jordan and Mandy's killers. 'Come on, let's go and have a coffee before we head back.'

They made their way to the coffee shop attached to the clubhouse and ordered. While they were waiting for their coffee to be served, Stella's phone rang.

'DS Bruno.'

'It's Ben Randel.'

'Yes, Ben.'

'I think we've got our Monday's mixed up. I know I booked to play on the first but I'm pretty sure now it was so wet we had to cancel. We didn't go to Sandy Creek until the following Monday.'

'I'm at Sandy Creek, Ben, and that lines up with what they told me,' said Stella. 'So, where were you on the afternoon of Monday, the first of June?'

'We spent the afternoon in the pub.'

'Which one?'

'The Old Spot. Do you know it?'

'Oh, I know it alright,' said Stella, not wanting to think about why. 'Which part of the hotel were you in?'

'The back bar. We were there until around four, four thirty. The woman on the bar will remember us. Her name's Rose Anderson. She's my wife's cousin.'

'Thanks,' said Stella.

Stella slipped her phone back into her pocket and picked up her coffee. 'That was Ben Randel. Says they were in the back bar of the Old Spot on the Monday afternoon Banks was killed.'

'Guess we can drop in and check that out on the way back.'

'Put's us back to square one, if it checks out,' said Stella.

CHAPTER 9

FRIDAY, the nineteenth of June, looked like it was going to be a sunny day, despite the strong southerly wind that felt as if it had come all the way from Antarctica. Stella climbed out of her car, wrapped her coat around her, and hurried across the car park to the warmth of the building.

Brian was already at his desk in the incident room.

'Got something, Sarge.'

Stella dropped her bag onto her desk and hung her coat on the back of her chair.

'That payphone call from the Port Adelaide Shopping Plaza was paid for with a credit card in the name of Ian Snedden.'

'Do we know this Ian Snedden?'

'We've got one in the database. Did time for assault in Yatala.' Brian scrolled through the record. 'He would have been in Yatala when Banks was there. Convicted around the same time.'

'Pull his case file. I want a full background on him before we have a chat with him.'

Stella felt a surge of optimism but told herself not to get her hopes up. It was still early days. She logged on and looked at the note she'd made after Steve Wright had told her Jordan Banks' toxicology report was clean. Scott Ridley's story possibly wasn't the truth and she wondered what that meant. She walked over to where DC Aplin, who'd worked on the Zimmerman case, was sitting.

'Helen, what do you remember about Scott Ridley?'

'Not much, apart from him being devastated about someone he'd trusted stealing from him.' Helen turned to DC Lyon, sitting at the next desk. 'What about you, Ken? You worked on a case involving Ridley, didn't you?'

'Caught one of his drivers red-handed with a truck load of stolen booze,' said Ken. 'I always suspected Ridley was behind it, though. Trouble was, we couldn't prove it. But that's not to say he wasn't.'

'It's possible he lied to me about firing Banks,' said Stella. 'Toxicology report says he was clean at the time of death, although Ridley claims he failed a breathalyser test when he showed up for work that day.'

'Faulty breathalyser?' said Helen.

'You'd think Banks would have protested if he'd been clean,' said Ken. 'I know I would have.'

'Any other witnesses to this breathalyser test?' said Helen.

'No,' said Stella. 'The woman working in his office told me she entered the details based on what Ridley told her. I'm wondering if his story is a cover to give him an excuse for why he didn't report Banks missing.'

'Ridley didn't strike me as someone you'd want to mess with,' said Helen, 'which made me wonder why Zimmerman did what he claimed he did.'

'You not sure he actually did it?' said Stella.

'The money was definitely gone,' said Helen. 'The Tax Office proved that, and he did confess.'

'Did you find where the money went?'

'He claimed he'd used it to settle his gambling debts but wouldn't reveal who he'd paid the money to. Reckoned that would put his family at risk.'

'Told me he'd owed money to some unsavoury characters,' said Stella. 'How much are we talking about?'

'Six hundred thousand dollars.'

'How come Ridley didn't go under?'

'It was over several years and he had insurance,' said Helen. 'It was only picked up because Zimmerman was on leave when the Tax Office turned up.'

'Did you suspect insurance fraud?' said Stella.

'We didn't push it that far, not after he confessed. We left that to the insurance company to follow up.'

Stella crossed her arms. 'So, Zimmerman could have had six hundred grand in cash sitting somewhere all this time?'

'I suppose,' said Helen.

'So, why is he growing veggies in his back garden?' said Stella. 'Did you ever meet his wife?'

'We didn't interview her but she was in court the day he was sentenced.'

'Remember what she looks like?'

'A bit like her,' said Helen, pointing to the photo of Mandy Webster on the whiteboard. 'Only thinner and with blond hair.'

'What's his wife's name?' said Stella.

'Give me a minute,' said Helen. 'I'm pretty sure I made a note of that somewhere.'

Stella waited, suspecting someone else had lied to her and paid for it with her life.

'Amanda.'

'Get on to the Registry Office. I want a copy of Zimmerman's marriage certificate and the details for their kids.'

Stella called Seaview High School.

'Is there a Mrs Zimmerman working in your finance office?'

'We've got a Jane Zimmerman. Is that who you're after?'

'How old would she be?' said Stella.

'Jane's close to retirement age, Sergeant. Do you want to speak to her?'

'If she's available,' said Stella, thinking a woman close to retirement age was more likely to be Dan's mother than his wife.

'Just a minute. I'll put you through.'

Stella heard a click and then the sound of a telephone ringing; she'd been transferred without any introduction.

'Finance office.'

'Is that Jane Zimmerman?' said Stella.

'Sorry, Jane hasn't been in all week. Can I help you?'

'No, I wanted to speak to her on a personal matter,' said Stella. 'I'll try her at home.'

Stella ended the call. It looked like Dan Zimmerman had lied to her as well. She called Steve Wright's number.

'Steve, can you run a paternity test on Mandy Webster's unborn child? I want to know if Jordan Banks is the father or if it's someone else.'

After speaking to Steve, she called Community Liaison.

'Who's taking care of Hayley Webster?'

Stella listened to the sound of a keyboard being pounded.

'She was collected by her grandmother, Sergeant. We got her details from the school when we picked her up.'

'Can you give me those details?'

'Heather Webster, 15 Young Street, Tanunda. Telephone number is 8234 5527.'

'Thanks.' Stella ended the call and tapped in the numbers she'd been given.

It was early afternoon when Brian parked in front of 15 Young Street, Tanunda, and they made their way along the gravel driveway to the front door.

'Didn't realise it got quite so cold up here,' said Stella, thrusting her hands deep into her coat pockets.

'Let's hope she's got the heater on,' said Brian, ringing the doorbell.

The door was opened by a woman with dark shoulder length hair, with a fair haired girl of about eight standing behind her.

'Heather Webster?' said Stella, holding out her ID. 'Detective Sergeant Bruno. We spoke earlier.'

'Please, come in,' said Heather. 'This is Hayley.'

'Hello, Hayley,' said Stella.

Hayley smiled but stayed close to her grandmother.

'This way,' said Heather, closing the door and pointing down the passageway. 'Let me take your coats.'

Stella felt the heat coming from the slow combustion heater in the living room as soon as she slipped off her coat. 'Oh, it's nice and warm in here.'

'We wouldn't survive the winter without that stove,' said Heather.

'Sorry we have to meet under these circumstances,' said Stella, sitting opposite Heather.

'What can you do?' said Heather. 'Life's not always easy or fair, is it?' She turned to Hayley. 'Do you want to stay or go to your room?'

'Stay,' said Hayley, sitting on the couch next to Brian.

Heather looked at Stella.

'That's okay,' said Stella. 'As I explained when I called, we need to get an understanding of your daughter's background.'

'What do you want to know?'

'Did she grow up here in Tanunda?' said Stella.

'Yes, she didn't go to Adelaide until after she'd finished school. Got herself a job doing office work for a transport company in Lonsdale. That's where she met Dan.'

'So, she worked for Scott Ridley Freighters?' said Stella.

'Right up until Hayley came along,' said Heather, 'and then Dan made a mess of things, but I guess you know all about that.'

'Yes,' said Stella. 'When did they get married?'

'Couple of months before Hayley was born,' said Heather.

'When did she leave him?' said Stella.

'Pretty much straight after he went to prison. She came home to us for a while,' said Heather. 'They'd been living with his mother. That should have been a sign, but she didn't see it until it was too late.'

'When did she move to Enfield?'

'Around the time Hayley started school,' said Heather. 'I don't know how she paid for it. There was someone else involved when she moved into that house, but she never wanted to talk about it.'

'Uncle Scott,' said Hayley. 'He used to sleep at our place and give Mum money.'

'Do you know his other name?' said Stella.

Hayley shook her head. 'He drives a big red truck. He even took me for a ride.'

'Was that fun?' said Stella.

Hayley nodded. 'It was really way up high. You could see the tops of all the cars.'

Stella smiled and turned back to Heather. 'How did she meet Jordan?'

'Now that I don't understand,' said Heather. 'She got back together with Dan for a while after he was released. Then, next thing you know, she's with this Jordan, but he was hardly ever around. Always away driving trucks.'

'Did she tell you who he was driving for?'

Heather shook her head. 'Said she didn't know.'

'It was Uncle Scott,' said Hayley.

'How do you know that?' said Stella.

'I heard Dad telling Mum when I was supposed to be asleep.'

'When did she get her new car?' said Stella.

'About a year ago,' said Heather. 'Whatever Jordan was doing, he was making a lot of money.'

'What did you think about her having a child with him?'

Heather looked at Hayley and Stella thought she might not answer.

'People said a lot of things about Jordan,' said Heather. 'I guess I don't have to tell you what he'd gone to prison for, but he was a gentle soul from what I could tell. He was really good to Mandy. They seemed happy together, happier than I'd ever seen her with Dan.'

'I liked him,' said Hayley. 'He was funny.'

'Mandy ever mention she'd been threatened?' said Stella.

'Only after what happened to Jordan,' said Heather. 'She rang me and said she was worried about what it all meant, and then a couple of days later she was dead.'

'Any idea how she was getting on with Dan?'

'Not really,' said Heather.

'Daddy's not really very nice,' said Hayley. 'He's bossy, and tells Mum what to do all the time.'

CHAPTER 10

DI WILLIAMS NODDED to Stella as he took his seat alongside DS Francese.

'A few people haven't been entirely honest with us,' said Stella, 'so we may have missed a few things that might otherwise have been obvious.' She picked up the printout of the information DC Aplin had obtained from the Registry Office. 'According to these Registry Office records and her mother, Mandy Webster was Zimmerman's wife. Not his cousin as she told us, and Zimmerman is registered as the father of her daughter.'

'So why was she living with Banks?' said Brian.

'I'm not sure she was,' said Stella. 'Most of Banks' personal stuff, including his car, was found at the Reynella house. I suspect he may have only been a visitor at the Enfield house. If you check the scene of crime report, you'll see they didn't find many of his prints in the house.'

'He was supposedly away a lot,' said Brian.

'She told us he'd moved in eighteen months ago, Brian. You saw her house. She didn't strike me as a cleanliness fanatic, and we only have her word for it that he was living there at all.'

'So, what's your theory, Sergeant?' said DI Williams.

'I think Zimmerman and Banks were running some kind of scam connected to the six hundred grand Zimmerman stole from Scott Ridley.'

'That's a bit out there, isn't it?' said DS Francese.

'Helen worked on the case,' said Stella. 'We've reviewed the case file and the court documents. The money was never recovered, and Zimmerman refused to disclose who he'd given it to or to provide any evidence confirming his gambling debts.'

'You think he still has it?' said DI Williams.

'Yes, and I think he and Banks came up with a way of putting it back into circulation.'

'The cash going through Mandy Webster's bank account,' said Brian. 'I wonder if it's Zimmerman who has the other card. She told us Banks hardly used it, but someone's been using it to take money out of that account on a regular basis.'

'Have you checked it since she was killed?' said DS Francese.

'I'll follow up with the bank when we finish here,' said Brian.

'And, there's something else that's not right,' said Stella. 'Scott Ridley told us he'd fired Banks for being under the influence on the day we think he was killed, but his toxicology came back clean.'

'You think Ridley's somehow involved?' said DI Williams.

'I don't know,' said Stella, 'but it's possible he isn't being straight with us, and young Hayley, who calls him Uncle Scott, told us he'd visited her mother in the Enfield house and given her money.'

'When was that?' said DI Williams.

'In the year prior to Zimmerman's release,' said Stella, 'but according to her mother, Mandy was working for Ridley when she met Zimmerman.'

'Small world,' said DI Williams. 'Perhaps he felt sorry for her.'

'I'm not so sure, sir. If we can trust what we've been told by an eight-year-old, Ridley was sleeping over, and this was after Zimmerman had been inside for four years,' said Stella. 'Then, when Zimmerman got out, he organised a job for Banks with Ridley, and persuaded Banks to make out he'd shacked up with his wife. Does that make sense to you?'

'Speak to Zimmerman,' said DI Williams. 'Let's see what he has to say for himself. Might help you put some pressure on Ridley to get the truth out of him.'

'What about this Ian Snedden that called Banks?' said DS Francese. 'He's got form, and was inside with Banks.

'Find out why he was talking to Banks,' said DI Williams.

Stella's phone rang as she was reviewing the data from Mandy Webster's mobile phone.

'Sarge, Zimmerman's done a runner. His mother says she hasn't seen him since last Tuesday, and he's not answering his phone.'

'Okay. Get an APB out on him.'

'She told me she'd heard him talking to Mandy on the Monday night before he left the house. Something about them getting back together now Banks was out of the picture.'

'He sent her a string of text messages along those lines,' said Stella, 'but it looks like she ignored him.'

'Is there a history?' said Brian.

Stella scrolled through the list of text messages on her screen. 'Think young Hayley might have been right, Brian. He was sending her messages wanting to know where she was and what she was doing nearly every day.'

'Was she replying?' said Brian.

'Every now and then,' said Stella.

'No wonder she was living in Enfield and not with him.'

'This could be a DV incident,' said Stella. 'Why didn't she report him?'

'Guess it's complicated,' said Brian. 'Oh, and there's one other thing, Sarge. His mother says he's a diabetic and he's taken his insulin supply with him.'

'Hmm, that's interesting,' said Stella, thinking about what Steve had told her was the cause of Mandy's death. 'Let me know when you've found him, Brian.'

Stella ended the call and then updated DI Williams.

'Do you want me to move on Ridley, sir?'

'No, Bruno. Wait until we find out what the Snedden link is.'

Stella looked around the incident room. DS Francese and DC Lyon were huddled over a laptop. She caught DC Aplin's eye. 'Take a look at this, Helen.'

DC Aplin walked over to Stella's desk and read through the text messages Dan had sent Mandy.

'I thought these two were separated,' said Helen.

'They never got around to finalising a divorce,' said Stella, 'even though it looks like she was having sex with other guys.'

'Have you got that paternity result yet?'

'Let's see,' said Stella, calling Steve Wright.

'Hi, Steve. How'd you go with that paternity test I asked for?'

'Just a minute. Let me see if the results are back.'

Stella waited.

'Probably not what you wanted to hear, Stella. Banks isn't the father.'

DC Lyon had traced Ian Snedden to a warehouse in the industrial suburb of Wingfield, where he worked as the general manager of Statewide Parcels, a courier company established by his father.

Sitting in their car parked across from the driveway leading into Statewide Parcels, DS Francese watched the flow of unmarked white vans into and out of the warehouse.

'Interesting they don't use any signage on their vans,' said DS Francese, opening the door to exit the car.

'Maybe they use independent contractors,' said DC Lyon.

They walked across the road and into the office at the street end of the warehouse, where a large man with dark hair and a full beard sat behind a computer in an open office.

'Can I help you, gents?'

'We're looking for Ian Snedden,' said DS Francese.

'You're not selling anything, are you? He doesn't see salesmen without an appointment.'

DS Francese smiled. 'Sorry, must be the suits.' He held out his ID. 'We're with the police.'

'He might not want to see you either.' The man smiled. 'Give me a minute. He's out in the warehouse.'

When the man came back with Ian, it was obvious to DS Francese they were related.

'Brothers?' said DS Francese.

Ian held out his hand. 'Yeah. He's Mike. I'm Ian.'

DS Francese shook Ian's hand. 'Detective Sergeant Francese.'

'How can we help you, Sergeant?'

'We're investigating the murder of someone I think you know. Jordan Banks.'

'Been a while since I heard that name,' said Ian, glancing at his brother. 'Someone I met inside.'

'Oh,' said Mike.

'What makes you think I can help you?' said Ian. 'I haven't seen him since I got out.'

'Recall anyone he might have made enemies with inside?'

'I can tell you he didn't make a lot of friends,' said Ian, 'but I can't say I heard anyone threatened to kill him. Besides, he would have been taken care of inside if it was going to happen.'

DS Francese nodded. 'Dare say you're right. Do you know a bloke called Ronnie Edwards?'

'I don't think so,' said Ian. 'Name doesn't ring a bell.'

'Drove a truck for Scott Ridley Freighters,' said DS Francese.

'We send stuff interstate with them.' Ian shrugged and looked at Mike. 'Can't say I've met any of their drivers.'

'Me neither,' said Mike. 'We usually have one of our boys deliver to their depot.'

'Bit of a drive from here, isn't it?' said DS Francese.

'Not as far as Melbourne,' said Mike.

'Fair enough,' said DS Francese. 'Just out of interest, where were you on the afternoon of Monday, the first of June?'

'What's that got to do with anything?' said Ian.

'That's when we think Jordan was killed.'

'You're not suggesting we had anything to do with it, are you?'

DS Francese smiled. 'Standard procedure, Mr Snedden. We're asking everybody who knew him.'

'We were here,' said Mike. 'We're here until six most days.'

'Do you have a business card, Mr Snedden, in case I need to contact you again?'

'Oh, sure.' Ian turned, picked up a business card from his desk and handed it to DS Francese.

'Thanks,' said DS Francese.

'How come you didn't ask him about the phone calls, Sarge?' said DC Lyon, as they walked across the road towards their car.

'Have you read the description in the witness statement from Reynella?'

'It was pretty vague, Sarge. Two men driving an unmarked white van, wasn't it?'

'Big men, one with a beard,' said DS Francese, turning and facing the warehouse. 'Plenty of unmarked white vans here, Ken.'

'Where to from here, Sarge?' said DC Lyon, as they climbed into the car.

DS Francese handed him Snedden's business card. 'Get the location data on this mobile and the registration details of any vehicles registered to either of them and this business, and then see if they were anywhere near Reynella on the first of June.'

Stella sat opposite Dan Zimmerman and his lawyer in the interview room and waited while Brian activated the recording equipment and walked them through the formal interview protocols. She wondered what was going through Dan's mind as she watched him cross and uncross his arms and look everywhere but at her.

'So, what happened, Dan?'

'I went to see Mandy after you came to see me.' Dan looked at the floor. 'I didn't mean to kill her. It was an accident. I asked her to come home with me but she laughed at me.'

Stella glanced at Zimmerman's lawyer. He wasn't taking notes.

'She said I was a loser, that I wasn't half the man Jordan had been.'

'And, that's why you killed her?'

'I lost it.' Dan looked up. 'He'd raped some girl, and she wanted to be with him! She was even having his kid!'

Stella took a few deep breaths. 'Walk us through what happened when you went to see Mandy.'

'What?'

'Just tell us what happened.'

Dan leant forward in his chair. 'We had things to work out. Things besides our relationship.'

'And what exactly was the nature of your relationship with Mandy, Dan? She told us she was your cousin.'

Dan shrugged. 'That was the story we agreed on when we set up the arrangement with Jordan.'

'What arrangement?' said Stella.

'We had a business arrangement, but they took it too far. She was supposed to be my wife, not his!'

Stella steadied herself. She could feel his anger bouncing off the walls. 'This arrangement have anything to do with the money you embezzled from Scott Ridley?'

The expression on Dan's face made Stella think of a rabbit caught in headlights.

'Yeah.'

'Want to tell me about it?'

'It's complicated.'

Stella waited.

'It started with a bloke called Snedden.'

'Ian Snedden?' said Stella.

'Nah, his old man, Jack. He was one of our clients when I worked for Scott. Sent a lot of packages interstate. Not all of it legit.'

'Drugs?'

'Drugs. Stolen goods. You name it. Anyway, he offered us an opportunity to become part of his operation.' Dan crossed his arms and leant forward onto the table. 'We needed the money to keep the business afloat. Why do you think we were hiding money from the Tax Office? Anyway, Snedden let us buy our way in by instalment. Made it easier for everyone. '

'Are you telling me Scott Ridley was in on it?'

'Yeah. We only got caught because the Tax Office paid us a visit when I was on leave. Scott should have called me in but he thought he could wing it. Anyway, all they could work out was I was making money disappear, so we agreed I'd take the fall. Scott made an insurance claim to recover the money and pay the taxman.' Dan leant back in his chair. 'They promised to look after me when I got out, but Mandy had to live the life of someone whose husband was in jail so she wouldn't blow my story. She wasn't happy. Five years is a long time to bring up a kid on your own on the pittance the government gives you.'

Stella wasn't so sure Mandy had kept her part of that bargain. 'Where does Banks fit in?'

'Had to find a way for Scott to get my share of the money to me without the Tax Office getting onto us again. Jordan was the perfect fit. No bastard wanted to know him after what he'd done, but he had a heavy vehicle licence. We set him up with a job, gave him a new name, and he agreed to move the stuff interstate and pass the money to Mandy.'

'Why did Mandy agree to be part of the arrangement?'

'You see all that stuff in her house? And her fancy new car? She said I owed her a new start in life after what I'd put her through.'

'Is that why you trashed her place?'

'I was looking for something.'

'Oh, what was that?' said Stella.

'The thing that got Jordan killed.'

'What was that, exactly?'

'He told me he'd been keeping a copy of his delivery logs as insurance so we wouldn't cross him.'

'What made you think Mandy would have it?'

Dan looked at his lawyer. 'I thought he was going to use it to demand more money or blackmail us. I told Scott about it. He said he'd take care of it.'

'And, did he?' said Stella, glancing at Brian.

'I don't know, but he asked me to look for it at Mandy's place after news broke that Jordan was dead.'

Stella thought of the state of the Reynella house, which had been turned upside down by someone looking for Jordan's records. 'Are these records paper or digital?'

'They're on an external hard drive, something he plugged into the computer in the cab of his truck.'

Banks obviously wasn't totally stupid, thought Stella, but he'd obviously made a mistake telling Dan. 'Did you ask Mandy if she knew where it was?'

'She said she didn't know anything about it,' said Dan.

'And, did you find it?'

'No.'

'Are you sure it even exists?'

'He showed it to me. It's on a red USB drive about the size of your hand.'

Stella opened her folder, which contained several photos from the Enfield crime scene. 'You said you didn't mean to kill her, Dan, so what happened in her kitchen when you went to see her?'

'We argued. She said she was going to tell you everything.'

'And, you couldn't have that, could you?'

'I wanted us to be together again,' said Dan. 'She said that was never going to happen. That's when I lost it.'

Stella slid the photographs the officers who had found Mandy had taken out of her folder and across the table so Dan and his lawyer could see them.

'Mandy was tied to a chair and pumped full of insulin. That hardly strikes me as accidental, Dan.'

Dan looked at his hands. 'At the time, I thought she had it coming, but now I can't live with myself. I'm ashamed of what I've become. Of what I did to her.'

Stella shook her head. She couldn't follow that logic and she wasn't sure she even wanted to try. 'Why insulin?'

'I didn't think it would be traceable.'

'Mandy was still alive when we found her. The hospital picked it up in their tests, but it was too late to save her.'

Stella slid the paternity test report out of her folder and across the table.

'What's this?' said Dan.

'We ran a paternity test on Mandy's baby,' said Stella. 'Jordan wasn't the father.'

'What? She told me he was.'

'Sure it wasn't your child, Dan?'

Dan shook his head. 'It definitely wasn't mine. I've had the snip.'

Stella knew Mandy had been protecting someone. She'd even told her mother Jordan was the father. 'Who do you think she was protecting by pretending Jordan was the father?'

Dan smiled. 'If I knew that I'd have killed him, too.'

'Are you telling me you killed Jordan Banks?'

Dan looked at his lawyer and then at Stella. 'You're not pinning that on me. I had nothing to do with what happened to him.'

'I wouldn't be so sure about that, Dan. After all, you just told me you told Scott about Jordan's records.'

As she watched Dan Zimmerman being taken into custody, Stella wondered where Jordan Banks would have put something for safe keeping. CSI had searched both crime scenes without finding anything like an external drive, and there hadn't been anything on Mandy's laptop resembling the records Dan had spoken about. They must have overlooked something, thought Stella, or Banks had hidden his records somewhere else.

Stella made her way back to the incident room and pulled up the crime scene report for the Reynella house. She figured it was more likely to be hidden there than at the Enfield property since it appeared to be Banks' real place of residence. She scanned the pages and clicked through the photographs, hoping something would suggest itself. And there it was. The perfect hiding place, which the killers had overlooked. She picked up her phone and called Barry Rice.

'Barry, where's the XR6 that was parked at Reynella?'

'In our shed,' said Barry, 'in the queue.'

'Move it up and see if there's an external hard drive hidden in it some place. A red one.'

Then she went to see DI Williams.

'Sir, I've got a confession from Zimmerman that covers more than the killing of his estranged wife.'

'What else has he confessed to?' said DI Williams, waving his hand towards the chair across from his desk.

'Told us the story behind his conviction for embezzlement, except it wasn't about the crime he went to prison for.'

'Oh?'

'According to Zimmerman, he was helping Ridley siphon funds from his business into an operation run by Jack Snedden, something that involved the distribution of illicit and stolen goods.'

'Is he saying his story about gambling debts was bullshit?'

'Yes, and he explained how Banks was passing money to him through Webster's account, money that he was promised for protecting Ridley and Snedden.'

'Have you mentioned this to Francese?'

'Not yet, sir. But Zimmerman's implicated Ridley and Snedden, possibly in the murder of Banks, but definitely in the movement of drugs and stolen goods through Ridley's freight operation.'

'Can he prove any of this?'

'Apparently Jordan was killed because he'd been keeping records of what he'd been delivering and to who,' said Stella, 'and he made the mistake of trusting Zimmerman, who spilled the beans to Ridley, who told Zimmerman he'd take care of it.'

'Do we know where these records are?'

'I've got Barry Rice searching the only place no-one's thought to look, sir. Banks' car.'

'Let me know if he finds anything.'

CHAPTER 13

BRIAN CLICKED on the link Sgt Rice had emailed him and opened a copy of the hard drive found taped to the underside of the driver's seat in Banks' XR6. The folder on the drive contained forty-three spreadsheet files, arranged in date order. He opened the file at the top of the list.

The spreadsheet contained two populated columns. The first column was headed: item number. The second was labelled: delivery address. Most of the addresses appeared to be a business address in Melbourne but there was one address listing a drop off point in Ballarat, highlighted in yellow. Brian checked the Melbourne address. It was a freight depot. The Ballarat address was a roadhouse.

Brian opened the next file. It looked similar, except the address Banks had highlighted was for a roadhouse in Wodonga. By the time he'd opened all forty-three files, which covered deliveries to Melbourne, Sydney, and Brisbane, he'd noted additional highlighted addresses in Bathurst, Ipswich and Broken Hill. All of them roadhouses.

Brian leant back in his chair and wondered what Banks was trying to tell him. The files contained no information on the items he had delivered, but he suspected Scott Ridley

Freighters' files might hold that information and the details of who had sent each item.

He wondered what someone would be sending, on a roughly bi-monthly basis, from Adelaide to roadhouses spread across the eastern states. Then he realised there was a hidden column between the two columns of the spreadsheet open on his screen. He moved his mouse and clicked unhide. The hidden column listed the name of the sender of each item.

Brian clicked through the spreadsheets open on his screen. Every item destined for a roadhouse had been sent by Statewide Parcels.

'Sarge, you need to look at this.'

Stella met with Dominic and DI Williams to discuss what they'd uncovered and to plan their next steps.

'Banks was recording the details of deliveries they were making for the Sneddens,' said Stella.

'That fits with Zimmerman's story,' said DI Williams, 'but we're going to need to find out what they're shipping if that info's to be of any value to us.'

'If Zimmerman's telling us the truth, sir, that would give Ridley or the Sneddens motive for silencing Banks,' said Stella.

'We've got nothing connecting them to the crime scene.'

'We might have something,' said Dominic.

'I'm all ears, Francese,' said DI Williams.

'The Snedden boys told me they were at their warehouse in Wingfield on the afternoon Banks was killed,' said Dominic, 'but Ian's phone data suggests he was in the vicinity of our crime scene for around two hours.' Dominic smiled. 'And, so was his brother.'

'Driving a white van by any chance?' said DI Williams.

'Traffic picked up one of Statewide Parcels' vehicles with a camera on Sherriffs Road that afternoon,' said Dominic, 'but that's not conclusive. We can't see who's driving, and it's not far from Ridley's. Could be someone making a delivery, but it's in the right time window.'

'Where were their phones on the evening of the ninth?' said Stella, sensing they were on the verge of a breakthrough.

'Hang on. I'll have to ask Ken.'

They waited while Dominic spoke with DC Lyon.

'Brighton, in the vicinity of the pub on the Esplanade,' said Dominic, slipping his mobile back into his pocket.

'That's where Banks' mobile was when it was used to send a text to Webster that night,' said Stella.

'Jack Snedden lives a couple of house away from that pub,' said Dominic. 'Could be a coincidence.'

'What would be the odds on that?' said Stella.

'Not high,' said DI Williams.

'Where do we go from here, sir?' said Stella.

DI Williams stroked his chin. 'Bring in the Snedden brothers, Francese. And search that vehicle.' He turned to Stella. 'Bruno, share that intelligence with our interstate colleagues. Perhaps they can tell us what's changing hands at those roadhouses.'

'What about Ridley, sir?'

'Have another chat with him. Let's see if he changes his story.'

CHAPTER 14

Dominic watched Ian Snedden through the two way mirror and wondered if he had any idea how much they knew about his movements. After several minutes of observing a relaxed suspect chatting with his lawyer as if they were sitting in a sidewalk coffee shop, Dominic exited the viewing room, pushed open the door and entered the interview room. He waited while Ken Lyon ran through the preliminaries.

'Before we start, Mr Snedden, let me remind you that obstructing a police inquiry is a serious offence, especially a murder inquiry.'

Ian smiled at him across the table.

'Where were you mid-afternoon on Monday, the first of June?'

'Why are you asking me that?' Ian looked at his lawyer, the expression on his face changing from amusement to confusion. 'I've already told you where I was that day. At the warehouse.'

Dominic opened his folder and slid an image of a white van going through an intersection across the table. 'Recognise this vehicle?'

Ian shrugged. 'I've seen hundreds of vans like that. What's so special about this one?'

'It's registration number,' said Dominic, sliding across a blown-up image of the rear number plate.

Ian crossed his arms.

'It's one of two vehicles currently registered in the name of Statewide Parcels,' said Dominic. 'It's being searched while we speak.'

'Why are you searching my van?' said Ian.

'Ah, now you recognise it?' said Dominic, choosing not to answer his question. 'Anybody else drive that vehicle?'

'Mike, sometimes.'

Dominic tapped the image of the van with the index finger of his right hand. 'See those numbers on the bottom right of the image?'

Ian glanced at the numbers and shrugged. 'What are they supposed to mean?'

'That's the date and time stamp telling us this photo was taken on Monday, the first of June, at three fifteen in the afternoon?'

Ian uncrossed his arms and rested his hands in his lap.

'Do you know where that photo was taken, Mr Snedden?'

Ian shrugged. 'Could be anywhere.'

'This photo was taken by a traffic camera,' said Dominic. 'That's the intersection of Sherriffs and Brodie Roads, where you come off the Southern Expressway.'

'Oh, that's on the way to Ridley's,' said Ian. 'His depot's off Sherriffs Road. It's not far from there.' Ian leant back in his seat. 'I must have done the run to Ridley's that day. Sorry. Must have got my days mixed up.' He smiled at Dominic.

Dominic didn't return the gesture. 'Make that trip on your own?'

'Yeah. Most times we send the stuff down with one of the contractors but, when they're really busy, I do it myself. We have to drop the stuff off at Ridley's before four.'

'So, you would have been on your way back to Wingfield in what, say, ten to fifteen minutes after this photo was taken?'

'I suppose,' said Ian, looking at his lawyer and opening his arms in front of him.

'Go back the same way?'

'Not always. Sometimes I go back through Brighton.'

'Where is this going, Sergeant?' said the lawyer. 'My client's already admitted he got his days mixed up.'

Dominic slid another piece of paper out of his folder. 'This is a record of the location data for your mobile phone on that day, Mr Snedden.'

Ian crossed his arms on his chest.

'This line here puts your phone where the photo of your van entering Sherriffs Road was taken.'

Ian moved in his seat.

Dominic slid his finger down the page. 'These lines here cover the signals your phone sent over the following two and a half hours. They place you at a location on the opposite side of Sherriffs Road to Ridley's, Mr Snedden.' Dominic looked Snedden in the eyes. 'I don't think you went to Ridley's that afternoon, Mr Snedden.' Dominic pointed to the numbers on the sheet between them. 'These numbers put you in the vicinity of the house Jordan Banks was renting.'

Ian shrugged.

'Want to tell me about that?'

'That data only shows my client's phone was in the vicinity of that address,' said the lawyer. 'It doesn't connect him to anyone at that address.'

'We have a witness that says she saw your client going into Banks' house,' said Dominic, 'with his brother.'

'Bullshit!' said Ian. 'I was on my own. Mike never left Wingfield.'

'Take his mobile with you for the ride, did you?' said

Dominic, sliding out another sheet of paper from his folder. 'Want to take a look?'

'He probably left it in the van by mistake,' said Ian.

Dominic decided he'd let Snedden think he'd won on that point. 'Do you have a credit card with BankSA, Mr Snedden?'

'Yeah. Why?'

'Got it with you?'

Ian pulled his wallet out of the back pocket of his jeans and extracted the card. 'This the one you mean?'

Dominic looked at the card and wrote down the number. 'Want to tell me why you called Jordan Banks from the payphone in the Port Adelaide Shopping Plaza on the morning of June the first?'

Dominic saw a brief flash of panic in Snedden's eyes as he waited for him to answer.

'No comment.'

'For the record, let me inform you, Mr Snedden, that your credit card was used to pay for a series of calls to Banks' mobile from the same payphone in the Port Adelaide Shopping Plaza,' said Dominic, 'and we have confirmed with BankSA that, at no time in the last twelve months, did you report your card stolen.'

'Look! He was the driver of the truck that took our stuff interstate. I delivered it to him. That's why I was at his house. That's why I called him, okay?'

'That's a bit unusual, isn't it?' said Dominic.

'We had an arrangement that didn't involve Ridley,' said Ian. 'Small stuff he'd drop off for us.'

'Cash payment arrangement?'

'Yeah.'

'What was he delivering for you?'

Ian smiled. 'Whatever our customers wanted delivered. It came prepackaged.'

Dominic gathered his papers and put them back into his

folder, hoping to give Snedden the impression he was finished, before starting on his next line of questioning.

There was a knock on the door and DC Rhodes stepped into the interview room.

'Sorry to interrupt, Sergeant, but can I have a word?'

'We'll take a five minute break,' said Dominic.

Dominic joined Brian in the corridor. 'What's up?'

'CSI just called. They've detected signs of human blood on the floor mats and in the back of Snedden's van. They're running tests.'

'How long?'

'Not sure,' said Brian, 'but it gets better.'

'What do you mean?'

'Silly buggers left one of Banks' mobile phones in the glove box of that van.'

Dominic chuckled. 'Which one?'

'The one he used to send messages to Webster.'

'That's helpful,' said Dominic.

Brian nodded. 'I've got something else, Sarge. Jack Snedden owns a boat. One of those runabouts people use to go fishing in.'

'Do we know where it is?'

'Keeps it on a trailer in his yard.'

'You know what to do, Brian.'

Dominic returned to the interview room and asked DC Lyons to reactivate the recording equipment.

'Do you know Dan Zimmerman, Mr Snedden?'

'I've heard Dad talk about him,' said Ian, 'but I've never met him.'

'Jordan ever talk about him?'

'Not to me.'

'Zimmerman seems to know a bit about you.'

Ian shrugged.

'In fact, he's made a statement, a confession I suppose you could call it, about what he did with the money he was supposed to have stolen from his employer.'

Ian sat up.

'And about the arrangement he had with Banks and Ridley.' Dominic smiled. 'He's dumped you right in it for moving illicit and stolen goods.'

'Then, he's full of shit,' said Ian.

Dominic opened his folder again and sorted through his papers until he found the photo of the hard drive CSI had located in Banks' car. He slid it across the table to Snedden. 'Do you know what this is?'

'Looks like one of those portable hard drives you can buy at the Post Office.'

'This one was found in Banks' car,' said Dominic, leaning back to watch Snedden's face. 'We've sent a copy of the contents to our colleagues interstate.'

Ian crossed his arms.

'Any idea what those contents might be?' said Dominic.

'Why would I?'

'Isn't this hard drive what you were looking for after you killed Banks?'

'I didn't kill Banks,' said Ian.

'So, was it your brother who killed him while you watched?'

'Fuck you! We had nothing to do with it!'

Domenic took a deep breath. 'That interruption we just had, Mr Snedden. That was DC Rhodes informing me our crime scene investigators have found traces of human blood inside your van, and one of Banks' missing mobile phones in the glove box. Want to tell me how that got there?'

'No comment.'

'Oh, and we're about to impound and search your father's boat.'

'You're wasting your time,' said Ian.

'Maybe, but you and your brother will be sitting in our holding cells while we do.'

CHAPTER 15

SCOTT RIDLEY FREIGHTERS was a hive of activity when Stella and Helen arrived and asked to speak with Scott.

'I hope this is important,' said Scott. 'I've got a business to run.'

'We won't keep you long,' said Stella.

'So, what do you want?'

Scott didn't sit and Stella noted he didn't invite them to sit either. 'You told me you fired Jordan because he was under the influence.'

'That's right.'

'Well, we have a little problem, Mr Ridley. His toxicology report came back clean.'

'What's that supposed to mean?'

Steve Wright had told her she'd be on thin ice relying on the toxicology report, given the amount of time the body had spent in water, but she wanted to see how Ridley responded to her implied accusation that he'd lied to her. 'There were no signs of any drugs or ingested alcohol in his system,' said Stella, 'so, I'm wondering how you knew he was under the influence.'

'I used the breathalyser,' said Scott. 'He blew zero six one. Didn't we cover that last time?'

'Yes, you told me, Mr Ridley, but you didn't actually have any evidence to back up your story, did you? For all I know, Jordan may not even have turned up for work that day.'

'Oh, he turned up alright. He was lucky I didn't beat the shit out of him. Do you have any idea how hard it is to get someone willing to drive one of these rigs interstate?'

Stella noted his agitation but ignored his question. 'When was the last time you spoke to Dan Zimmerman?'

'I haven't spoken to that thieving little bastard since they put him away.'

'That's not what he's telling us,' said Stella.

'Why would you believe anything he says?'

'Because I have access to his call log, and he's confessed to killing Mandy.'

'Fuck!' Scott clamped his hand over his mouth. 'Excuse my French, ladies. I never saw that coming.'

'Are you sure?' said Stella.

'What's that supposed to mean?' said Scott, sitting on the edge of his desk.

'I've had a chat with Hayley.' Stella waited. Scott didn't say anything. 'You're Uncle Scott, aren't you?'

Scott dropped his head onto his chest. 'Guess I should have thought about that.' He looked up. 'Someone had to look after them while Dan was inside.'

'We know Jordan wasn't the father of her baby. Was it yours?'

'Guess you'd better take a seat. It's a long story.'

'You might want to call your lawyer, Mr Ridley,' said Stella. 'Dan's spilled the beans on the arrangement you have with Jack Snedden, and we have Jordan's hard drive.'

'What?'

'We know about the operation you're running with Snedden. Dan's made a full confession,' said Stella, 'and, we know who killed Jordan.'

Scott finally sat behind his desk and put his head in his hands.

Stella turned to Helen. 'Let Uniform know we're ready.'

CHAPTER 16

STELLA WAS the last to arrive in the incident room, where DI Williams had asked them to gather for a briefing.

'DS Francese, let's have a rundown on the Banks investigation,' said DI Williams, as soon as Stella sat down next to Brian.

'The Snedden brothers are denying any involvement,' said Dominic, 'but it looks like we'll have enough evidence to make the charges stick. Forensics have confirmed the blood found in their van matches with Banks and they're working on the boat we think was used to dump his body out at sea. Then, there's the fact they had one of Banks' mobile phones, and the location data we have from theirs.'

'Do we have anything placing them at the Reynella crime scene apart from that location data?' said DI Williams.

'Analysis of the hair samples picked out of the blood on the floor at the Reynella house,' said Stella. 'We have a match with hairs from Mike Sneddens' beard, which definitely puts him at the crime scene.'

'And we have a witness who says she saw both of them at the house,' said Brian, 'even if her description is a little short on detail.'

'Okay, get that written up, Sergeant, so I can pass it on to the DPP. Any further developments on what Ridley and the Sneddens were up to?'

'Ridley is denying all knowledge. Says the arrangements were set up by Zimmerman, who's insisting Ridley was in on it from day one,' said Stella.

'What about the arrangements between Ridley and Banks?' said DI Williams.

'Ridley's claiming no knowledge of the cash payments Banks' was receiving,' said Stella, 'but Ian Snedden told DS Francese he was paying Banks in cash.'

'We might never get to the bottom of that,' said DI Williams. 'What about Jack Snedden? What's Statewide Parcels sending across the border?'

'Methamphetamines, according to Victoria,' said Ken.

'We need to find out where that's coming from,' said DI Williams. 'Are they making the stuff or shipping it for someone else? That operation has to be shut down.'

'Might be better to pass that to the Drugs Taskforce,' said Dominic. 'They have more resources than we do.'

'Good call, Sergeant. Get what we know written up so I can take it up with the Chief Inspector.'

'Yes, sir,' said Dominic, nodding to Stella to let her know she'd be doing most of the work on that report.

DI Williams looked at the detectives sitting in front of him. 'Well done, people. Let's reconvene in fifteen at the Seven Stars. First round is on me.'

STELLA HAD THE WEEKEND OFF, her first free weekend since the Banks' case had started. She spent the morning watching Josh play for his school soccer team. After the game, Josh caught the O-Bahn into the city centre with some of his friends, for an excursion Stella suspected was little more than an excuse to spend time with his latest girlfriend.

While he was gone, she took the opportunity of being alone to sit in the sun-drenched living room and enjoy a glass of Chardonnay. It felt good to be alive.

As she sipped her wine and enjoyed the view, she couldn't help thinking about Mandy Webster and wondering why she'd lied, when she could have so easily told them the truth.

The case had been one of the more confronting investigations Stella had worked on and it worried her that it had led to Mandy's death. If she'd been honest with us up front, thought Stella, Mandy would still be alive, and Hayley would still have a mother and be looking forward to the birth of her baby brother.

Stella shook her head. She'd never understood domestic violence and was glad she was no longer in Uniform, where you had to deal with it every day. She wondered what made men like Dan Zimmerman think they could do whatever they liked to the women in their lives, and gave thanks for men like her brother and Shaun. She hoped Josh would follow their modelling and treat the women in his life with respect.

She sat and stared at the hills in the distance and wondered if things would have turned out differently for Mandy if Banks' killers had done a better job of tying a weight to his torso before dumping it into Gulf St Vincent, or if she and the others had thought about what they were going to say when people started asking questions.

But, there you go, she thought. That's why we catch them.

Ryan Holiday PI Short Stories

Rosie

Framed

Novella

The New Girlfriend

Living Alone series

After She's Gone

Cooking 4 One

Sanity Savers

Living Alone (Collection)

Living Alone Journal

Everyday Business Skills

Everyday Project Management

Everyday Productivity

Everyday Money Management

Writings of the Mystic

Sharing the Journey: Reflections of a Reluctant Mystic

My Life is My Responsibility: Insights for Conscious Living

I Am Affirmations: The Power of Words

Beyond the Words: Reflections on I Am Affirmations

Mystical Journey: A Handbook for Modern Mystics

Sharing the Journey Coloring Books

Mandalas

Mandalas by 3

Sharing the Journey Coloring Journals

Sharing the Journey Coloring Journal

Sharing the Journey Coloring Journal ~Discovery

Sharing the Journey Coloring Journal ~ Reflection